FROM GRAVES TO GARDENS

HEATHER CAMACHO

RENEWED HEARTS | BOOK ONE

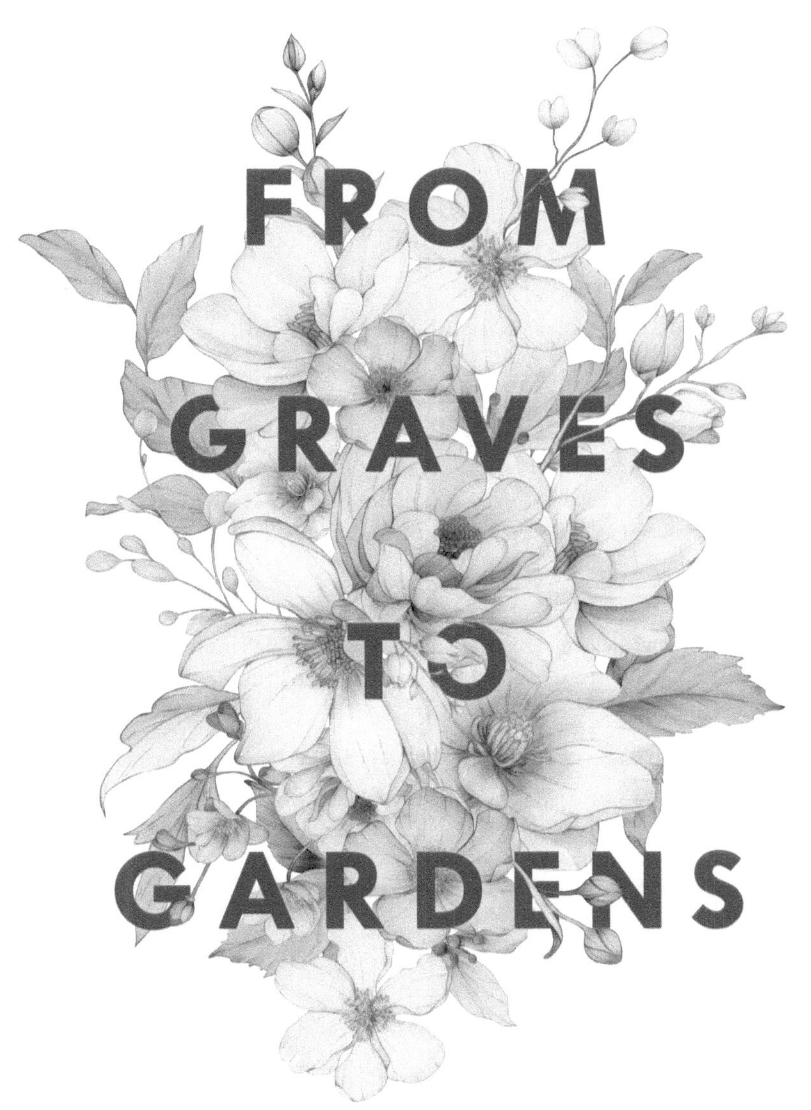
FROM
GRAVES
TO
GARDENS

HEATHER CAMACHO

For Mr. Halloran — *I have told myself since high school that I would dedicate my first book to my favorite teacher and now I have. The things you do and endure for your students really matter. Thank you for teaching me how to English good.*

For Kevin — *The boy who came to me in a dream with fear in his eyes, begging for my help. If your story touches just a single person, I'll know I was successful.*

For God — *Whom I hope to impress the most, and without Whom I could not have written this.*

KEVIN

1

GROWING UP, I DIDN'T HAVE A DAD WHO GAVE ME SAGE ADVICE about life, instructed me on how to talk to girls, or even sent me to my room hungry when I wouldn't finish my dinner. What I had was more like a wicked stepfather. A Craig Wyatt, to be precise. And the only thing he ever taught me was how to stay out of striking distance when he got wasted.

Last night, he and my mom coupled their drunkenness with something worse that he apparently hadn't yet come down from. I found the remnants of their over-indulgence after getting home from work and had gunned straight for my bedroom, where I'd been ever since.

This morning, the morning of the first day of my last semester in high school, Craig slammed his fist into my bedroom door like a sledgehammer, jarring me from what hardly counted as sleep. Trusting my extra locks, I turned to my side.

"Get up, boy," he shouted.

The door handle jiggled as he swore incoherently and attempted entry. He could try all he wanted, but I'd learned to take precautions. I'd never get an ounce of rest in this house with him roaming around, if he could just pick a simple knob-lock and walk right in.

"Do you hear me?" The pounding continued. "Come on out here. Your lazy mother is still in bed, and I want breakfast. Don't you people know a man needs a hot meal before work? If she ain't makin' it, then you are!"

"I'm not your servant," I muttered through the grogginess of another sleepless night. And I would find out just how "lazy" my mother was when I got home from school and counted her new bruises.

"You'll do as you're told!" he snapped back.

As I squeezed my pillow around my head and clamped my ears, trying but knowing I could never truly drown him out, I resorted to shouting, "Buzz off, Craig!" I knew it was the wrong move before I even said it. Issuing challenges to him never worked out in my favor, but it felt good to have that fleeting second of control.

"This is my house, boy. You think I can't get into your room and make you do it?" He made a sound resembling laughter, and then his footsteps receded.

This house was the furthest thing from his. My mom first rented it when I was a baby and then later bought it, paying it off with a small family inheritance, a long time ago. Things were looking up for us for a while in those days. My mom was already an addict, but she had it under enough control that I didn't know yet. We had food on the table every single night, not just occasionally. That was right around the time Craig became a regular fixture, and our façade of normalcy fell apart for good. She had met him years before I was even born, if I remembered correctly, but their involvement didn't get serious until about six years ago.

With Craig on the move, I had a brief window of opportunity

to get dressed and sneak out of the house for school before he came back and did something irreparable to my door. There was no saying what he might try after my outburst, but if my room was open — and empty — when he got back, there would be no cause for damage.

Hopefully.

I threw off the covers and got out of bed. The first thing I did was open my window and glance at the sky. Still black. Still trying, like me, to wipe sleep from its tired eyes.

Taking me by surprise, Craig appeared in the backyard outside my window, his dark figure triggering a motion light on the side of the house, spotlighting his intoxicated endeavor. Back and forth, he rocked haphazardly on his feet. Talking angrily to himself, he approached the storage shed, which housed an assortment of tools, Mom's long-abandoned gardening supplies, and all their recreational stuff. Craig became increasingly frustrated when he lifted the padlock and failed repeatedly to satisfy the combination. Swearing like a drunken sailor, he staggered over to a window and clumsily tried to pry it open. When it didn't give, he fell back and sputtered. He looked too exhausted to mess with it anymore, so I pulled my clothes on. I was just tying my shoes when I heard the first crash.

Returning to my front-row seat, I saw a hole in one of the shed windows and Craig recovering from having thrown something through it. He then reached his arm in and groped for something, withdrawing empty-handed. Picking up another object from around the shed, he took more swings at the unyielding padlock, yelling for it to open. Wood split and debris sailed all over the yard. It finally occurred to him to focus his efforts on the lock itself, and while he was toiling away at that, I made my move. There was no point in staying around to watch the rest.

Once outside, I sprinted to my truck and roared away, not knowing if the theory about my door and Craig would pan out. For now, a broken door was a risk I was willing to take. Missing school over another Craig ordeal was not. If I played all my remaining cards right, at the end of this semester, all of this would be over. The nightmare that was my life would finally end, and I could wake up. Graduation spelled sweet deliverance for me, and it couldn't come fast enough.

After leaving my house so early, I had at least an hour to burn. It wasn't the first time I'd loitered in the parking lot, waiting for school to open. There were many occasions during my junior year, after I'd gotten my truck, that I slept in it at the far end of the lot. I was more than willing to do a lot worse things to stay away from home as much as possible.

Shifting into park and killing the engine, I glanced out at the approaching daybreak. I'd beaten the sunlight there. Only the welcoming pink streaks of morning stretched out across the sky so far. Then, little by little, the sun peeked out, diluting the colorful palette above.

My phone went off about a hundred times, all notifications from Craig. If it wasn't a text berating me for leaving in the middle of his *"conversation,"* it was a call and a new voicemail of his disgusting slurred words. When all his contact attempts came to an abrupt halt, I concluded Craig must've finally passed out. With any luck, he wouldn't remember this morning by the time he woke up.

As the minutes ticked by, and the sky got brighter, other cars arrived. Soon enough, I was just a drop in the bucket, just one of the many nameless faces at Corpus Christi High School, eager to start the morning so we could be done with the day.

TO ENFORCE the impression that I meant business and nothing else, I sat alone at the last empty table in first period Advanced Placement Biology. Though it was behind two chatty girls, I considered it a bonus to be at the very back of the room. All I wanted to do was fade into the background, mind my business, and get the rest of the school year over with.

The five-month countdown to freedom was officially on.

As the warning bell fired off, Mr. Hallinger stood vigilantly beside the door and watched the minute hand tick by on the large white clock above it. Whoever wasn't there already only had minutes to go.

I knew all about the strategy implemented in room 204 once the late bell rang. How many times had he locked me out for being tardy last semester? Even if I hadn't skipped the entire school day so often, Mr. Hallinger's method alone was enough for me to fail his class.

Realistically, I shouldn't have taken any AP classes, but I wasn't thinking clearly when I signed up for it. I discovered it counted for double credits and jumped on it. Our school's weird, ninety-minute-long class structure worked out for me in the end, because the first and second semesters were the same, each semester fulfilling a needed class and credit. I would be behind, and royally screwed, if classes were all-year long.

Then, before I knew it, it was too late in the year to change my mind, so I had to accept an Incomplete in order to avoid an F that counted for two. That meant I had to take it over from scratch, and since time was quickly running out, I had to pass. Without these last credits, I had no hope. Like it or not, I had no choice but to adhere to Mr. Hallinger's conventions. Given how early I could get to school, anyway, being late was no longer much of a worry.

I had my sights set on Texas A&M Central University next, for their Bachelor's program in aviation. As far as I was concerned, Killeen might as well be Timbuktu. College would get me away from everyone and everything that had ever done me wrong, and I couldn't wait to never look back.

For the first time, my future looked something other than dim. I'd already passed all my preliminary exams and qualified for a partial scholarship. It wasn't a full ride, but it was enough to get me started. Working my way through the rest wouldn't be difficult. I was already used to working like a horse with little to show for it. At least at school, the money I earned would actually be mine. Never again would I have to pacify Craig by funding his habits, nor would my mother and her own bad choices hang over my head like a never-ending storm cloud.

Adios, Corpus Christi. I won't miss ya.

While everyone else in class was socializing, I started drawing on a blank page in my sketchbook. Hallinger wouldn't cover anything I didn't already have notes on for a while, so why not? I didn't need to be taking new notes in order to be listening.

The drawing distraction was nice but short-lived. My attention was diverted when Sarah Stevenson, a girl I recognized from the halls, walked through the door at the last second.

Mr. Hallinger whistled, the note low and dramatic. "Down to the wire, Stevenson. I think there's still a spot for you right back there." Hallinger pointed my way, and I shot my eyes down. Of course, the only empty seat left in the room was the one next to me. Sarah headed my way as the bell finally sounded.

"Alright, now that everyone is here…" With his arm emphasizing the white board behind him, Mr. Hallinger reiterated his welcome message aloud to us. "Welcome back, seniors! I know we're all going to have a great final semester together. How do I know this? Because I know that each and every one of you will strive to make it to class on time, —" at this, he winked at Sarah, "— and will respect one another as well as me, so that the learning in this room can flourish. Oh, and pay attention to where you sat today, as that is now your permanent residence, and the person immediately beside you is your new lab partner."

Part of the room sighed with relief. Some groaned with annoyance. As for me, I kept my head down and my hood up. My focus was on the class, not the strawberry blonde only an elbow's length away. She would do her share if I had anything to say about it. If she thought to try coasting by on her looks to avoid doing any actual work, she was mistaken. Things at home were rougher than usual, if such a thing was possible, and I could not afford to lose any momentum.

Determined more than ever, I paid no attention to Sarah. Keeping my eyes on the sketch in front of me, I bent my arm around it protectively. As she slung her backpack onto the floor between us, it hit my chair, and I scooted further away.

"Oh, sorry," she whispered, dragging the backpack around to the other side. I offered nothing in response and remained silent for the rest of the period.

Near the end of class, Sarah leaned over, just as I was putting the finishing touches on my drawing. "Hey… You're Kevin, right? How come you didn't take notes?" When I didn't answer, Sarah bumped my elbow, causing my hold on the sketchbook to shift and my pencil to skid across the page.

Now irritated, I erased the stray line. "Yes, I'm Kevin. No, I didn't take notes."

"I'm not going to let you just copy mine later," she warned in a hushed, accusatory tone.

"I don't need them." Wanting to shut down her assumption, I reached down into my backpack and took out a black and white composition book labeled "BIO." Opening it firmly so the pages would lie flat, I slapped it onto the table. *I see your notes and raise you forty pages.*

From the corner of my eye, I watched her tilt her head in order to read it.

"Oh," she quietly acknowledged. "Nice."

I adjusted my hold and scowled, put off by her arrogance. I might've needed a scholarship to escape town, and I may have needed a viable partner for this class, but I didn't walk around asking for handouts. If Sarah pulled her weight on whatever assignments we were stuck doing as a team, everything would be just fine. The only thing I would need was extra durability for my nerves. We weren't even through the first day and Sarah Stevenson was already well at work on all of them.

2

On the second day of class, the girls and I were chatting away our free minutes before the period officially began. We were talking about nothing of consequence when Sammy fished a nail file out of her backpack and pointed it suspiciously at me before starting on her nails. "Where were you yesterday morning, by the way?"

My face threatened to warm, but I faked it away with only part of the story. "Yesterday morning was chaotic. I overslept and had to rush." The rest of it was that I spent extra time in my car inhaling a banana and juice box, then did my morning bolus in order to bring my blood sugar back up before I really felt awful. My glucose number might've temporarily suffered, but at least I made it to class on time. But I didn't tell them that. I didn't tell anybody about my Type 1 Diabetes.

Birdie nodded, accepting my explanation. "Oh, that stinks. Sleeping through your alarm is the worst."

Sammy refused to let it go. "Sounds kinda sus to me. You're never late anywhere."

"Things happen. Even to us perfect specimens." I fluffed my

hair in jest, inciting laughter that caused them to forget the subject.

"By the way, Sarah. We're really sorry you got stuck with a rando for a partner. I hope you aren't upset," Birdie said sympathetically in her eastern Texas twang.

"It's okay. You guys didn't know, none of us did. One of us always would've been the odd-man out, anyway."

"So, you aren't upset?" She wanted to know for sure.

I sighed as I leaned heavily into my thoughts. Was I upset? Yesterday, I thought I was. After taking one look at Kevin and then observing his total lack of respect for the class, I really wasn't too happy. Without his involvement, I'd be left with all the work and the risk of damaging my GPA. I didn't have any plans for my future — yet — but good grades kept the doors open for me. Closed doors made decision-making exceptionally more difficult.

"Too bad Jenna refused to take the class with us. Who picks film study with her boyfriend over AP Bio with her besties?" asked Birdie Jo playfully.

"Any sane person," Sammy quipped.

She was right about Jenna. It would've been nice to partner with her, but maybe this didn't have to be so bad. I had only one bad first impression of Kevin Sloan, but I didn't think it was fair to judge him based on that alone. I knew virtually nothing about him, except what I had seen of him so far, and that he supposedly had a negative reputation. If I paid closer attention to gossip, I might've known why.

Although we attended the same school, we'd never spoken until yesterday.

Suddenly, I had it on my heart to do something about my new situation with Kevin. Somehow, I had to make these upcoming months tolerable for us both. "You know what? No, I'm not upset. In fact, I think this will work out fine," I finally said, feeling confident in my conclusion. "I've just decided he's going to be my friend and the best lab partner ever, whether he knows it or not."

Sammy chuckled. "You would try to befriend a chupacabra if you could."

"And it would work, too. Only you, Sarah."

Kevin's stark figure appearing in the doorway caught my eye, and I lowered my voice. "Guys, stop. He's here."

Birdie Jo leapt to her feet and moved around the right side of the desk as Kevin approached. Sammy stayed put, comfortably perched on the edge as if it were her natural spot.

He didn't seem happy to see them, but I wasn't sure what his happy looked like. I had nothing to compare his permanent look of displeasure to.

"Hey, Kevin," I said, keeping my expression friendly.

"Hey," I was surprised to hear him say. Taking advantage of his engagement, I made quick introductions.

"Kevin, these are my friends, Birdie Jo MacLean and Sammy —"

Sammy pushed off the table. "Samantha Ballard, actually. Only my friends call me Sammy," she said, sizing him up. He gave a brief and unenthusiastic wave before scooting his chair away from her and lowering into it. She smirked and then winked at me as she walked around to her seat.

"It was nice to meet you," Birdie snuck in before Hallinger leaned against the doorway and welcomed us all to day two.

DESPITE MY FRIENDLY, clean-slate greeting to Kevin upon his arrival, he had not yet said another word to me. With his prickly demeanor in full swing, his hood was pulled up again. His hair spilled out from under it, framing him like a grumpy Backstreet Boy. Based on the little I saw of his face, I thought he might be good looking.

He sat quietly, hunched over another drawing. I opted to sort my notebooks and pens on the table, trying to see what he was working on without being obvious. But once I caught a glimpse, I was stunned. Most of the drawing was abstract, edge to edge, covered in various shapes and shades. What really impressed me was a highly realistic bald eagle, drawn much larger than to scale. Its wings were open wide, taking up most of the page, with its talons nestled tightly beneath it. The whole thing looked like chaos, all done up in grainy monotone strokes. The combination of a realistic bird and an unfiltered surreal background was remarkable.

"Wow, that is incredible!" The sudden compliment escaped me without a thought. "That's not the same one you were working on yesterday, is it?"

He shook his head, his attention remaining firmly in place on the paper in front of him.

"That is some serious skill. Have you been doing it a long time or are you naturally gifted? Or both?"

Kevin's gaze flicked up at me, and I welcomed him to the conversation with a smile. Finally, I had picked up on something worthy of his attention.

He pulled back his hood and ran a hand through his hair to sort it out. "Say what?" That hair was the same rich brown as his eyes and crinkled against his furrowed brow. His cheekbones were predominant, with a strong and masculine nose.

Unsure of the heat in my cheeks, I realized he was really good looking. "I said your art skills are insane. Have you been doing it for a long time?"

"Oh. Yeah." It appeared that he was a man of few words, but I wasn't giving up now.

"And you did all of this just now? Dang, that's impressive. Where do you get your inspiration?"

He tensed up, looking like he didn't want to answer. "I don't get inspired. I just start drawing and something happens."

"That's very cool, Kevin. That's probably the mark of a genuine artist. If I try really, really hard, I can draw a mean stick-figure, but that's about it."

After a last quick glance at me, he looked away, aggressively closed his sketchbook, and stuffed it into his backpack.

Okay then. Where did I go wrong?

Turning back toward the front, we finished out the period in uncomfortable silence. Very much in my head, I considered my new lab partner, trying not to sweat his repeated brush-offs. Clearly, this egg would be hard to crack, but I would accept the challenge. I wanted to know more about Kevin Sloan and wondered what other talents lurked beneath his cloak of mystery.

DAY THREE PROVED I still had a lot of work ahead of me.

"Alright, class," came Mr. Hallinger's loud teacher's voice. "Open your books to page thirteen and start reading until you get to unit two. I highly advise you to take notes because you will need to include this stuff on your — drumroll please — first project!" A chorus of student grumbles rang out, competing with

Hallinger's excitement, and he hushed them with his hands. "I know, I know. How dare I? But don't worry. We'll review the reading before class ends and thoroughly cover each unit before moving on. We'll wrap up each one with a partner presentation."

Around me, everyone began opening large textbooks. Even Kevin had one. Confused, I leaned toward him. "Wait. When did we get those? I don't have one." Kevin didn't respond. "Can I just share with you today?" I leaned even closer and, having pulled my notebook with me for a better angle, accidentally brushed against his arm.

Abruptly, Kevin shot up and walked to the front of the class. Sammy and I both watched him with curiosity as he crouched down in front of the cubby beside Hallinger's desk and worked a book out of the heap. I blushed with embarrassment when I realized I was the only one who hadn't noticed the instruction on the board to grab a book from the front. Kevin probably thought I was dense now, but that was okay. I could easily prove I wasn't.

Upon his return, he slid the book down to me like we were in an old western, and the desk was a bar.

Jeez... So the guy doesn't like to converse or share. Got it. "Thanks."

Turned slightly in her seat, Sammy looked at me questioningly, hiking an eyebrow in his direction. Discreetly, I lifted my shoulder and gave my friend a look that conveyed I had no clue what his deal was, either. Secretly, I felt like I would soon find out.

3

THE WEEKS WENT ON, AND BY THE BEGINNING OF FEBRUARY, WE'D been assigned our first major project that was due the following week. Despite all the moaning and groaning, I actually didn't mind. This would give me an idea of what it would be like working with Sarah under pressure, and how it would be for the rest of the year.

As if reading my mind, Mr. Hallinger's expression called me out as he walked by distributing the project syllabus.

"All work must be new." He tapped the paper down with one finger in front of me, and my jaw tightened. He gave me a knowing look before continuing on as he spoke to the class.

"This is gonna be a fun one," Sarah mused in her usual upbeat tone, scanning the bullet points of the project. "How do you want to split this up? How about you draw a diagram to explain the energy transfers and I'll do the rest? And I can write the speech cards, too."

For no good reason, her offer irritated me. "No. We'll do it together."

She blinked. "Seriously?"

"If we're supposed to do these projects as a team, then we'll do them as a team. I don't want to risk my grades over your social life."

She blinked, perplexity making her forehead crinkle. "Wait, what? Who said anything about my social life?"

"Isn't that why you want to split up the work? Because you have better things to do?"

Her face contorted in contempt. "I'm confused. What are you trying to say?" She held firm against my challenging remark.

Putting my foot in my mouth, I looked away. "Forget it."

"Uh-huh. So, what do you propose, then?" she asked, hunting for my eyes until I gave them to her.

"Well, if you're asking me, I think we should meet up at the library after school tomorrow. See how much we can get done sooner rather than later."

"Why tomorrow?"

"I work tonight," I informed her, feeling the edge of her scrutiny.

"Okay. Tomorrow, then. At 4:30? Come with your notes, and we'll combine what we have. But I don't want to bother with the library. You can just come over to my house. I have everything we'll need there."

"For real?"

"Unless you really have your heart set on the library…"

"No, it's cool. I'll go to you."

"Alright then." With that, Sarah seemed satisfied. She tore a piece of paper from her notebook and scribbled her address on it before handing it to me. Pocketing it, I turned toward the front, mystified by what had just happened. Suddenly, I had plans to go to Sarah Stevenson's house? What world was I living in? I could feel her watching me still, and I didn't like it.

Throwing my hood back on and stretching out my legs to sink deeper into my seat, I folded my arms over my chest. Just a few more minutes to go until I could get her out of my face, but I suspected she wouldn't be far from my mind.

4

How freaking long was it going to be 4:04 p.m.? I still had twenty-six minutes until Kevin was due, and those minutes were dragging on. Since getting home, I'd already cleaned, fixed my hair and face, talked to my mom about my plans, set out all my project stuff, and taken care of my blood sugar — all with time to spare. There was nothing left to do but wait and pray.

God, please don't let me make a fool of myself. Help me understand the meaning of my interest in Kevin...

The past month with him had been so uncertain and new, and that strangely excited me. I wanted to put my best foot forward for him and show him I was a friend, not a foe. He seemed like the type that would bolt at the first available opportunity, and I felt compelled to soothe something in him. Or, at least, be a decent human being while trying. If he had any other friends, I hadn't seen them.

He actually surprised me by not only wanting to work on the project together, but being comfortable enough to work on it at my house. One would think that meant he was slowly coming around. All the unrequited *"Good mornings," "See you tomorrows"* and my warmest smiles must've been well spent.

The doorbell rang — at last. As I ran down the stairs, I almost missed the last one. Catching myself, I shook a tremor from my hands and took a deep breath.

I am not the girl that trips. Why am I so anxious? I've got this.

Don't I, Lord?

Smoothing down my shirt and squaring my shoulders, I opened the door for Kevin.

When we were face to face, he cleared his throat. "Hey."

"Hey. Come on in." My words came out less steady than I intended, but I played it off with a smile. My signature move.

Behind me, Kevin looked around my house. "Where is everyone?"

"My parents are at work," I told him.

Prying further, he asked, "Is there anyone else?"

Confusion marred my smile. "Like who? The man who sneaks around living in the walls, stealing all the peanut butter?" That one actually pulled up the corners of his mouth. *Score!*

"Nah. Any siblings or maids or anything?"

"Ha, nope. Unfortunately, I'm an only child. And the only maid around here is me." His nod told me he understood, but the solemnity in it said something more. Interesting. Depths were exposing themselves.

Taking the lead, I turned toward the stairs. "Everything's up here. Let's go."

Disappearing into my room ahead of him, I took up my usual spot at my desk, facing the window.

"Where should I sit?" his voice cut through the air as he approached. Turning around, I saw him glance awkwardly at my bed, then around the rest of the room. In all that hustling I did before he arrived, I hadn't thought to bring in a second chair?

"Oh, I'm so sorry. And I thought I was prepared." My minor oversight was exposed as I jumped to my feet. I brushed past him in the doorway, making eye contact the moment our shoulders touched. Like a scene in a movie, it came and went in slow motion, but with a sense of energy.

Bypassing any silly thoughts, I took my mom's desk chair from her office down the hall and wheeled it back to my room.

"I got it," Kevin said, taking it from me. I quietly let him have it and sat back down. He drew up across the desk from me, my window at his back.

I grabbed my backpack, laid it out, and rummaged through the contents. During the process of pulling out my binder, a bunch of tiny colorful candies tumbled onto the desk.

"Crap," I said harshly under my breath. That wasn't supposed to happen. While digging through my things, I must've torn the bag open.

"Skittles?" he asked, reaching for one.

"Yeah, sorry. Major sweet tooth." I laughed nervously, hoping he wouldn't question me further as I hastily swept the rainbow-colored offenders away. "Anyway, I thought we could start by deciding how to divvy out the work. Do we actually want to break up the prompts, or just work on them together, or…"

"Let's just go through everything together."

Silently, I watched him shift uncomfortably.

"Because I want nothing to get lost in translation, then we both botch the speech or whatever. It's best we stay on the same page," he added.

"How much time are you able to dedicate to this over the weekend?" Now it was my turn to feel awkward. Obviously, we needed to get the project done, but that wasn't my only motivation for spending time with him. I was eager to know who Kevin Sloan really was.

"I'll make the time I need. The scores all count." His voice sounded bitter, piquing my curiosity.

Settling into my seat, I rearranged the books and other supplies I'd set aside for today's use. "So, did you fail the class before? Is that why you're taking it again?" Even though I kept my tone gentle, I soon felt bad for asking. The look in Kevin's eyes changed and something twisted in my gut. We felt on the verge of genuine conversation; otherwise, I wouldn't have pushed. Forward was the only way to go.

As I tried to figure him out, I surveyed his outward appearance. His gray t-shirt was plain and form-fitting, which really made his muscles stand out. I never would have guessed at the build hiding underneath all those freaking hoodies he wore to school, but dang, I didn't mind what I was seeing now.

"I had to drop it." His voice brought my thoughts back to the topic at hand.

"Why?" The simple word triggered an expression that conveyed the answer was *anything* but simple. He sighed and leaned back, hands clasped behind his head, completely unaware that his relaxed posture aided in showing off his frame.

Staring is rude, staring is rude, staring is rude!

But those arms are so nice.

"I was absent too much the first half of the year. I made my other credits up already, but I had to retake AP Bio. Since I didn't fail it, I withdrew with an Incomplete. Had to bust my butt, but I finally caught up. Now, as long as my GPA doesn't fall, I'll still get my scholarship."

I nodded, feeling appreciative and surprised by his engagement. "I gotcha. So, you have college plans after graduation?"

"Yep. Once this year is up, I'm out of Corpus Christi for good."

Swallowing hard, it rattled me how much I disliked the sound of that. "Where will you go?"

His eyes brimmed with determination. "As far as I can."

The longer Kevin held my gaze, the larger the lump in my throat grew. I didn't know how long we remained there like that. His honey-brown eyes, nestled behind long dark lashes, were so beautiful, and yet I thought I saw the glimmer of a hidden sadness behind them. It nearly pained me not to reach out and comfort him.

Talking with Kevin like this was nice. Outside of school and apart from his sour attitude, he was actually kind of pleasant. Stumped as to why, he brought a stirring of emotions to the surface. Something about him kept drawing me in, like a desperate siren calling a sailor through the chaos of a hurricane.

Downstairs, the front door announced my mom's arrival, shaking me to my senses.

KEVIN

1

"SARAH, I'M HOME," CALLED HER MOM FROM DOWN BELOW. THE sudden interruption had me feeling disoriented, so I straightened up and grabbed a pencil to look busy.

Sarah slid over and made a few clicks on the computer, printing something out. The loud machine put us into full distraction mode by the time her mother walked in.

"Hey, there." Sarah's mom came forward and reached her hand out.

I stood abruptly, likely looking as awkward as I felt. I had done nothing wrong, but nervousness still overtook me.

"I'm Lynnette, Sarah's mom. Just call me Lynne."

I took her hand and shook it. Lynne's smile was lovely and warm, reminding me of Sarah's. "Nice to meet you, ma'am. I'm Kevin."

"He's my new Bio partner," added Sarah.

"Ah, yes. The one you were telling me about."

I could no longer see Sarah's face as she whipped toward her mom. "Mother, really?"

"What? Is it a crime to talk to me about your classmates? Sorry, I didn't know. Anyway, I'll just be downstairs if you need anything." She smiled again at me. "It was nice to meet you, Kevin." As she was heading out, she stopped short of the door. "Oh, Sarah, have you checked your —"

"Yes! Thanks, Mom."

When we were alone again, Sarah seemed every bit the embarrassed daughter. Indeed, when she turned around again, her face was beet red, and she couldn't meet my eyes. I sat back down, propping my elbows on the table, and hid a smile behind my hand.

Wouldn't I love to be a fly on the wall the moment I leave? And I'd give just about anything to know what she'd already said, if Sarah had, in fact, talked to her mom about me. Interestingly, I was more curious than nervous about the idea. When had such ease swept over me? I didn't understand it, but I didn't hate it.

Sarah fidgeted with a little pink eraser. "What's your favorite color?" she asked, completely changing the topic.

"I don't have one."

"Oh, I'm sure that's not true. If you had to pick."

"What is this, Twenty Questions?" I rubbed the side of my neck.

"It's just harmless fun. Come on, you can do it. Have a bit of fun," she urged, her joyful nature seeping into me.

I sighed, losing the battle of resistance against Sarah's forces of friendliness. "I don't know… black."

"Black? The absence of color is your favorite color?"

"You made me pick something! It's the color of charcoal or pencil marks on paper. I like that."

"Oh, hmm… Well, when you put it that way, it makes sense. I accept your answer."

I laughed. "Alright then. What's yours?"

"Pink."

I rolled my eyes. "Typical girl."

"Am not," she insisted, nudging my shoulder with her fingers.

Something zinged through me, and I smiled nervously. *No, you're really not.*

"Tea or coffee?" she asked, hardly missing a beat.

Shaking my head, I made a face. "Yuck to both."

"Aw, I love tea. It's so healthy, too. Herbal blends are my favorite. Anything sweet tastes bitter to me, no matter how I brew it. But I totally agree – coffee is super yuck."

"It definitely is. And tea is how I imagine a humid swamp might taste." Her laugh was intoxicating. I wasn't sure how to keep making it happen. I'd never considered myself a funny guy. All I knew was that I didn't want this new fun to stop. I quickly scoured my brain for something to ask her. "You ever watch *LOST?*"

"That's a random one. I most certainly have. Why?"

"What did you think of —"

"The ending?" she eagerly finished for me.

"Yeah! People either hate it or love it, and most people don't love it. Where do you land on the scale?"

She blew out a deep breath and sat up straight. "Personally, I'm a love it kinda girl."

"For real?" How could something so trivial make me feel things on the inside? Her liking a TV show or not didn't matter to me, but discovering another thing we had in common heightened my already on-edge emotions.

"Yep. Considering the craziness they pulled on that show, especially in later seasons, I was perfectly okay with the way it ended. It actually made me pretty happy to see them together again. In all the chaos, it was so simple and gentle. That feeling of finally going home. The characters deserved that."

Wow. Oddly insightful and concise. "You've answered this question before, haven't you?"

"Not to any actual person, but I've debated it many times in my head."

How cute was that? "I couldn't agree more. Great ending, for all the reasons you said."

"Take that, haters. Consider the scales officially tipped."

Naturally following her, I laughed easily, which was something I wasn't used to at all. My defenses, which were always well-cemented into place, crumbled like clay around her. I tried my hardest to keep her at a distance the past few weeks, but getting close to her was proving to be so much better. Maybe it wasn't best for me long-term, but it was nice at the moment.

I didn't understand the power of talking to her. Maybe it was just that I was talking to someone new for the first time in ages. Aside from my buddy, Russell, I kept to myself. When I didn't, I usually ended up in trouble. Trouble was something I couldn't afford anymore.

Still, with Sarah, as each new revelation sparked another, waves of something shot through my gut. As far as I knew, that something was telling me I'd better be more careful.

"What's your middle name, Kevin Sloan?"

I snorted, seeing an opportunity to shift the conversation away from the personal line of questioning. "Forget it. Twenty Questions is over."

She clutched my forearm. "No, please. I promise I won't laugh."

I grinned like a fool, like I already accepted that I couldn't resist her pleading. "Ezekiel," I confessed, unable to remember the last time I'd told someone. Don't think I ever had.

"Is it really?"

"Yep."

"That's a really cool one. It's a biblical name. Did you know that?"

"Nope."

"He was an Old Testament prophet."

Whatever that all meant. "Oh, cool."

Eventually, we were going back and forth explaining our scars. The battle wounds of childhood already seemed so far away. Without thinking much, I showed her the spot on my right hand where one of my mom's exes had put out his cigar.

"What's it from?" she asked, reaching out to touch the puckered skin. I flinched and her question barely registered. It preoccupied my mind to take in the simple gesture without feeling stupid.

Then, before I could realize I shouldn't be telling her so much, the truth spilled out. "My mom's ex-boyfriend did that."

Her eyes grew cold. "He did?"

"He used my hand as an ashtray for his Cubans one day while getting after me for something. Said since I didn't seem to remember how to behave, he would help make it easier."

"Oh, my… How old were you?"

"Probably like six."

"I'm so sorry."

The look on her face made me feel like crap. I hated pity and told no one about all the bull I dealt with at home. And I really didn't want Sarah feeling that way. Not for me, nor for anyone else. But why start lying now? "It is what it is. I don't worry about it."

"I think that makes it even worse."

"What do you mean?"

"Never mind. I didn't mean to comment," she said. Then she grabbed my hand, softly kissed the scar, and held it tightly.

Looking into her hazel eyes, I thought for a second that I could get lost in her — so very lost and unable to find myself again. Eventually, I would lose track of where I ended and she began. For the first time, I wanted to be close to another person. Her gaze alone made my skin feel tight and warm. I could only imagine what an actual kiss might do.

"What are you thinking about?" Sarah asked.

My heart drummed wildly. "You." My eyes sank to her lips when they parted slightly in surprise. I was struck with the desire to lean in and press my mouth against hers, but I didn't get the chance to consider it further.

"Sarah! Does your friend want to stay for dinner?" Her mom's voice came from downstairs. Sarah dropped my hand and retreated, and immediately, I felt starved for her touch.

Tapping her phone to check the time, she balked. "I had no idea how late it was."

I flicked my watch up to see for myself, I agreed. "Dang. Me neither."

"Well… Do you want to stay for dinner?" Sarah became suddenly shy, looking up at me through thick lashes.

I did, actually. But what I wanted didn't matter. Even if I didn't have things to do, it wouldn't be a good idea. "I gotta get going. Still got chores to do at home." I must've been mistaken by the disappointment in her eyes. "Sorry."

"No, it's okay. I understand." She offered a meager smile and looked at the papers scattered around. "But we didn't get any work done."

"I guess we didn't." I tore the corner off a piece of paper and wrote my number before I got up to leave. "Let me know when you want to meet up next." Despite my better judgement, I hoped I wouldn't have to wait long.

KEVIN

6

IT WAS PITCH BLACK AND NEARLY SEVEN WHEN I GOT HOME THAT evening. Mom was passed out on the couch, and Craig sat in the recliner with a beer in his hand. The TV blared something stupid in the background. The severely old carpet was littered with a mess of dirty laundry and various stains, some known and some unknown. I felt such shame in this place. It was a live depiction of trailer trash, minus the trailer part, and this was only the living room.

Every time I walked through the front door, that fact got thrown in my face all over again.

I didn't even have the door locked behind me before Craig started in. "Where you been all day?"

Just like that, I was set on edge.

The last nine years with Craig had been worse than any that came before him, and none of those years were something I'd consider "good." I wished and pleaded countless times for Mom to divorce Craig, but despite my protests, he's the one who seemed to last. My mom, Marie, had never made it that long with one man before, and it would just figure the one she married would be evil incarnate.

"Studying," I said, forcing the waves of my nerves to still. "I have a biology project due soon. I might be busy with it all weekend."

Craig pried himself from the moaning recliner and sauntered my way. Instinctively, I moved my backpack down over my shoulder and let it slide to the floor.

"Oh, is that so? You'll be busy, huh? You mean you're trying to avoid helping me fix the shed?"

"I can't help it, Craig. I have school."

"Isn't that convenient?" Craig wiped his hand under his nose and coughed. "Aren't you 'bout nineteen now? You don't need no more school. You should be working for your living."

"He's only seventeen, Craig," Mom chimed in, shakily sitting up from her half-stupor on the couch. I could tell by the deep, passive tone of her voice that she hadn't had a drink or anything else in a while. Regardless, I preferred her passed out over her trying to come to my rescue. It never went well for either of us and only made me hate her more when she gave up.

"I'll help with the shed, just not sure when. I can't fail this class."

"Ain't no *time* like the present! I say you go out right now and make up for being gone all day."

"But Craig, it's already so late. I'm sure he's hungry," came my mother's feeble intercession.

"It's pathetic the way you coddle him, Marie. That's no way to raise a man. No wonder he can't even be helpful around the house. He's as useless as you've raised him."

Mom pushed to her feet. "Don't you say that about—"

Without warning, Craig turned and forcefully slapped my mother's face. She fell back onto the couch and nursed her already red cheekbone with her hand. "You better watch how you speak to me, woman. I won't tolerate that tone."

I stepped forward, placing myself between them. My fists were tight at my sides, and all my hatred for Craig boiled up inside me, seeking any excuse to give him a pounding and claim self-defense.

Sensing my false bravado, Craig sputtered an offensive laugh. "Well, would ya look at that? Look how grown he thinks he is." Craig came toe to toe with me, and the mixture of tobacco, alcohol, and whatever else felt like acid on my face. My mom got back up and tried again to protest.

I held my hand out. "Mom, stop. Just stay there."

Despite my efforts, she shuffled around me, negating any protection I could offer. "No, son. I don't need your help. Just go on out back and work on that shed. It won't fix itself."

I glared at her in disbelief.

"You see, boy? Mommy don't want or need your help, because she knows a good lesson when she receives it. Unlike you, she knows how to fall in line."

"Hitting her in the face for defending her son is a good lesson?"

Craig's face grew dark and grotesque. His voice was unpleasant and unwelcome, like a meat grinder full of rocks. "Learning not to disrespect the man of the house is a *very* good lesson, and you'd better learn it, too."

I tensed up, anticipating Craig's next actions. The first time he swung at me, I hadn't been big enough to retaliate properly. My arms were too lanky and under-muscled, and cloudy, tear-filled eyes thwarted my every attempt. It was like those recurring nightmares people have where they scream and no sound comes out, or where they will themselves to run or fight but end up stuck, throwing spaghetti-armed punches.

For me, the nightmare felt all too real, but I'd put a lot of miles between eight-year-old and seventeen-year-old me. Starting from the time I took my first advanced physical fitness class, I began pumping all the iron I could and running regularly. Storing up a stockpile of wrath for years, I was ready to go at a moment's notice. I knew I could lay the tweaker out flat now. Craig only had to make the first move.

Again, Craig laughed. It was a disgusting, drawling excuse for a round. My fury was about to breach its breaking point. If Craig said another word, I wouldn't be able to contain my fury. Wouldn't even care to try.

The pit of my stomach grew cold and hard. It wasn't the first time Craig had hurled such sickening insinuations around. I couldn't fathom what pleasure it gave someone to be so heinous, but I wanted no part in it. Wanted nothing more than to be rid of Craig, *and* my mom, for that matter. Screw them both.

"I'll be outside working on the shed," I said, grabbing my backpack and storming to the kitchen, ignoring anything else that came out of Craig's mouth from behind me. I dumped the pack on the island and pounded through the back door.

When I approached the shed, I picked up the first heavy thing I found, which was a remnant of a two-by-four. Gritting my teeth together to stifle my yell, I took a hard swing at a window, sending shards of glass everywhere, building upon the destruction that Craig had started when he was on one of his trips.

Pitching the board through the busted window, I didn't care

what else it hit on its way inside. I bit back stinging tears of desperation that I hadn't let fall in years. Craig wasn't worth it. Even my mom wasn't worth it.

Out of nowhere, Sarah's beautiful face flooded my mind. The image of her brought a stream of positive thoughts that eased my fragile nerves until I saw reason again. When my phone vibrated in my pocket, I just knew it would be her.

Sure enough, Sarah's text read,

SARAH

So how 'bout tomorrow?

I might've been smiling. It almost kinda-sorta seemed like she wanted to spend time with me.

KEVIN

I gotta work. I'm not off 'til Sunday.

SARAH

Oh, I can't. I have church.

Church? Oh, yeah. She wore a cross necklace. Of course, she was a Bible-thumper.

SARAH

But perhaps after...? :)

A genuine smile spread across my face for the hundredth time that day. There was no denying it; thanks to Sarah, a burst of happiness chased away the terror in my life. It's like she turned on a light inside me, and for a while, the darkness couldn't penetrate. Suddenly, I could handle Craig because he meant less than nothing, and if I had to make time to work on the piece of crap shed, so be it.

Sarah, though... She somehow already meant something to me, even though I didn't know what that something was. The first days were shaky, but this afternoon with Sarah was the best time I'd spent with anyone in who knew how long.

And when my stomach fired off a zealous growl, I really wished I'd stayed for dinner.

SARAH

7

ON SUNDAY AFTERNOON, KEVIN AND I MADE PLANS TO MEET UP AT the University library, the only one open and luckily available to the public. Typically, I didn't make plans on Sundays, but a school project was a reasonable exception. My parents could go on our traditional post-church brunch without me for once.

We could've gone to my house again, but the last thing I wanted was my parents loitering near my room and finding all sorts of dumb excuses to intrude, and I really, really wanted another conversation with Kevin like our last one.

I had spent the last few nights replaying our time together over and over in my head. One part of me couldn't believe I had been bold enough to kiss his hand like that, while another part was annoyed I hadn't been bold enough to just kiss him on the mouth.

Shoulda, coulda, woulda, right?

Being forward wasn't usually my MO. Most often, I was content to sit back and let things happen, but in the mysterious and exciting case of Kevin Sloan, I wished I'd been more proactive.

I recalled thinking much too hard about what he'd meant when he said he was thinking about me. He could've meant he was thinking of me in a practical sense, like in regard to the project, but deep down, I wasn't so sure.

Pulling into the library parking lot, my stomach pitched into a wild frenzy. I brought in and released a deep breath as I gathered my things. I could already see his truck parked a few spaces down. This morning I'd asked him if he wanted a ride, to which he'd promptly said no. Now it clicked, and I bet that had something to do with the drama he mentioned at home. No wonder he suggested the library in the first place, or why he didn't mind coming over. He just didn't want me at *his* house.

Entering the library, I scanned the tables for Kevin. As I explored, doubt made its presence known. What if whatever we'd felt at my house was all in my head, and mine alone? What if, when I sat down with him today, he was not happy to see me? I couldn't reason with the polar extremes vying for dominance in my heart, but they all hushed to nothing when I finally found him.

Kevin sat at a study table under the row of windows at the far end of the library. He absentmindedly twirled a pencil between his fingers like a drummer with drumsticks. His other hand propped up his head, and his arm was bent at the elbow atop the table. He had a book open but wasn't reading it. From the looks of it, even from a distance, he was somewhere far away in his mind. When I reached the table and he turned abruptly, his glossy eyes confirmed it.

"Hi," he said, completely unaware of the toil inside me.

"Hey. You beat me here."

"I'm a fast runner."

I plopped all my stuff down. "Seriously?"

He smiled and sat up straight in his chair. "You make it so easy. No, I drove."

"Duh, I *knew* that. I saw your truck when I pulled in." By giving him a humored smile, I made myself comfortable. *He* made this so easy.

One roll at a time, I laid a poster board out on the table. "So, to dive right in, this is what I was thinking…"

It was adorned with different colors, charts, and index cards with text taped in various sections. There were blank sections fully labeled for Kevin to draw the diagrams and even a reference sheet for the syllabus, pointing out how the required material would be displayed.

"Wow, when did you do all this?"

Chewing my bottom lip, I shrugged. "I couldn't really sleep last night."

Because I was too busy thinking about you…

KEVIN

8

I DIDN'T SLEEP, EITHER. ALL NIGHT, MY THOUGHTS KEPT BANGING around my head so erratically I couldn't keep my eyes closed. One minute, I was mentally raging about Craig, and the next, I was recounting each detail of Sarah's face and the petal-like feel of her lips, even though she'd only kissed my hand. We could just be vibing, but that didn't stop me from anticipating seeing her today.

When I got to the library, I pulled my book out in an attempt to shut off my mind. That plan failed miserably. The more I thought about things, the more I wasn't sure I *wanted* her to be into me. How would it benefit anything? What if we kept spending time together and she tripped me up? Ever since I set myself on the path to get out of town, my greatest fear was that something outside my control would derail me and I'd get stuck in Corpus forever.

I could not live with that. I would not stay in this town and be my mother's son anymore, with an evil shadow of a father figure always lurking, striving to torment me. I'd had enough of living a trashy life. Maybe that trash piled up a bit more than it should've because I helped it along, what with my bad habits last year, but I was not into that junk anymore. I gave up. I just wanted out.

But Sarah was… so beautiful. And funny and incredibly smart. She captivated me with her intellect and her life stories. This simple biology poster board impressed me, and it was something she threw together without any effort.

Realization then reared its ugly head. Even more troubling than the idea that Sarah could hold me back from my dreams was the fact that I might step in the way of hers.

What was I, except for baggage? I had brought my grades up this past semester to secure my future, yes, but I didn't care about academic performance before this. Not to mention my many family issues. All that was only a fraction of what I would bring to a relationship with her or anyone else, and it boiled down to one thing — drama.

Things made a lot more sense when I kept my hood up and my head down. I never should've gotten this close to someone this near to the finish line. I didn't have *time* for this.

Now that I was with her again, daunting confusion swam back and forth in my brain. Why did she smell so good?

"You actually think it's okay?"

On edge that I might've said that last part out loud, my gaze snapped up. "What?"

"The poster board. What do you really think of it?"

A puff of relief escaped me, and I laughed nervously. Quickly recovering, I said, "Oh yeah, it's awesome. Nice job with it."

"Great! Then we'll use this as our rough draft and just go back to polish everything for the real display. And you can't forget those drawings. Sound good?"

"Perfect."

"Alright. Let's plot out the speech."

I kept myself cool and focused as I dove right in. Her eyes drifted toward me more than once. I could feel it every time but refused to engage. If end-goal concentration was priority number one, then follow-through was key. She couldn't know that she was all I could think about, no matter how disappointed she might look right now. That alone was throwing me for a loop, but I wouldn't — I couldn't — care.

Luckily, we worked well together. In the midst of our back and forth, I was able to draft our presentation speech. "Here. How's this sounding so far?" I was slightly nervous that it wouldn't be as good as she could probably do. I awaited her response, watching her lips move silently as she read.

"Yeah, that sounds good to me. This word is "'duty' or 'duly'?" She adjusted the paper and pointed at a particularly janky scrawl.

"Duel, actually."

"Oh." She held the page up to her face and nodded. "Duh. I see it now." She laughed at herself and returned it to me. "You're pretty good at writing, too. I'm sure glad you're taking care of that portion."

"Why?"

"Because you're clearly good at it, and I'm not."

"Nobody's ever said I was good at writing before." That wasn't completely true. Once, my sixth-grade teacher had made a similar comment, but I hadn't believed her, either.

Sarah wrinkled her nose and eyed me teasingly. "I smell bullcrap."

I shrugged. What more could I say? It was the truth.

"Well, if that's really the case, I'm happy to inform you. I don't suppose you also need further enlightenment regarding your mad drawing talent, do you?"

The second compliment caused me to look at her with

surprise. She couldn't possibly mean it. Drawing was one of the only things I loved in this world, but I'd never thought it was much of a *skill.* "I only do it so I don't punch people." My smile widened and I returned to my paper.

"You should show me more of your work sometime," she said, not letting it go. "And what about writing? Have you ever written anything outside of school?"

"Like what?"

"Poems or stories or song lyrics or anything? Any haikus about photosynthesis? Or perhaps, an Ode to Hoodie?"

Ha! Nice one. "Nah, not my style to be all sappy like that."

"I wouldn't say creative writing has to be sappy. But that's too bad. I'd love to read it."

"Well, I have written a couple of short stories in the past, but mostly I just draw."

"Are you gonna go to art school?"

"Nope. I'm going to be an airline pilot."

"Oh, wow. That's really awesome. You know, you surprise me, Kevin Sloan."

That smile of hers gave me shivers, lending support to her statements. The teasing was cute, too. One sensation at a time, she brought my recently discovered ease back to the surface. That ease would serve as nothing but a distraction if I let it.

I shouldn't ask, but... "How?" My palms got sweaty, and I snuck them under the table and ran them down my pants leg.

"You're not what you put out there. I think you know that."

"I guess." I'd never really thought about it.

"I don't blame you. It's hard to be yourself. High school totally sucks, and if you have the mindset that you need acceptance, you're going to find more disappointment than anything. Trust me, I know," she added dryly at the end.

"How do you know?" I wondered, almost incredulous. Sarah was gorgeous, smart, funny, sociable, financially sound, and had a home life that anyone would envy. What could anyone give her crap about?

"For example, how many devout Christians do you know at our school?"

"None."

"At least one," she corrected, somberly indicating herself.

"Oh." *Way to go, dummy.* "I'm sorry."

"It's okay, I'm used to it. But you see my point. You shouldn't be worried about putting yourself out there more, though. You have a lot to offer."

I scoffed. If only she knew. People with my sort of upbringing generally didn't consider themselves brimming with possibility.

"You don't have to believe me." Sarah tucked wayward strands of amber behind her ear. How soft her hair looked. Somehow, I maintained enough good sense *not* to reach out and touch it.

"Thank you," I said awkwardly, being unable to come up with anything better.

"Think nothing of it. Just know that you're going to be responsible for all the project writing *and* drawings from now on." She winked.

Whenever Sarah smiled, it did something to me I couldn't explain, but I really liked it. From the delicate, tan freckles on her nose to the soft rise of her cheekbones and the shine of her eyes — I felt like it was all for me. It made me want to make her smile all the time. "You surprised me, too."

"Oh, yeah?"

"Yeah, I was wrong about that social life. Look where you spend your Sunday afternoons." I shook my head in mock shame, earning a laugh and a knuckle jab to my arm. It was the simplest of gestures and the least skin-to-skin contact imaginable, but it sent a sizzle throughout me.

"There you have him. Kevin Sloan, everyone — artistically talented and *so* funny," she chaffed.

"I like you, Sarah," I blurted, momentarily forgetting all reason. The confession poured through me with a life force of its own. Only once the words were free did my throat seize up on me.

So much for not caring.

SARAH

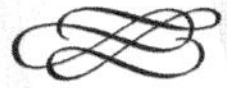

9

"You like me? In what way?" My heart trembled as I awaited his response. It killed me that I couldn't read his expression at all.

"Never mind. I'm just talking."

With his words, my hopes came crashing down. Something was either holding him back, or he really didn't mean it like I hoped.

Hold up. Hope? Is that what I'm doing? Hoping for Kevin to like me-like me?

"Should we finalize the entire speech now and then finish the display board tomorrow, go for the whole thing now, or what?" His words pulled me from my confused mind.

"Um…" I flicked my wrist up to check the time. It was already well after when my parents and I usually had brunch. I wasn't prepared to go this long without a proper meal.

"Or do you have somewhere to be?" He questioned me without looking up. His tone was dull. I hated it.

"No, I'm just seeing what time it is. I'm actually pretty hungry. We should pack up and take a lunch break. Based on what we've worked so far, we could be done by the end of the day tomorrow."

"Really, that long?"

Now it sounded like, instead of having all the time in the world to work on this project, he already wanted out. To be done with me.

Fidgeting with my hands, my lack of sustenance was catching up with me, and my patience wore out. "We can try to cram it all if you need to," I offered briskly.

"I'm game, whatever you want."

Ha. You don't mean that.

I liked everything I was learning about the real Kevin, but the trouble was, if he didn't want to be that person with me, I couldn't force him. I'd have to settle for whatever he gave me. Best I could do was attempt to mirror his platonic manners and nurture a simple friendship — and that was treading optimistically. More and more, the prickles of his unfriendliness were returning.

"I know we haven't been the fastest hands in the west, but it's been fun, right?"

"Yeah."

Losing that optimism by the second, I gave up and closed my book. If he wanted to push me away so soon after bringing me in, fine. A month ago, I thought nothing of him at all. I could stand to just be his lab partner, if that's the way he wanted it. But I wasn't going to starve and screw up the rest of my day for him. We could still get the project done on time, even if I stopped for a break. "Alright, I'm gonna head out for lunch."

"Okay."

"I'll probably just run down to Whataburger. You're welcome

to come if you'd like. We can even drive separately." I pause. "Or I can give you a ride."

"Yeah, that'll work."

"Cool. Let's go, then." I probably bristled more than I should have, but it was hard not to. Wherever our two steps forward had gone, I didn't know.

When we got to my car, Kevin was quiet and I didn't know what to say, so I asked him to pick a radio station as we left the lot. He leaned over and, from the corner of my eye, I could see him struggle with it. My car had a touch-screen display, and I figured he must not be used to it.

Pushing at the screen, something loud and ridiculous blasted through the speakers. Both of us groaned at the audible assault, and when he thought he was turning down the volume, he actually reduced the air conditioning.

"Why is your smart car making me feel so dumb?" he shouted.

Laughing, I turned the volume down from the steering wheel, and Kevin was able to reverse his damage on the AC touch dial, restoring the pleasant flow of air.

"Do you maybe just have some CDs somewhere?"

"What's a CD?" I asked.

"What?! You serious?"

"No, not at all. Look in there." I laughed, nodding toward the glove box. My mind thought nothing of it as my eyes remained fixed on the road.

With a curious tone, Kevin said, "Whoa. This certainly doesn't look like T. Swift's Greatest Hits."

"That's because I don't listen to —" My smile disappeared as I glanced over and saw the zippered pouch sitting open in his lap. His hands were drawn up like he was afraid to touch it. There were no CDs in that pouch, but there were needles and vials of clear liquid.

"Don't touch that. Put it back, please. Right now!"

"Okay, okay. My bad." Kevin folded up the pouch and zipped it shut, gently returning it to where he found it. He shut the glove box, not even bothering to reach for the actual CD case, which I caught a glimpse of deeper in. "I'm sorry. It's cool, though. I saw nothing."

My face scrunching, I kept my eyes forward. "What do you think that is?"

"I don't know. I have no opinion. You don't gotta worry about me telling anyone anything."

Really? That's what he thought? "Don't be ridiculous, Kevin. Do I look like a druggie to you?"

"No, you don't *look* like a druggie. But you wouldn't be the first person I've seen hide it super well, believe me."

"Well, I don't do drugs, okay?" I rolled my tightened shoulders and let a harsh breath go. I hated this part of getting to know someone; that's why I got really good at avoiding it. Now, he would give me that same look others did when they found out — that disgusting look of pity they didn't even know they were giving. I was decent at managing my disease, but others' reactions to it were not so simple. Not even my closest friends knew I was a Type 1. "That's my insulin."

"Oh."

"Oh?" I took quick peeks at his face, but he remained emotionless, staring out at the road ahead.

"So, you're diabetic."

It was a statement, not a question, and he offered nothing further. Not knowing what to make of it, I finally agreed with his silence and drove the rest of the way without another word.

There was a decent lunch rush at Whataburger, but after we ordered, we lucked out with a table on the deck upstairs. When we sat down, I placed my plastic order number tent in front of me and opened my tote in my lap. With no reason to hide it now, I withdrew my glucose monitor and pricked the side of my left middle finger, watching the number generate. When it told me my number, I prepared a fresh syringe to inject what I needed to bolus my blood sugar. All the while, I could feel Kevin watching, but he gave me the courtesy of his silence.

Afterward, I sighed and took in the scene around me. The downtown waterfront view was awesome from here. Feeling the salty sea breeze and cradling warmth of the sun from our slice of shade put me in the best mood. "I love it up here." I looked to Kevin, wondering what he was thinking as he, too, looked out there. "I'm sorry I snapped at you," I said sheepishly.

He stretched his arms out over the table. "It's okay. I should've just put it away without making jokes."

"So you could go on thinking I shoot up? Listen, this is on me. I shouldn't have freaked out." I sighed. "The thing is, I go to a lot of trouble to hide it from everyone. You're the first person to just find out."

"Really? Why hide it?"

"It's embarrassing. People don't understand it, and their reactions make me uncomfortable."

"How so?"

"Usually by asking questions," I said with a smile.

"Oh, sorry."

"Don't be. It actually isn't bothering me to talk to you about it." I leaned into the ease I now felt and kept going. "Most people usually fall into one of three categories. Either they think having diabetes means I'm basically dying, or it's my fault even though neither type 1 nor type 2 are self-inflicted, or they have so much sympathy they don't know how to respond at all. It gets real awkward real fast."

"Wow."

I nodded. "So, you see why it's a lot easier just to keep it to myself."

"Don't your friends know?"

"Nope. Not even Sammy."

"Dang," he said. For a moment, when our eyes met, all we did was stare. The more I searched his countenance, the more I was convinced he didn't show pity.

He tipped his head and eyed the chair beside me, where I'd put my tote and insulin bag to rest. "What was that earlier? Is that part of it?"

"Yeah. I tested my blood sugar and took insulin. It's just something I have to do before meals. Or workouts. Or if I'm sick. Plus, every morning…" I trailed off when an employee in orange and white stripes came by with our food. I hadn't meant to ramble, but it was hard to stop once I started. Telling Kevin about my diabetes was a strange sort of liberation, and then doing a whole bolus in front of him was quite another. But yet again, I wish I knew what he was thinking.

"How often do you have to do that?" Kevin asked before taking a bite of his number 5; all the way.

"Every day, but if I'm careful, I usually only need 2-3 doses of insulin."

"How do you know if you need any?"

"I always do since my body can't make its own. But my glucose monitor will tell me if I need more or less, plus, I can physically feel it. If I were to run out or just neglect to do this for too long, I would die. It's important, but by now, it's pretty second nature to me. It's not something I'm ever going to enjoy having to do. I just accept it."

"Does it hurt?"

I breathed deep, pulling apart my onion rings and taking small bites. "When I was little, I thought it did, but you get used to it real fast. I'm kinda numb to it now."

He made a sound of empathy as he nodded. Then, his face crinkled in confusion. "What about the candies in your backpack? Isn't sugar bad for you?"

"That's gotta be the number one misconception about type 1, ever." I chuckled, taking a swig of my lemonade sweet tea. *At least, he doesn't think I'm dying.* "I have candy and juice boxes everywhere I go, just in case my blood sugar drops in a bad way. We absolutely can and need to have sugar. It's just that our bodies cannot process it the way yours does. The way it's supposed to. Ergo, the injections. As long as I have insulin, I can eat whatever I want just like everybody else."

About an hour later, we were back at the library. From there, it didn't take us long at all to finish putting together our final presentation board. We worked with strong focus, barely stopping for breaks or chatting, each of us seeming to strive for something neither of us spoke about. Although there had been some bouts of lightheartedness, already things felt different. The illusion I'd briefly allowed myself to believe in seemed to have never existed.

Back at home, I was wasting away in my discontent. I had to shove my phone away in order to curb the letdown when I heard nothing from Kevin after parting ways. Today's visit had been a lot of up and down emotionally, and I didn't know what I needed to even myself out. I wanted to talk to him more, but I also wanted to be okay with letting it all go.

If only candy and juice could do for my feelings what they did for my blood sugar. I was tired of feeling low.

SARAH

10

For matters of the heart, I had God instead of candy. Turning to Him, I went to prayer, asking God for the wisdom I lacked in dealing with Kevin. Any assistance from above would be fuel in my arsenal since this wasn't a typical situation for me.

Sometime after my conversation with God, I fell asleep. My phone rang, waking me abruptly. I was already in a funk when I fumbled to answer. I must not have effectively calculated my carb ratio at lunch earlier, because my blood sugar felt like it was running high.

"Hello?"

"Hey, girl, hey," Jenna said, her upbeat voice carrying through the receiver like a bullhorn. "How's it going?"

"Fine," I yawned. "I fell asleep."

"Oh, boring. I wanted to stop by and see you earlier, but you didn't answer when I called. It feels like it's been ages. I thought we were going to make plans this weekend, but I didn't hear from you."

"I'm so sorry, Jenna, I completely forgot. I had a biology project due."

"Ah, right. I heard something about that."

I'll bet you did... From Sammy and her big mouth, no doubt.

I was reminded again about how things could've been different. If Jenna had taken AP Bio with us, then I would've had my choice of lab partner on that first day. I could have avoided the Kevin roller-coaster, remaining unaware of his eccentricities.

The same also went for his pleasant, more positive traits, too. If I didn't know the good and bad about him, I wouldn't know anything. And I didn't like that thought one bit.

"I've been busy, I'm sorry. We'll do something this week, okay?"

"Sounds good. Dan and I were hoping to introduce you to a friend of his from the team. In fact, Dan's having a party on Friday. I know it's not your scene, but you totally have to come. It'll be the perfect opportunity to get to know him."

Jenna Rodriguez, the relentless matchmaker, was at it again. She and Daniel Schellers had been dating since the beginning of junior year. Jenna's happiness with Dan meant she was utterly convinced her friends needed to find someone to be happy with, too. Starting with me, apparently. This was not Jenna's first attempt.

As I groaned in protest, Jenna was quick to dispute it. "Just hear me out first…"

Today's Bachelor of the Month was Jared Tomlin, running back for the varsity football team and one of Dan's *"sweetest"* friends. "I really think you'll like him," she said, her voice dripping with dreamy hopefulness.

There was no point in beating around the bush. "I'm aware of who he is. I'm not interested."

"Sarah, why do you always shut everyone down so fast like

that? You haven't gotten to know him, so you have no idea if you're interested."

"I know I'm not interested in a boyfriend."

"Now, I know that's not true," Jenna argued.

"What makes you think so?"

"Because hopeless romantics aren't meant to be alone. And if you would stop fighting me at every turn, I think I could help you find someone awesome."

But I already found someone awesome. "I'm just not looking for anybody, Jenna."

"Oh, whatever. Don't you want someone to cuddle with on the couch, steal popcorn from at the drive-in, and smooch every once in a while? I mean, dang, are you even human?"

Yes. Yes. Also, yes. And — yes, last I checked. I answered each of Jenna's questions in my mind and realized my zealous friend was right. "You never give up, do you?"

"I want to see you happy, girl."

"I know you do, and you know I love you, right?"

"Right. Naturally. Buuut…?"

"But I don't want to be set up. I'm not interested in getting involved with anyone right now."

She sighed into the phone. "Does this have anything to do with that Kevin guy?"

"Why would you think that?"

"You've been spending a lot of time with him outside school lately. I don't know. Maybe you're not just studying, wink-wink."

"You know I don't do any 'wink-wink' with anyone, Jenna."

"Oh, come on. You know what I mean. Are you into the guy or not?"

Thou shalt not lie. But how about a partial truth? "I don't exactly know right now."

"Seriously?"

"Seriously, *what?*" I snapped.

"Nothing, I just didn't think… Never mind. Alright then, what about this? While you're deciding if you like Kevin or not, how about you consider Jared, too? At least let me give him your number. That way you can get a feel for him yourself. If you still don't like him or don't want to pursue anything, I promise I'll leave it alone. Deal?"

"Fine. Deal." Whatever it took to get Jenna to stop practicing her Cupid skills on me.

Admittedly, despite my resistance to her efforts, Jenna had a point or two or three. I *wanted* somebody, as well as all those wonderful things Jenna brought up. But I wanted it with the right guy, and the only matchmaker I trusted with my heart was God.

God, please give me strength and guidance.

Here's the thing. I wasn't mad at Kevin for accidentally finding my insulin, nor had I taken any issue with his questioning me about it afterward. At first, I wasn't thrilled by it, but he accepted it with such respect and grace that I actually felt relieved to talk to somebody other than my parents or endocrinologist about it. In fact, I wished he'd asked more. Since Pandora's Box was already wide open, he might as well have gotten his curiosity out, but the dialogue had stopped at the restaurant. Eventually, he'd withdrawn again, giving me every reason to think, if I ever had a shot with him, it had come and gone. It drove me nuts that I couldn't figure out what had gone so wrong so fast.

What bothered me the most was that I couldn't deny my feelings for him, and those feelings were overwhelming my rationality.

KEVIN

11

When I got to class on Tuesday, Sarah was already seated. Her attention was split between her phone and her two friends at the table in front of us… The two chatty girls who I came to know as Samantha Ballard and Birdie Jo MacLean. When they weren't turned around talking, they weren't too bad.

As I approached our table, her eyes remained glued to her phone. Her cheeks lit up and something in me came to a screeching halt. What, or who, could she be interacting with on her phone that caused that reaction?

"Hey," I mumbled as I sat down.

"Hi," came Sarah's simple reply.

Mr. Hallinger caught everyone's attention with his announcements and promptly called people up for presentations. He loved sitting in the very back row, waiting for someone to mumble, just so he could constructively yell out so-called encouragement like, "FROM THE TOP! LOUDER!"

Mr. Hallinger felt like he was building character and improving valuable speaking skills, but to the class, he was downright evil. He didn't bother me personally, because his rules were easy enough for me to follow, but I could see how his methods rubbed some the wrong way.

It completely panicked me when Sarah volunteered us to go first. It wasn't that I hated public speaking, it was that… No, yeah. It was that. I hated public speaking. Getting up in front of people, even if I knew everyone here by name and face, was not my jam.

As agreed, Sarah took the lead and explained our research and findings while I detailed the display itself. Nervously, I stumbled over a couple of words and shifted on my feet. My little flubs must not have been too bad because, in the end, Sarah and I both got an A. Hallinger clapped with the rest of the class and nodded his approval as we made our way back to our table.

My last, first important grade of the semester was safe in the books. My step on the road to freedom had begun successfully, even if it had been an emotionally taxing one.

Forty long minutes later, after all the other groups presented, I was ready to jet. Sarah's phone went off the entire time, and here and there, she'd peek at it and respond. Right at the end, before the bell rang, I heard it vibrate again. As she brought it out of her pocket to read, I couldn't stop myself from sneaking a glance at her screen. Someone named Jared was texting her.

Who the heck was Jared?

Annoyed that I was annoyed, I closed my sketchpad and put it away. Somewhere deep down, I'd been hoping, if I had it out, I could lure her into conversation. It wasn't the first time I'd taken a gamble recently and lost.

After all our time together over the last few days, I hadn't heard from Sarah at all. Although I'd told myself to ignore her if I did, I still craved her attention. After seeing that text come in on her phone, I now wondered if her lack of communication had anything to do with Jared. And that idea did not sit well with me at all.

I redirected myself as I looked at the clock. Only minutes to go before this class ended and I could head to the next one. There was a need for space and clarity. Somehow, I had to do a better job of keeping her out of my head. Finishing school was all that should matter.

When the bell rang, Sarah headed out faster than anyone else, waving to her friends and inciting my jealous brain in the process. I could only imagine where she was off to so quickly, and as much as I wanted to follow her and find out, I suspected whatever I saw would only grate me more. To spare myself any assumed trouble, I took my time leaving.

I wasn't even trying to listen when I heard "Hey, Sarah," come from outside the room. And then, looking up, I watched some guy walk up and put his arm around her.

"Hey, Jared," Sarah's words answered faintly, her voice almost masked by the other sounds in the hall before they disappeared from view.

Instantly triggered, I overrode self-restraint and got up. Stepping off to the side, I rested against a row of lockers, out of the way of the masses. Sarah and Jared were standing by the stairwell talking, his big ape arm still draped over her shoulders.

I stared intently, silently willing her to ditch her company. She didn't so much as glance my way. Instead, she gave her new friend that amazing smile of hers. The same smile that made me feel like I never had before.

They were talking about his friend's upcoming party, apparently.

"So, what do you say? You wanna go to the party with me Friday night?" he asked her.

She didn't think about it for long. "Sure, Jared. It's a date."

Jared used his free hand to reach up and tuck fallen hair behind Sarah's ear. My stomach turned and my blood boiled as visions of smashing Jared's face came to mind. The world around me grew very dark, and all at once, I knew only one truth: Even if I was into her before, I had missed my chance.

KEVIN

12

I SPENT THE ENTIRE DAY EAGER TO GO HOME, NEEDING TO PUT AS many miles between myself and temptation as I could. But once I got there, I found no respite.

Craig continued giving me crap about the shed, and now the busted window *on* the shed, which resulted in yet another fight about money.

Or rather, how much of it Craig could squeeze out of me this time.

"Things have got to change around here. My good will ain't free no more. It's time for you to get a job and start paying your keep."

"I already have a job," I reminded Craig. For the last two years, I'd been working for Tanner Automotive, the local body shop. In addition to his pay for general labor, I could keep any tips I earned, and Blake Tanner let me take leftover parts I could use for my truck for free. Secretly, I had banked sizable savings. One that I vowed to never let my mom or Craig find out about.

"That dinky little thing don't pay for nothing. It's time to forget about Tanner and school and get a real job. I think maybe

I'll talk to Reg and get you on at the plant where I can keep an eye on you myself."

"I'm not quitting school or my job. I'll replace the window myself so you don't have to worry about it."

"Ha. We'll just see about all that."

I stole a glance at my mom who stood silently slumped over a pan of burnt eggs, then left without another word. I had a shift at Tanners — and apparently a window to buy.

When I got to work, Russell was already there tinkering with some rich dude's classic Porsche. A really sweet, fire-engine red one.

Russell Grandy and I had been friends since the fourth grade. He taught me how easy it was to stay loyal to someone who stayed loyal to me. Russ was the type of person who always had my back, even if the guy couldn't have his own. His home life was ten thousand times better than mine, but for whatever reason, he was happier being in trouble. And for him, school was no exception.

Once I understood that partying and cutting class would trap me, I changed my thinking right away.

We didn't have any classes together now, and work was most of the hanging out we did, but we stayed relatively close. Of all the old crew, Russell was the only one I talked to anymore at all.

I shared the latest news. "Craig wants me to quit work and school so I can make him more money."

Russell made a sound of disgust and threw a small cloth to the ground. It landed beside our feet with a heavy plop. "That guy is a piece. What are you gonna do?"

I finished tightening a bolt under the hood of the little red car. "Replace that stupid window he broke and keep doing what I'm doing."

"Yeah, bro. I don't know how you put up with him. Tell me again why you don't just move out?"

"I need the scholarship more than I need money. I can deal until then."

Russell shook his head in sympathy. "You should make those extra deliveries I was telling you about. There's plenty of money to go around there. You could easily leave without having to work too hard, with no time lost for studying or whatever."

I stood up straight over the hood and rolled my shoulders. Russell had tried to recruit me before, but I had no interest in Tanner's illegal car part trade. "Thanks, man, but I'm still not interested."

"I don't get why not. It's easy money. It would literally solve all your problems. You should at least consider it."

"Maybe," I lied. Not wanting to talk about it anymore, I leaned back over the engine. Russell seemed satisfied to let it go, and for a few minutes, we worked in silence.

"Oh, hey, did you hear about Dan Schellers' party?" Russell later asked.

Wanting to talk about that even less, I inwardly cringed. "Yep."

"You gonna go? I was thinking about it. It's not our usual people, but you know what, a party is a party."

"Hadn't planned on it."

"Well, you should consider going. More than college or money, you need a solid night out. How long has it been?"

Honestly, I couldn't even remember. Back in the day, I really enjoyed a good time. I could put a few back all weekend and still be at school on time come Monday… until my habits made a liar out of me. Eventually, drinking became less fun and started reminding me of home, to the point where even thinking about alcohol made me feel sick. Talk about a sobering realization.

But how nice it sounded to step back into the comforting arms of drunken oblivion again. Or I could at least cozy up to her kid sister and get a nice buzz. As long as I didn't overdo it, maybe a night to take the edge off was exactly what I needed to further fortify myself against Craig.

And Sarah.

Earlier in the hall at school, Sarah agreed to attend the party with Jared, yes, but that didn't mean I would run into her.

Before I could think better of it, I replied, "Let's do it."

SARAH

13

THE NIGHT OF THE PARTY, SAMMY, JENNA, BIRDIE, AND I SPENT the evening getting ready at Birdie Jo's house. It was finally time for me to forget about everything else for a while and give a date with Jared a fair try.

My friends and I were chatting in the mirror while applying our makeup. My hazel eyes took on a green hue with light brown liner, framed by black mascara on my lashes. Besides that, I only opted for a glossy ChapStick and a dab of perfume on my wrists and neck. Due to equal parts laziness and modesty, I preferred to keep my face natural.

Jenna gulped down some of her wine cooler and cleared her throat. "So, Sarah… Truth or dare?"

I shook my head. "Nope, that's not happening. Last time you tried to get me to hijack the neighbor's car."

"And it would've worked, too, if not for 'you rotten kids!'" Birdie held her fist out, putting on her best comically villainous impression. We all laughed.

"Come on, live a little. I'll be fair." Sammy's coy smile did little to reassure me, but what did it matter?

"Whatever. You know what? I'll play." Ignoring the racing of my heart and the rattling of my conscience, I snatched the bottle from Jenna's hand and took a swig. The rancid liquid burnt as it went down. Not worth it.

In shock, my friends whooped before Jenna snatched it back.

Birdie leaned in. "Sarah Stevenson, I'm surprised at you. I don't think I've ever seen you drink."

"Will you have to go do a bunch of Hail Marys on Sunday to make up for it?"

"Jenna, I'm not Catholic. But I'm pretty sure that's not how Hail Marys work."

Sammy lightly smacked Jenna's hand. "Wow. What's wrong with you? Zero points for tact."

Jenna's eyes went wide, her hands going up in apology. "That was rude, right? I'm sorry. You know I've never understood your God stuff."

"It's fine. My God and I aren't easily offended." I gave them all a smile of peace. I was used to most people, my friends included, not understanding my stance on most things. Being the most spiritual one among us, I knew to take their inadvertent mockery with a grain of salt. Even Birdie, who had grown up Baptist, would forget her church-roots from time to time. I had faith that, in His own *way*, in His own perfect timing, God was working on each of us.

"But for the record, I'm not really going to drink. I just felt like being a little crazy for a second, and believe me, I'm already over it. That stuff is so nasty." My face matched my feelings, both of which were disgust.

"I'm sorry, anyway." Jenna threw her arms around me. "You still love me, right?"

"Of course I do!"

"And me?!" Birdie chimed in, wanting to be part of the recovery even though she hadn't been part of the offense.

"You know it!" I assured her, too, hugging them both.

"Well, don't leave me out," Sammy said, making a shark with her hands and wiggling into the middle. The group hug concluded when her head collided with Jenna's, and laughter ensued.

"Anyway, y'all, we've got a party to get ready for." Birdie took up the seat at the vanity and twisted a curling iron around her blonde locks. Then, looking at me in the mirror's reflection, Birdie smirked. "Now, how 'bout it, Sarah? Truth or dare?"

Grinning, I rolled my eyes. "Screw it. Dare."

Jenna was all over it. "Heck yes! I dare you to let me pick your outfit for tonight! I'll be totally fair, I promise."

Birdie laughed, and I sighed. "Fine." I would go through with it and hope Jenna truly meant to keep that promise. *Please, don't put me in one of Birdie's old pageant costumes...*

Clapping her hands together with glee, Jenna took off into Birdie's walk-in closet. After a few minutes of oohing, aahing, and snickering, she surprised us all when she came back with a beautiful, black, cocktail-style dress. Nothing too formal or revealing, but just fancy enough to look very much unlike my usual casual style. The arms flowed delicately off the shoulders, and the whole thing shimmered like a New Years Eve party. She also had a pair of black, knee-high boots tucked under her arm. I wouldn't look frilly and frivolous like a Miss America contestant, so I was happy.

Bullet dodged.

"This is it, then. You'll look amazing! Jared will love it, for sure."

Rolling my eyes, I took the ensemble from her. I donned it in the closet and then opened the door wide for the big reveal. I smoothed my hands down the material and twisted this way and that so they could see everything. "Well? Is it okay?"

"More than okay!" Birdie exclaimed. "You can totally keep that dress, Sarah. It's so beautiful on you."

Sammy agreed. "It's not typical Sarah, but I love it."

"You're gonna make Jared one happy dude after just one look," Jenna beamed, and all I could do was smile and nod along. I didn't know what to say. I couldn't voice my true thoughts, because I wasn't sure how to acknowledge them to myself, let alone others.

If Kevin was going to the party tonight, what would *he* think of my outfit?

As we finished getting ready, eventually our game of Truth or Dare circled back to me. This time, I asked Sammy for a truth.

"Loser, taking the easy way out. That's fine. I'll just have to get creative —"

"I got one!" Birdie interjected. "Sarah, what's the deal with you and Kevin Sloan?" She pegged me with her suspicious expression and practically sang her question like we were on a playground at school.

"What?! Kevin Sloan?" Jenna looked from Sammy to me, desperate for an explanation. "Is there a *deal*, Sarah?"

"No!" I felt heaps of traitorous warmth coloring my face. "There is no deal."

"Lies! You're blushing! Why didn't you tell us anything?" When Jenna's attention took hold of something, it wasn't easy for her to let it go.

"I already told you before. There's nothing to tell."

"Hold up. This isn't the first time this has been discussed?" Sammy inquired. ·

"It came up once before, barely. There's really nothing going on. I thought there might've been at one point, but…" I shrugged. "Guess it was a fluke."

"Oh, please," Birdie said incredulously. "That's it? I've seen the way you look at him. He looks at you the same way, you know."

"Really?" I couldn't help my question as I sat on the edge of the bed with the others. Had Birdie meant it? Kevin had a special way he looked at me?

Jenna pointed, latching onto my momentary weakness. "So, it's true!"

"See? You do like him," said Birdie, now sounding more sure than ever. "That's okay. Whoever you like is totally your choice. We just wanna hear all about it."

"Look, guys, you can ask all you want, but there's nothing between me and Kevin. There was a time when I thought he liked me, and fine, maybe I did like him a little bit. But there's *nothing else* to it." I got up from the bed and grabbed Birdie's brush and got aggressive with my hair. "Besides, I'm going out with Jared tonight, remember, Jenna?" I tried the words on, like the outfit I was told to wear, and they just weren't me. I felt nothing special for Jared. There were no butterflies or eagles in my stomach, making me both excited and scared to see him. There wasn't even a spark of true interest. Jared was probably a great guy, but he wasn't the guy for me.

The more I thought about it, the more the idea of me and him together protested like hot lava in the pit of my stomach.

Or maybe that was the alcohol.

Not able to read the room, Jenna pressed on with the inquiry. "Yeah, hold on. So, you *did* actually like Kevin? Why?"

I was at a loss for words as my cheeks heated to a new shade of pink. Explaining it all now sounded so cheap since I'd already given up on the idea of me and Kevin.

Hadn't I?

"Please, let's just forget it," I beseeched.

Jenna gasped, still on fire with intrigue. "What if Kevin goes to the party and sees you with Jared? Think he'll, like, rage with jealousy?"

"Better not. He had his chance." I doubted he would be there, anyway. He'd said parties weren't really his thing anymore. That meant I could relax and focus on getting to know Jared fair and square, with no distractions from Kevin.

Before leaving, I checked myself one last time in the mirror, straightened my dress, and tried hard to console myself. *Kevin missed out.*

SARAH

14

Dan's party was in full swing when we got there. Music poured out of every room and people were all over the place. Most were standing around or sitting down chatting, all with various drinks or snacks in hand. Some were dancing while a select few were making out for all the world to see.

Earlier, Jenna left Birdie's before the rest of us in order to meet up with Dan before things got started. When she saw us arrive, she ran up squealing, already tipsy. She had about half a dozen fresh hickeys on her neck.

"Jeez, Jenna, did he even come up for air?" Sammy teased, making all of us laugh. She had a knack for voicing the stuff that everyone else thought, but was too shy to say. Sammy was not shy *at all*. It was one of the many reasons we loved her.

I attempted to not stare at the bruise-like kisses on my friend's neck. I'd never let a guy Hoover me like that. It was far too intimate. Between Dan's partygoers and my own friends, I couldn't believe how little desire for privacy so many had. Jenna would say that was just me being jealous, but I would say she was reaching. Even if I had a boyfriend of my own, we wouldn't be doing *that*.

Dan soon came around the corner with Jared beside him. Jared's smile grew wide when he saw me. A glint bounced off his eyes from the party lights.

"Ladies, you all remember Jared, offensive-champion," Dan announced.

"We sure do," said Jenna. "Don't we, Sarah?"

"Yep. Hey, Jared." There he was, with all his frat-boy charms. He had the looks, the build, and the athleticism, but I just couldn't find it in me to care. Not the way he seemed to want.

"Hey, Sarah." He looked me over, his brows raising. "Wow, that dress is killer on you."

"Don't you love it?" Jenna encouraged. I wish I could've elbowed her then and there.

"Definitely," Jared confirmed without hesitation, his eyes locking on mine. I thanked him, more out of embarrassment than flattery, and wondered how the fake smile plastered on my face was doing.

Jared stepped closer to me. "Do you want to go sit down and talk?"

"Sure." After all, I was there to move on, right? Time to see what face-to-face conversation with this guy was like.

Weaving through the masses, Jared led us to a sitting room elegantly decorated in a masculine Victorian style. The music was softer in here, and only a few others loitered around us, playing with the pool table beside a wet bar at the other end of the room.

"Can I get you something to drink?"

I hesitated a moment.

"They have a tap if you want that. Shots of just about anything. Or even Sprite or water. Ladies' choice."

"Sprite sounds good."

"You sure? I can probably make that extra special for you." Jared winked, and I smiled at his silliness.

Jared disappeared down the hall to the kitchen, and I looked around, curious about Dan's parents' old-fashioned taste, and whether the furniture pieces were authentic antiques. If the lack of comfort provided an accurate guess, I would say they were.

Feeling too warm, I peeled off my outer layer and re-shouldered my purse. I could see Birdie and Sammy across the way, chatting with a couple of guys, some plates of finger food in hand. Sighing, accountability berated me. I probably should have skipped those drinks back at Birdie's, especially since I hadn't eaten.

No time like the present.

On my way to the bathroom to address my blood sugar, I bumped into Jared. With two drinks in tow, he just barely avoided spilling them.

"Oh, hey!" he said, smiling. "Couldn't stand to be away from me, huh?"

Perspiration broke out on my neck, and I played it off by fanning myself. "I was just going to fix my makeup." Fibbing like that, I felt like a sweaty deer in headlights.

"Take it from me, it all looks great. You don't need to change a thing." He handed me a red plastic cup, sloshing around with blue, fizzy bubbles. "One Sprite *a la* Jared. From what I just heard around the water hole, you'll really like this."

Inspecting it, I wasn't so sure. "Why is it blue?"

"Isn't that cool? Some little coloring tablet the guys in the kitchen were passing around. Apparently, there are all kinds of colors. I picked blue to make it look like an ocean for you."

It had one of those cute little cocktail umbrellas in it and two grapes skewered by a tiny sword. The blue of the liquid made the whole thing appear tropical and inviting. "How cute is that? I almost don't want to drink it." The sweet drink would give me a temporary boost in blood sugar, at least, but it was no substitute for a proper meal. I collected the cup, ready to accept a cool-down.

"Don't worry, me hearty, there's more where that came from." Jared put his arm around my back and we returned to the sitting room.

It wasn't long before my drink was gone. We were prattling on, not talking about anything substantial. Still, I laughed more than I'd expected to, and Jared really seemed interested in me. He remained respectful, engaging, and offered me a refill when he noticed my empty cup. I snatched the mini sword as Jared took the cup from my hands and savored the grapes one by one. *So tasty,* I revered, hoping there'd be more.

As I sat alone, I thought, maybe I *could* like Jared. Trying to was surprisingly fun.

Kevin didn't like me, but Jared did. Jared had given me adorable little pirate-sodas with snacks in them and told me again how much he liked my dress. He was present and open with me, and that alone counted for *something*. He asked about my classes and my interests beyond high school, and I could tell he cared about my answers. I really liked his way of telling stories, which made everything sound ten times better than it probably was. Even his tales of football sounded exciting. That particularly impressed me, considering how little I cared for sports.

Jared came back with more drinks. This time, there was not one, but *two* tiny swords stuffed with fruit inside my cup.

"Thank you!" I said, eagerly wiggling my fingers out to take it.

He laughed gingerly as our talk picked up where it left off, and inch by inch, he scooted closer. When our thighs were touching, he reached out and put his hand over mine. The gesture surprised me, but my shoulders fell in quick disappointment when there was no jolt of electricity.

Unlike when I'd touched he-who-shall-not-be-named.

A.K.A. Mr. Broody.

A.K.A. Kevin-freaking-Sloan!

Oh, interesting and beautiful Kevin. In his plain, gray tee with silky, dark hair. With all his scars and amazing talents and his irresistible, crooked smile that I hardly ever got to see. With his soft inside and hardened exterior, there was more to him than what he projected in order to keep people away. I knew, because I'd seen it.

That's what I want.

Jared was nice and even nicer to look at, no doubt about it, but he just wouldn't do.

My mind kept bringing up Kevin, and so vividly, too. If I didn't know it was all in my head, I could've sworn he was standing outside the room watching me. He couldn't possibly be there, though, because it made me feel warm and tingly all over when he was near.

Actually, I *did* feel warm and tingly. *Odd.*

Jared squeezed my hand. "Sarah?"

I looked up at him, feeling a little swimmy in the head. "Hm?"

"I'm really into you."

"I know," came the words, so flippantly from my mouth.

Shock momentarily coated his features before he smiled. "And how do you feel?"

I thought about it for a moment, or at least I tried to. Pleasant thoughts began slipping away as I realized just how poorly I felt. I tore my hand out from underneath his, shaking, and covered my pounding heart. "Actually, not that good."

His smile faded, and his deep blue eyes turned sad under his blonde spikes. "Oh. You don't like me?"

Panic stretched its ugly, sharp fingers around my heart and squeezed. Earlier, I'd tried to fix my glucose but had gotten side-tracked. But why in the world was I suddenly feeling *this* badly? There was a strong tremor in my hands, and my heart pounded too hard in my chest. In my head, thoughts were mixing up into mush.

Is this my blood sugar or something else?

On impulse, I sniffed my drink, a little too late to be asking. "Jared, be honest with me. Was there any alcohol in these?"

Jared went straight as a board, pulling slightly away. "Well, yeah. I thought you knew that."

That accounted for some of the issue, but not all. I'd had blood sugar dips and spikes before, some pretty bad when I was first figuring it all out. Whatever this was, it felt a lot worse. "Why did you give me alcohol, Jared? There's a reason I didn't ask for any!"

He recoiled and blinked in surprise. "I told you I was going to do something special to it up front. I thought you knew what that meant!"

Realization dawned, falling like a cluster of cement into my gut. He had said something funny about preparing the drinks earlier, but I'd assumed he was just trying to make me laugh.

"What about those colored tablet things? Do you know what they actually were? Did you see any packaging?"

Jared's jaw clenched, and he met my eyes sympathetically. "No, not really."

My stomach bottomed out. "What do you mean *not really*?!"

"I thought it was just food coloring, I swear, but I'm not a hundred percent sure. I had them in my drinks, too, and I hardly feel a thing."

I felt like the world's biggest idiot. A wave of nausea and shame overcame me simultaneously, and I desperately wanted to run away. I couldn't remember a time I'd ever let myself get so careless. If this was the kind of thing they did at these parties, it's no wonder I'd always avoided them before. There was no way to know how I would react to an unknown substance I'd never had, so I wasn't sure how to correct it. And the harder I mentally groped for a solution, the worse I felt.

"I have to go." My emotions were spiraling. Blood drained from my face as I stood up on shaky legs. If I could get to my friends, one of them could take me home.

"I'm so sorry, Sarah. I just thought you would like it. If I'd known, I never would have..." He scowled at himself and shook his head. "Forget it. This is my fault. What can I do?" he asked, cupping my arm at the elbow.

Over Jared's shoulder, Kevin appeared. I was almost-kind-of-sure of it this time. I blinked, trying to see if my mind had made him up. Was he real or was he another side effect of Jared's undisclosed concoction? "Kevin?"

His focus was intense, his hand outstretched. "Let's go, Sarah," he said, very much real.

Sliding away from Jared, I wobbled. "What are you doing?" I

whispered, though my words sounded much louder when they hit my ears.

"Come on," Kevin said sternly. He was mad? I hesitated for only a second before reaching out for him, but Jared forcibly moved past me and got into Kevin's face.

"What do you think you're doing?" Jared demanded.

"We're leaving."

"She's not feeling okay. She shouldn't go anywhere," Jared insisted, staring Kevin down.

Kevin eyed him, his jaw ticking. "What did you have to do with that?"

Jared's brow rumpled in contempt. "You serious? Who do you think you are, dude?"

"Forget it. We're out." Bypassing Jared's anger, Kevin turned with me in hand and we started to walk away.

With Kevin's back turned, Jared shoved Kevin's shoulder, causing him to stumble forward. He caught himself on a wall, losing his grip on me in the process. Luckily, that actually kept me from falling flat on my face. I recovered, leaning on the edge of the couch, not feeling okay *indeed*, and I could see that Kevin's resolve to leave was quickly deteriorating.

"I'm talking to you!" Jared's loud voice drew in a handful of people who wanted to watch the fray. Staring each other down, Kevin and Jared squared off like two angry bulls.

"Guys, don't." My plea came out weak. Exasperated, I could no longer summon any power to put behind my voice.

Jared's fist came for Kevin and he took the hit to his jaw. His head snapped to the side, but he didn't appear concerned.

Wavering on my feet, I moved behind Kevin, linking my fingers through his in a silent plea for peace. "You're right, Kevin. Let's go," I said, my shaking breath hitting his ear.

"Stay away from her," was his final command to Jared.

Tugging my hand, Kevin led us away, breezing past the small sea of onlookers. He didn't stop until we burst out through the back door. Then, without missing a beat, he backed me against the side of the house and ran his fingers through my hair, cradling the side of my head. Before I could comprehend his closeness, his mouth was on mine. The fire that had slowly been brewing from the moment we first met grew brighter and higher, stoked by his kiss.

Comprehension was slipping away fast. My head was so heavy with a cloudiness that filled my skull and pressed at the edges. My limbs felt weaker by the second.

The drinks. Jared. A fight. The wonderful blaze of Kevin's kiss… It was all quickly falling victim to my total system shutdown. Kevin's heat was all over me, yet I'd never felt so cold.

God, help me!

KEVIN

15

THE DEEPER SARAH AND I KISSED, THE MORE SHE CONFORMED TO my touch. When she suddenly went slack against me, I stiffened, pulling away.

"What is it?" Her head lulled down and her lips moved with no sound. I steadied her in my arms, dread coursing through me. "Sarah?"

Slowly, her eyes fluttered open. "Not soda. Something… Jared." Sarah forced out her words and then, right in front of my eyes, her consciousness slipped. I held her as she sagged to the ground.

What exactly did Jared do?!

"No, no, no! Sarah, please." Jared put something in Sarah's drink?

I'll kill him.

Trying to cradle her gently in my arms, I unsuccessfully groped for my phone in my front right pocket. I was hardly aware of it when Samantha burst through the door.

"What is all the yelling — Sarah? What did you do to her?!"

She punched my shoulder. The action jarred me, and while I was able to keep a steady hold on Sarah, I lost my balance and fell from haunches to rear.

"Back off! I'm trying to help her!"

"Tell me what's going on right now, Kevin, or I swear!" Samantha angrily demanded to know.

"She passed out trying to tell me something. I think she was drugged. I need you to call 911."

The color drained from Samantha's cheeks, and her eyes glossed over. "Oh, my God…"

I didn't know what else I could do for Sarah like this, and I worried I would hurt her further if I moved. Samantha herself seemed frozen in place. "Call 911, *now!*"

Wincing under the sound of my voice, she turned and ran back inside. Not long after, a handful of people came pouring out to see what was going on. Ignoring them, I wiped the cold sweat from Sarah's forehead and cupped her cheek, desperately willing her to wake up. She didn't stir at all. Seeing her like that broke the heaving thing inside my chest, taking it to bits one piece at a time.

I shouldn't have pushed her away. I could have spared her from this.

My adrenaline plateaued and panic gripped me, all the while uncertainty wreaked havoc on my heart. Repeatedly calling her name did nothing. Patting her chilled cheeks did nothing. I was too scared to shake her, or even to move. All I could do was wait. Even with all the practice I'd had, what with all my endured misery through the years, I had never felt *this* helpless before in my life.

The hideous feeling bubbling up inside me was familiar, threatening my cognizance. Every fiber of my being required I ensure her safety, even if I didn't know what "safe" meant right then. I had to try.

When I heard the ambulance sirens in the distance, I could have wept with gratitude. I had to get her to them. Fast.

Pushing to my feet with Sarah in my arms, I saw Samantha and the swarm of stunned and curious eyes gather around me. Her friends flanked her sides, their faces all wet and swollen from worried tears.

"Don't cry. Sarah's going to be fine," I barked at them, hoping that just saying it would make it true.

On my way through the house, I saw Jared. My eyes narrowed on him, furious that he might have caused this. Jared looked away and I instantly knew I'd do something about him later. As soon as I knew Sarah was really okay and I had the whole story, Jared would pay *oh, so dearly* for this.

"There you are," came Russell's voice as he pushed his way over. "Whoa, she doesn't look good at all. You okay, man? What happened? Everyone heard those sirens and half the party started bailing."

"She's *fine!* The ambulance is for her. Just get everyone out of my way."

"Sure thing, man. I've got this." Russell ran ahead and shouted for everyone to move. It felt surreal to push through the parted crowd, protecting Sarah in my arms as if escaping from a fire.

The sirens were loud until the ambulance was finally out front, a firetruck pulling up behind it. I had a hard time keeping my composure as the EMTs arrived with a gurney and took her away from me. They placed her on the gurney and started their assessments, simultaneously hooking her up to tubes.

While everyone else, Russell included, cut ties and took off,

Sarah's friends hung back. They all shared looks of frightened concern.

A tall, slender guy with a clean-shaven face walked over. "Can you tell us what happened?" he asked the small lot of us.

Stepping forward, I said, "I think something was put into her drink. She fainted before she could really say anything. She's diabetic, too, so I don't know if maybe that had something to do with it."

I was crumbling quickly, nearing a breaking point. I shoved my hands in my hair and tried to calm myself down. The paramedic came forward and put his hands on my shoulders, talking to me in an even tone. "What's your name?"

"Kevin."

"Kevin, I can see you care a great deal, and I'm sure you've done your best here. I know this is scary, but you're doing great being strong for your friend. Now, is there anything else you can tell me? Did she have any alcohol tonight?"

After sharing a glance with the others, Sammy nodded shamefully.

"Did you see her eat anything since then?" we were asked.

"I don't think so," Birdie Jo said.

"I don't know, either," I added. "I wasn't with her the entire night." *But I should've been.*

"We didn't know she has diabetes," Birdie blurted out, eyes full to the brim with tears.

It hit me then that I'd forgotten what Sarah had told me. Not even her friends knew. I felt bad about how she might feel once she discovered her secret was out, but there was no way to take it back. If she was upset about it later, at least she was around to be upset.

From the corner of my eye, I saw Jared approach. "What are you doing here?"

Ignoring me, he made straight for one of the first responders. "I'm not sure what this is, but I think she had some. I just thought it might help."

Crouching down, the woman dug around in the pack at her feet, then withdrew a small plastic bag. She held it open, gave thanks, and tucked it away. Jared gave a clipped nod and then quickly turned, keeping his eyes averted from the rest of us.

Beside us, Sarah was loaded into the ambulance. Seeing her like that wreaked havoc on my insides, but I pushed past it and stepped forward to follow. Then, the paramedic from before brought me to a standstill.

"One last question," he said. "What happened after she fainted? Did she hit her head or anything when she lost consciousness?"

"She just started to fall, and I lowered her down. I didn't know what to do, so I just held her until we heard the ambulance. Should I have done something differently?"

"No, you did great, Kevin. Thank you. Just try to relax. We've got her now, okay? We'll take good care of her. Best you can do is go —"

"I'm not leaving. I'm going *with* her."

"We'll meet you there," Jenna said as she and the others jogged down the street to where they had parked.

Not trying to change my mind, the sympathetic paramedic directed me up into a seat off to the side. The whole way to the hospital, there were beeps, cords, tubes, and a lot of medical jargon, and through it all, my eyes were never far from Sarah's beautiful but lifeless face. The silver glint of her necklace dangled off the side of the gurney, and a pendant stuck out. A plain, beveled cross.

Feeling ineffectual and abnormally desperate, I thought about asking God for something for the first time in my life. Bowing my head, letting it bob and weave with the movements of the drive, I prayed.

I'm not sure what to say. Dear God? I don't even believe you exist, but Sarah does. So, if you do exist, if you are up there listening right now, then I beg you, please... Please, don't take her.

KEVIN

16

Back and forth, I paced around the waiting room. "You called her parents?" I asked again of the nurse behind the desk.

"Yes, they're on their way. And they can choose whether to disclose any details from there. It's best if you just go home now."

The nurse's tone was gentle, but the suggestion fell on deaf ears. From the moment the ambulance arrived, one person after another had told me that same thing. Since I wasn't family, I wouldn't be given any information about Sarah — I got it. I was upset over being denied, but there was no way I'd be leaving.

Everywhere I turned, someone wanted to get rid of me. My mother kept me around out of obligation, and my stepdad ensured I stuck around as free labor or a punching bag. Neither *wanted* me there. My teachers didn't care for my attitude or my track record and couldn't wait for me to graduate. I had only one real friend, and I'd repaid him tonight by snapping at him.

Sarah was the only person I had ever imagined myself being genuinely happy with, and I tried to end things with her before we could begin, afraid of risks that I'd imagined in my mind. Damaged though I was, how could I have let go of the one person who enjoyed being with me for no other reason than she liked me?

"I'm not going anywhere." My declaration to the nurse's suggestion was simple and resolute.

"I understand. Then your only option is to wait over there until her parents arrive."

So, I kept pacing. Much of the time, my thoughts took me to a dark place, picturing what horrible things could happen to Sarah. Had I actually done anything helpful? My mom had never let me call 911 for her. Not even two years ago when she was crying, fully clothed, huddled in the shower under the cold water, after Craig had dislocated her shoulder. Again.

All the terrible thoughts threatened to consume me. Thoughts of my past, questions about my future... Only with great effort did I force everything out, firmly rubbing my neck, hoping to relieve some tension.

Soon, Sarah's parents showed up, followed by her trio of closest friends, as if they'd waited for them before coming in. They all blew right past me, heading straight to the desk. Following them, I leaned in to listen.

"Mr. and Mrs. Stevenson?" asked the nurse.

"Yes." The couple hurried closer, Lynne pushing herself against the quartz countertop. "Where is Sarah?" It was obvious she had already been crying. Her swollen and streaked face was in stark contrast to the vibrant and friendly woman I knew. We'd only met one time, but I liked her. She was kind. She seemed truly invested in her daughter's life and wellbeing, like any decent mother should.

The nurse stepped out from her station and got in close, lowering her voice. "My name is Jessica French. I'm one of the nurses who helped when your daughter came in tonight. Would you like to step into a private room to talk?" Jessica glanced at me and the others who had just come in.

"No, it's okay if they're here," her mother stated, pulling the others in tight under her arms like a protective hen. "Please, just tell us."

She nodded and continued. "The doctors are with Sarah now. An ambulance brought her in from a party tonight. She lost consciousness prior to their arrival, so priority one has been getting her stable."

"But what happened?" asked Lynne.

"We won't be sure until after her toxicology screenings come back. The doctor will update you himself as soon as he's able to."

Sarah's dad looked white as a sheet. "Toxicology screening? I don't believe this. Is she awake yet?"

"I'm so sorry, Mr. Stevenson," Jessica said benevolently. "That's all the information I have."

Sarah's mom turned to her husband as she quivered. Sarah's dad took her into his arms. "My baby, Jeff... my baby girl..." Fresh tears spilled freely down her face. Her dad looked blank-faced and strained, his eyes also watery.

Wow, what a sight.

I remember spending the night in the hospital once, after a drunken fight had turned into emergency appendicitis. The doctors told Marie it'd been worse than they thought and they could have lost me during surgery. The possibility of almost losing her son didn't seem to affect my mother, and she'd instead harped on the size of the bill.

"Can we see her?" Jenna cried.

"I'm sorry, but that's not possible just yet. As soon as Dr. Blake comes out, he'll be able to tell you everything, including how soon she can have visitors."

"Thank you." Hand over her face, Sarah's mom sobbed, her dad's tears falling silently down his face now, too. He directed his wife toward the seating area, and that's when she saw me.

"Oh, Kevin…" She walked over and the shattered look in her eyes nearly took me to my knees. "Were you at the party, too? Did you see anything?"

I nodded nervously. "I came with her in the ambulance."

"Please, Kevin, what happened?" she pleaded.

Completely overwhelmed, I froze, words refusing to comply with my desire to explain. For once, I had nothing to hide. I'd done my best — even the EMT had said so — and yet I couldn't form the words to defend myself or put Sarah's mother at ease.

"It's okay," she said, softening. "You won't be in trouble. Whatever it is, I just need to know. Please, tell me what happened."

"Stevenson?" All heads turned. Dr. Blake had come out and everyone rushed to him. Everyone but me, who collapsed into the nearest chair and slung my head down into my hands. The bulk of my adrenaline had passed, and now I just felt like crud on so many levels. I squeezed my eyes to hold back tears, pressing my palms against the sting.

"Doctor, please. What's the news?" Her father's tone was hardened and stoic.

"The medical team has stabilized Sarah and will move her out of the ER shortly."

"Oh, that's great news. Right?" Lynne asked desperately.

"I believe she's out of the woods. While her high blood sugar certainly didn't help matters, it wasn't the cause of this incident, and is now under control. The substance we found in her system matched what was given to the paramedics when she was picked up, and *that* is to blame for this. She is very lucky. If she hadn't gotten the immediate help she did, things could have gone a lot worse. Somebody's fast actions helped in curbing the worst."

Lynne nodded fast as she listened, her composure looking like it was in short supply, before breaking down completely. Her husband clutched her as her body shook with emotion.

Through tears of her own, Samantha piped up, "That was Kevin. He stayed with her until the ambulance came." I could feel the eyes in the room turn to me, but I didn't dare look up.

"When can we see her?" asked her father.

"As soon as she's settled in her room, I will send someone to bring you in."

A little over an hour later, a new nurse came through the doors and down the hallway with a smile on her face, and told Sarah's parents they could go in.

"What about us?" Birdie asked, voicing the concern they all shared.

"Whether visitation is open to non-family will be up to her parents," said the nurse.

I stood and approached Sarah's dad, beating down the apprehension soaring through me. "Excuse me, sir. Please, you have to let me see her, too."

He ushered me to the side and gave the nurse a gesture to wait. "Look — Kevin? I'm not as familiar with you as my daughter must be, but if it's as the doctor says it is... Then I owe you thanks more than anyone. But I think it's for the best if you kids go on home and let us deal with this as a family tonight. Perhaps we can have her call each of you when she's made it back home."

"I can't leave until I see her."

"I don't want to make this complicated, son, but I could have lost my daughter tonight. My wife and I need this time with her right now. I'm sorry." His firm hand squeezed my shoulder before he walked away.

Sarah's mom hugged each of her friends, then she came over and hugged me, too. "Thank you for being there." She placed a sad kiss on my forehead.

When the couple disappeared with the nurse through the double doors, and the rest of us were left behind, Samantha approached me. "This is just so insane. That all happened so fast."

The others gathered and the interrogation began again.

"How did you know what to do?" Birdie asked. She and Jenna had their arms linked. Leaning on each other like that, they looked piteous.

"I didn't." I couldn't take credit for blind, stupid luck. It would only reinforce the fear I could barely withstand.

"She had a little to drink at my house before we even left, but she said she had everything under control. Why'd she keep drinking if... if it could've..." Birdie's voice faltered and she sniffed.

"She didn't know what she was drinking. This is *Jared's* fault." Spitting it through gritted teeth, I thought back to how I'd found Sarah yelling at him. So, that really was it, then. He'd loaded her up with who knows what, for who knows what reason, and her body couldn't handle it.

Almost as if uttering his name had summoned him, Jared came through the automatic sliding doors of the ER. All heads turned his way. Rage pumped through me and my clenched fists.

"Kevin, don't do whatever it is you're thinking of doing." Samantha tried to take hold of my arm, but I yanked free of her, already honed on Jared. He started backing up

He continued backing up when I didn't stop advancing, and

the doors slid open again. "How is she?" Jared's look of concern would not save him.

The words barely breached his lips before I made contact and shoved him. Jared hit the ground outside the hospital with a groan. It wasn't good enough, but it was a start. I hovered over him in a threatening stance, daring him to retaliate. Samantha threw me off course by inserting herself in the way. She gave me a forceful push to the forearm. "Knock it off! We're all here because we care about Sarah. You can see that much, can't you?"

"But this is *his fault!*"

"How? You never told us what happened."

"When I found them together, Sarah was yelling at him over her drink. And now we all know why, huh?" As I moved around Samantha, she moved, too, keeping me separated from my prey.

Samantha hurried the conversation along. "*Then* what happened?"

"After this douche sucker-punched me, Sarah and I left. When we got outside, she fainted almost immediately... Before she passed out, she said the words 'Not soda. Something. Jared,'" I choked out, directing my attention back to Jared as he tried to get up. "She has diabetes and you poisoned her!"

"I swear I didn't know that could happen. So many people were taking that stuff, myself included."

Eyeing Jared incredulously, Samantha scoffed, "Does Sarah look like the type of girl who does what everyone else is doing, Jared? I mean, really."

"I don't know, okay?! I should have asked, I am fully aware of that now. How many times can I say I'm sorry before you guys believe me?"

"I don't think a number exists," I said, cutting the words through my teeth.

"She's okay, right?" Jared's voice sounded like sandpaper against a rock.

"She's okay." Samantha leaned down and helped Jared off the ground. He winced but stood upright. "Thanks to Kevin." I realized Samantha was being a decent person, but I couldn't stand to see Jared get anyone's sympathy, and I couldn't stand to be in this place any longer. If I didn't leave and clear my head, I would steamroll through them both and finish what I started.

And if Sarah's parents wouldn't let me in to see her anyway, there was no point in hanging around. Especially not while the others were here. I'd have to sneak back later, on my own. I didn't mind resorting to less-than-honest means if it resulted in seeing her tonight.

Decided, I left without another word or glance to anyone, even as they called out to me.

One way or another, I *would* see her tonight.

17

WHEN I AWOKE TO THE SOUND OF MY MOTHER'S VOICE, I DIDN'T know what was going on.

"Sarah?! Oh, Jeff, she's awake! Hurry and get the nurse!"

"Mom?" My voice was merely a rasp. My head felt cluttered and my stomach churned. When I pried my eyes open, the world around me was an intrusion, the bright lights too harsh on my vision and the variety of beeps assaulting my ears. Once my eyes adjusted, I realized where I was but couldn't recollect the details of how I got there. "What's going on?"

My mom squeezed my hand but didn't have time to answer. The door to the room opened and my dad followed a nurse inside. The two walked over to my bed, my dad taking up my other hand. I'd never seen him look this way before.

"Hello, Sarah. How are you feeling? Do you mind if I take a little closer look at you now that you're awake?" The nurse was already withdrawing a pen-sized flashlight from her coat pocket and shining it in my eyes. "Good," she muttered. Then she uncovered one of my legs and tested my reflexes. "I'm seeing all good things here." She inspected the machines I was hooked up to.

"And some fantastic readings, too." She finally turned to look me in the eye. "You have made great progress, Miss Sarah. Tell me, do you recall what brought you here tonight?"

I closed my eyes, uncomfortably aware of all the attention on me. I tried to block them out in order to think. What *did* I remember last? My face flushed with shame as memories came back, at least up until they'd fragmented. After Kevin had kissed me, I couldn't piece things together too well…

Holy crap, Kevin kissed me!

That memory flooded completely unfiltered into my mind.

Leaving that part out, I began explaining what I could remember. "I was at a party with my friends. I thought I was drinking Sprite, but someone had been adding stuff to it and I…" A hard lump worked its way down my throat. My mom gave my hand an extra squeeze.

"You hadn't checked your blood sugar?" It was less of a question than a statement.

"I can't believe myself. I'm so sorry, Mom. Dad… I don't know what to say."

"Well, it wasn't your blood sugar that caused this, though it was unfavorably high when you arrived," the nurse explained.

That was at least somewhat of a relief. "What about the other stuff?"

"They said a boy from the party turned some in to the paramedics, so they were able to identify it early," my mom explained.

A boy from the party? It couldn't have been Kevin because he didn't know. My attempt at explaining things probably didn't translate well in the moment. It must have been Jared. I had to remember to thank him for doing that.

My dad squeezed my forearm. "We're just so glad you're okay, sweetie. We were terrified for a while there."

"I'm so sorry." The lump returned twice the size as before, and I had to choke the words out. "I have never done anything like that on purpose."

The scenes that surfaced were replaying in my head — everything leading up to that kiss was easy to place. Kevin had found me with Jared and barely passed on fighting him, then he had angrily carted me off. I had been glad to go.

"We will discuss your health and what happened at the party, but not until you're back home," he said. "We just need you better first. Okay?" My dad's tone was stern yet reassuring, and I believed him. My mom held my hand between her own and could do nothing but silently lament and force a smile.

I nodded and then yawned, overcome by sudden drowsiness. The nurse then told them I needed rest, and after my parents promised to come back first thing in the morning, I fell back asleep before they were out the door.

During the night, the sound of my room door opening woke me up. I eyed the splinter of light cast on the wall beside me, and when Kevin stepped into the room, that streak of light cast across his face.

I lifted a little. "Kevin? It's the middle of the night. What are you doing?"

He chuckled. "You keep asking me that."

"Do I?"

Kevin moved beside my bed, his worry evident as his eyes took me in through the darkness. "You did at the party. You looked surprised to see me."

"I was. I mean, I was also very much intoxicated by then." How strange it was to hear those words from my mouth.

"What do you remember?"

"Everything after... a certain point... is either foggy or just not there." It was incredibly embarrassing to know I'd fainted like a real damsel in distress after we kissed. I wouldn't mind if he brought it up, if only to clear the air about it, but I sure wouldn't be. What if I'd only imagined it?

"Probably better that way. You shouldn't have to relive it." A layer of dejection coated his somber features.

My every instinct urged me to embrace him. I gripped Kevin's hand, but I quickly let go. "I'm so sorry, Kevin."

"Why are you sorry?"

"Because it's crappy you were put in that position. You shouldn't have had to rescue me."

"I didn't. I hardly did anything at all."

"No. What you did mattered. Thank you for being there."

He threw down his gaze. "I should've gotten there sooner."

"What could you have done?"

"Kept you away from Jared like I wanted to in the first place." Kevin's confession came out in heated emotion, and when I made no immediate remark, his jaw went taut.

"You couldn't have stopped me," I finally said.

"Why? Are you saying you actually like that douche?"

"Well, no. Definitely not now."

"But you did?"

"I tried to."

"Why?" he asked.

I folded my hands in my lap and watched them as though mesmerized. The tighter I wound my fingers together, the less they trembled. "Because he was there. He was up front with me about his feelings the whole time. I never had to guess at anything. And despite everything, I know he's not a bad guy. I've already forgiven him for his part in what happened tonight." I let my breath go, slow and deep. I watched the tension in Kevin's muscles but couldn't discern the exact cause, and my inability to figure it out had nothing to do with the lack of lighting.

Kevin's hands fisted and relaxed at his sides, and he faced me head-on. "Just because he was honest? Is that what it takes? Then here's some honesty. After everything that happened, I talked myself into forgetting about you because I saw my chance slip away when you accepted Jared's invitation. Russell and I agreed to go to the party tonight with the simple intention of kicking back, doing how I used to do. But as soon as I saw you, I knew there was a problem, and not just because you were yelling at him. Ultimately, I realized I couldn't keep pretending I didn't want you, even if that scares me to death."

"What are you saying?"

Kevin's chest slowly rose and fell. "I don't have much to offer and I'm not good at relationships, but there's something about you that makes me want to try." Kevin sat on the bed's edge and faced the wall. "If you'd been with me tonight instead, then none of this would have happened."

The moon shone through the slotted blinds, and the machines I was tethered to painted Kevin's features with their faint light. His gaze was directed straight ahead out the window, following the reverse path of the moonlight that gently cradled him. His nostrils flared and his mouth was a thin line pressed together. Kevin's confession had shed him of an armor I had never realized he'd been wearing, exposing an extreme layer of vulnerability. If I'd only bothered to look harder, maybe I could've seen it for what it was.

"You've been quiet a while. What are you thinking?" he asked, his voice low and clipped.

"So many things. But first of all…" Sitting up, I wrapped my right arm around Kevin, leaning my head on his shoulder. "None of this was your fault. Second, I'm just as scared as you are. If I were to tell you that I like you more than I've ever liked anyone else, how I've thought about you constantly since we met, you would know how easily you could break my heart."

"You don't know how messed up my life is. I'm probably the worst guy in the world for you, Sarah. But maybe I could make you happy."

My chest simultaneously rattled with joy and fear. Tears stung my eyes. "Maybe you could." I placed my hand around his cheek to draw his face to mine, and he winced. I gentled my touch, realizing my mistake. "Is that where Jared hit you?"

"Yeah, but it's nothing. He hits like a little b—." Before he could complete his crude thought, I finished what I started by pulling him close. When our lips touched, Kevin welcomed me softly, which in turn, softened him. "—baby," he finished, releasing a breath.

Kevin twisted, deepening our contact. This time, his mouth roved over mine. His arms slipped around my waist and drew me near. Every sense of wonder and thrill that ever existed in the universe coursed through me at that moment. I heard nothing but the sound of my beating heart competing with the beeps now filling the room, making a show of my excitement. As far as I was concerned, *this* was our first kiss.

As quickly as the adrenaline came, it crashed, and I felt my borrowed strength deplete. Severing the earth-shattering kiss, I apologized.

"Are you okay?" he asked, backing up.

"Better than okay." I sighed dreamily as I settled back onto the pillows.

"Are you sure?"

"Totally sure. Just feeling wiped." Closing my eyes, I forced myself to breathe slowly until my pulse and the monitors regulated.

Kevin grabbed my hand, kissing the top of it like I'd once done to him. Smiling, my eyes fluttered open again. "So, are we really going to do this?" His petition was laced with nervousness we both felt.

Someone burst through the door and threw on the light, thwarting my response. I jumped, and Kevin bolted to his feet.

The heavy door automatically closed behind the nurse, whose name was Jessica according to her badge. She scowled when she saw us, planting her hands heavily on her hips. "Hey! You're that Kevin kid, aren't you? How the heck did you get in here?"

"I'm so sorry, he was just about to leave," I was quick to assure her.

"Is he harassing you? Is he trying anything unscrupulous?"

"No! Not at all. Kevin is being very scrupulous." I bit my lip as I tried not to smile.

"Uh-huh," the nurse said dryly, then zeroed in on Kevin. "I distinctly remember saying you had to wait until her parents said you could visit. *In the morning.*"

"Technically, it is morning," he said. When the nurse pinned him with a glare, Kevin cleared his throat. "I'm sorry, ma'am. You did say that."

Looking sternly between the two of us, Jessica settled on me. "Do you know what kind of position this puts me in? Your parents will have a cow, not to mention my boss." Then to Kevin, "How did you get in here, anyway?"

"Look, I'm really sorry. I didn't want to cause any trouble. I just had to see for myself how she was doing. Please, just forget you saw me and I swear I'll go home this time."

After what felt like hours, Jessica sighed. "I hate to admit, I'm a little impressed by your determination. You must really care about her." Jessica tapped her foot for a minute before throwing one hand down and the other into her short, blonde hair. "Ugh. Okay, listen, you two. It's too late in my shift for these shenanigans, so I will *consider* pretending this never happened if you both promise me it will not happen again. Visitors can't be sneaking around patients' rooms after hours like this."

Kevin and I shared a surprised look before we both nodded. "Absolutely, we promise," I declared.

"Yes, ma'am," Kevin agreed emphatically.

"Can't believe I'm doing this," Jessica muttered to herself. "Just so you know, nobody else would be so accommodating. If any of the others had come in here instead of me, you'd be out on your rear with an armed escort." She turned to emphasize her statement with a pointed finger at Kevin. "If you even hint to anyone that I let this slide, I'll put you on security's glamorous no-entry list. Hurry and say goodnight and leave the way you came. If I see you, I'll have to call you out. Now, I'm going to grab a coffee from the cafeteria then do my rounds. Got it?" And then she was gone.

Returning to me, Kevin bent down and gave me another kiss. It was firm and brief and less than we needed, but I was still happier for it.

"I'll see you tomorrow," he said, a smile changing the sound of his voice.

"Goodnight," I whispered, basking for a few seconds longer in the possibilities this night might speak of the future.

SARAH

18

Just one night in the hospital was enough for me to gain a new appreciation for my own bed. On Saturday, after verifying my blood sugar was under control, and once my system was detoxed, I was free to go — under two conditions. I needed to take it easy for another day or two, and I *had* to be extra diligent in caring for myself from now on.

No one had to tell me twice!

Before being discharged, I had a visit from my endocrinologist. Per his strong recommendation, my parents had me outfitted with a device that would continuously monitor my blood glucose. My first endo had offered it to me in the past, but younger Sarah thought they were ugly, intrusive, and embarrassing. But mature and desperate-to-go-home Sarah was now the willing recipient of a brand new Dexcom. The idea of having the funky-looking protrusion sticking off my body twenty-four-seven still didn't sound appealing, but I admitted that controlling my diabetes had been too easy to forget lately, and that's not how I wanted things to be. I conceded it was better to be a little self-conscious of my monitor than risk an episode like that again.

Oh, and it went without saying that I would *never* drink alcohol *ever* again. I hadn't consumed much at all, but the thought of it made me queasy, especially with the distressing taste still looming at the back of my throat.

Too awake now to go back to sleep, I rolled from one side to the other and tucked my blanket up under my chin as I peeped out the window. Sunshine had crept in a while ago, but I couldn't bring myself to announce I was up yet. The silence was much too cozy.

Even though my friends had been calling and texting, asking to come see me, my parents wouldn't allow anyone over yet. Their primary concern was my health, and since we now had a collective handle on that, they weren't as upset anymore. They were simply taking the doctor's orders very seriously.

Mind wandering, my thoughts settled once again on Kevin. My boyfriend? I wasn't totally sure yet since we hadn't discussed it since. The sooner I could tell my parents, the better, but I wanted it confirmed for myself first.

I could just picture how much Jenna would freak out over our relationship when she found out. Not only did I not go for her pick, but I ended up with the one for which I'd previously denied having feelings. Of course, that was dependent on whether or not he and I *were* actually starting a relationship.

Partially rolling over, I grabbed my phone off the nightstand before returning to my blanket cocoon. Clicking on Kevin's name, I composed a brand-new text, having deleted our thread when I considered myself over the idea of him.

SARAH

Hey.

So eloquent.

I plopped the phone down on the bed, still unlocked, and watched the new conversation for signs of life. I couldn't see when he read my messages, but I could see the moment if and when he responded.

More than once, I closed my eyes and took a deep breath, willing myself not to focus on the phone. With that not working, I tapped the screen like a mouse tempting the fate of a trap just to sneak a piece of cheese.

When finally those little bouncing dots greeted me, I snatched my phone before the trap snapped shut and shot upright in my bed, ready to behold my prize. The dots blinked and disappeared three times before any reply came.

KEVIN

Good morning. How you feeling?

My heart beat frantically and I felt instantly flushed. I had a megawatt smile plastered on my unkempt face and thought at any moment I might either cry, throw up, or faint from giddiness.

SARAH

Fine. Slept so much better at home. How about you?

Waiting, I watched the dots resume their teasing dance.

KEVIN

I'm good. Be better if I could see you today…

My cheeks hurt from smiling, and I anxiously chewed my lip. It sounded promising for him to say that, but I didn't want to assume anything. Feelings often differed in the bright light of day. If he'd changed his mind or if things weren't how I hoped, I couldn't take it gracefully. My heart already ached too much.

In response, I said:

SARAH

Doctor said for me to rest like an invalid for another day or two, so my parents won't let me have visitors yet.

I was adding to my text when he sent:

KEVIN

Oh. Yeah, you should rest.

I shook my head at my phone.

SARAH

That being said...

I purposefully pressed send before I was done. I could play the dot-dot-dot game, too. My smile pained me but never ceased. Onward I typed,

SARAH

They're leaving for church soon and I'll be here by myself, 'resting.'

Send. *Dot, dot, dot.*

SARAH

Could you come by so we can talk?

Send.

Now I waited, expecting to pay remarkably for every single second I dragged that text on. To my surprise, and palpable relief, his response was near immediate.

When?

Excitedly, I slammed the phone down and clutched my pillow, shoving my face into it and giving a shrill, muffled laugh. I took another deep breath and settled myself, picking the phone back up like I was chill.

10:30 in the backyard under the big oak tree.

Throwing the covers off, I hopped off the bed, then crept to the door. Crouched, as if standing tall would somehow ring an alarm and attract the attention of my parents, I slowly eased my bedroom door open. I listened, detecting their voices just at the bottom of the stairs.

"—wake her and say goodbye, at least?" Mom.

There was shuffling. A door closed. The closet, I assumed. More shuffling. Dad was probably putting on his Sunday coat.

"No, Lynne. Let's just let her sleep."

"Alright, I suppose. We could bring back her favorite breakfast tacos from Julio's, then."

"That's a good idea. Come on. No sense in being late."

Their steps click-clacked across the hardwood, and the front door opened, closed, and locked behind them. Leaving my door ajar, I scooted — still on my knees — to my window and peeked out from the small opening the blinds afforded above the windowsill. Already seated, Mom closed the passenger door just as Dad was reaching for his. As it opened, he glanced up at my window, a deep, soft look on his face. Not ceasing momentum, he redirected himself until situated inside the car and closed the door. I watched them ease out of the driveway and onto the road before I dared move a muscle.

Once their dark blue Sportage disappeared beyond the trees after the first stop sign, I bolted upright and took off. I had a list of things to do in only a short time, but first things first. Opening my Dexcom app, I clicked to see what my long-acting needs were for the day, never feeling more alive in my life. My recent brush with death had already been forgotten.

KEVIN

19

Mornings were still cold this time of year, but I didn't bother pulling on a hoodie. The world was lucky I'd dressed at all, since from the moment Sarah invited me over, I'd been running on autopilot, with all thoughts of anything but her void from my mind.

I'd thrown on the first pair of pants I could find and shoved my feet into my shoes like slippers, squishing down the heels and completely forgetting about the laces. I didn't know what my hair was doing, and only when I'd parked beside her house did I lean into the rear-view mirror and attempt to slap down the stuck-up clusters atop my head.

Taking the keys from the ignition, I looked at my watch. It was 10:21. The only new notification was from Craig.

CRAIG

Where do u think u r going? Get back here and help me with this shed!

Great. Of course, it was too much to hope I'd got outta there unnoticed, and I still wasn't done paying the piper. These distracted days had added up, preventing me from keeping my word to finish the shed repairs. I couldn't spare as much time with Sarah as I would like this morning because of that, but some was better than none.

KEVIN

Just grabbing beer. Be right back. Do we need any more nails?

I made a mental note to stop at the corner store by the house and bring home a case of beer. It wouldn't be the first time I'd resorted to such pacification. The last question was merely thrown in as a deterrent. I knew we had nails and screws galore, but if I gave the impression I was on the job and coming back with one of Craig's favorite things, he would shut up.

It was always easiest to manipulate him in the mornings. For however long he stayed sober, he wasn't vile and violent. Just rude. Still, Craig's kind of rude was on a whole other level.

Pocketing my phone after switching it to silent, I got out of the truck and closed the door. I scrubbed a hand down my face and leaned on the door for a moment. A glacial breeze whipped me and kept going, rustling the trees and kicking leaves up around my ankles. February mornings still had a strong taste of winter, even in south Texas. It tempted me to rub my hands over my arms to assuage the cold, but I refused to move, accepting it, letting it clear my mind. I didn't want to see Sarah with any hint of Craig clouding my thoughts, so I simply held fast and hoped the frigid current would make it leave.

I checked my phone again. There were two more replies from Craig, but I didn't open them. Forget him for now. The clock said it was 10:26, and I reasoned that I'd waited long enough. Shoving my phone away, I rounded the front of my truck and headed up the driveway, nerves bundling up in my gut and twisting in all directions.

When I reached the back gate, I manipulated the latch until it gave and let myself in, closing it behind me. The backyard was much bigger than I expected. Usually, the nicer the neighborhood was, the smaller the yards got, but that was not the case here.

Glancing around, I found Sarah instantly, just as she said I would. She sat on a wooden plank swing that hung from a large tree in the middle of the yard. That tree provided such an expansive canopy, it shaded much of the area with only thin streaks of sunlight making their way through. As I walked to her, all the flowers and plants around me seemed to lean toward those beams of light, yearning for their turn in the warm sun.

"Hey," she said when she turned to face me.

"Hey, yourself." I looked around and stuck my hands in my pockets. "Pretty nice yard."

"Thanks. My mom spends too much time out here. Sometimes I help," she giggled.

"It's nice," I reiterated. If only my mom occupied her time doing things like this. Growing things and creating life instead of... what she does.

When my eyes caught hers again, I smiled effortlessly. She stood up from the swing and smoothed out her dress. Her cheeks pinked ever so slightly, and instinctively I reached out. Heat bloomed from her cheek beneath my palm, and she closed her eyes and leaned into it, placing her own hand over mine. I was in awe as I brought her in for a hug.

Pulling back, I left my hands at her hips. "I couldn't wait to see you," I admitted with a nervous laugh.

"I can tell," she smiled back.

I followed her amused gaze and discovered my shoes were

still undone. Not only undone, but my feet were still not fully seated inside them. How I didn't notice that is beyond me. My shirt was hanging funny and my belt wasn't threaded right, so it wasn't doing its job. Obviously, I was a mess, but how could so much have escaped my attention?

"Ah, I'm sorry." Feeling sheepish, I turned away to fix everything.

"I'm not. It's cute."

"Cute?" My tone was incredulous as I spoke over my shoulder, re-looping my belt and anchoring it. "Don't you mean trashy?"

"Do you think I only like you for your style?" she asked jokingly.

Shirt and belt righted, I faced her again as I hooked a finger into my shoe. One after the other, I pulled out the heel, making way for my foot. "Why do you like me?" I probably sounded like an insecure idiot, but I suddenly cared more about her answer to that question than I did my next breath.

"That's what I wanted to talk to you about," she told him.

Never had anything before made me feel so discouraged. Did she already mean to dump me? We'd barely put twenty-four hours into our new relationship.

"I know how I feel about you, Kevin. And if what you said the other night is true, then I know how you feel about me, too. But where do those feelings leave us?"

"Together," I said without hesitation. Searching her eyes, I hoped I hadn't been mistaken, my confidence deteriorating by the second. "Right?"

Sarah teared up. Either I'd said something incredibly right or incredibly wrong.

KEVIN

20

"Yes. Together." It was confirmed at last. Sarah leaned her head on my chest, and my arms immediately wrapped around her. She breathed into my white T-shirt as my chin rested atop her head and joy enveloped us both. Already, I was so used to this.

A little while later, I was gently pushing Sarah on the swing. My mind brought me back to the party, and I got curious. "Have you spoken to Jared?"

"Do you really want to know?"

"Yeah."

"Yes, I've talked to him. He messaged me just yesterday."

"What'd he say?"

"He asked me how I was doing and apologized. Like a dozen times."

Pfft. "A dozen more still wouldn't cut it," I muttered.

"It's funny. You guys both seem to feel solely responsible for what happened, no matter how many times I insist that's not the case."

"Because we are."

Sarah sighed and plunked her feet down, abruptly stopping the swing. She turned. "You're not. And Jared's not."

"Tell me how he's not at fault for sneaking you the junk that made you sick."

"Jared had his role in it, yes, and that's what he apologized for. I forgave him the moment I was conscious. Grudges give you wrinkles." Sarah playfully fluffed her hair, eliciting a joyful sound from me. "So, how long can you stay? Do you want to do something else?"

Looking at my watch, I puffed my cheeks and blew out. "Want to, but can't. I have to finish up the shed today."

"Aw, okay." Rising to her feet, she faced me as I stepped in front of her and welcomed her hands in mine.

"I'll miss you," I blurted out, stepping outside my comfort zone.

"It's weird to hear you say that. But *good* weird."

"I've said it a few times, but I've never really meant it before."

Sarah smiled as she tipped up on her toes to meet me for a kiss, and we said our goodbyes.

Once in the truck, I flipped the radio up loud and cheered a sound of victory to myself. There was nothing left to question. We were official. Now that Sarah and I were on the same page, I could shift my focus without worry. Bring on the shed.

In my excitement, I almost drove right past the corner store. I parked at the front and ran in, too preoccupied to see Russell at the cold case beside me, taking hold of a six-pack of his own. Unlike mine, his was Big Red.

"Yo, Sloan!" Russell caught my attention at last by waving his hand in front of my face.

"Russell, hey. What's up?" I closed my side of the refrigerator and turned, Craig's six-pack hoisted under my arm.

"I've been standing here talking to you. Did you hear anything I said?"

"Ah, no, I didn't. Sorry."

"I was asking about that girl from the party. How's she doing?"

"She's fine. She made a picture-perfect recovery. Thank you for helping that night, by the way."

"Oh, that's good. I've never seen you look so jacked up. I was worried she would keel over and you'd go off the deep end."

Heh. "Me too. We're actually together now." I smiled.

"No kidding? Well, good for you, man." Russell held his hand out to congratulate me. I took it up with pride and smiled. "I'm glad that worked out."

I then watched Russell's gaze rake over the case in my hands.

"So, are we celebrating? Or is Craig on your back again?"

"It's for him, but he's actually not been that bad. As long as I finish the shed today and ply him full of these, it'll be all good." I laughed it off and headed toward the checkout. Russell followed.

"Dude, forget that guy and his shed, and whatever the next thing is. Put that ugly old beater of yours to good use and come work with me."

"Don't talk trash about my truck." I dropped the case onto the counter and the proprietor of the store gave me a once over before nodding his familiar approval. In this neighborhood, anything went. Nobody was asked for ID as long as they had cash to spend.

I stared through the window at the "old beater" in question as the guy behind the counter tallied my bill. A cop car and fire truck blew by, their sirens ringing in my ears one second and gone the next.

Russell elbowed me and laughed. "Fine, fine. But I mean it, your talents are wasted at home."

"Yeah, right. What talents?" Surely, he didn't mean drawing?

Now there was a thought. Maybe Tanner would pay me for new branding. It was something I'd considered offering before. His logo was completely irrelevant to his current business, considering he'd begun entrepreneurship as a corn and cotton farmer, of all things. It didn't sound like such a bad idea to offer to design a new one for the shop.

"You're too loyal to waste it on that douchebag. Aside from your own transportation and an inside connection, that's really all you need. I already know you can keep a secret."

I handed over twenty bucks for my fourteen dollar case of beer. A twenty I'd earned as a tip from detailing a Miata at the shop that week — a twenty that I, for a split second, imagined was a hundred while my mind entertained Russell's alluring offer.

Alluring and way too dangerous.

Picking up the beer to leave, I stood just out of Russell's way, pivoting toward him again. "Russ, I love you, man. I know you want to help, but I'm not interested in getting caught up with anything like that right now. I really can't afford any risks."

Any more *risks,* I mused, my thoughts instantly returning to Sarah. I forced away the stark consideration, unwilling to let my insecurities creep in and chase away my newfound happiness.

"That's the beautiful thing, bro. It's essentially risk-free." Russell collected his purchase, and the two of us walked out. "I've been doing it nearly a year now, and nobody's ever come sniffing around even once. If it was easy to get caught, do you think someone like me would do it? I don't think so. And Tanner isn't a dumb guy. He knows what he's doing, and he already trusts you."

"It sounds like it's already such a perfect system without me."

"See, that's what I think, but since I'm such a good friend, I don't want to see you worrying about lame stuff like money and school. You could pay your way through any college you want in no time, no scholarship necessary." Russell took advantage of my silence and pushed on. "Maybe save a little more to put money down on a nice house for you and the new wifey," Russell ribbed me again.

Somewhere in the furthest reaches of my mind, I let those ideas play out. If I were independent of my mom and Craig, how would that be a bad thing? I wouldn't even want to waste money on a house. I'd be perfectly happy with a small apartment. Sarah could come and go as she pleased, and we could graduate together, pressure free. I might not even need to move away from town if I did that. Maybe by then, once school was over, she could see herself moving in with me…

Reining myself in, I shook my head loose from the slippery thoughts. "I'm good with my plans, Russ, seriously. Don't worry about me."

"But I do," he said sternly, in the most caring tone I'd probably ever heard from Russell. I opened my door, slid the beer to the passenger seat, and then offered Russell my hand.

"I know. Thanks, man."

A few minutes later, I was still subconsciously toying with the possibilities Russell had dangled in front of me when I turned down my street and saw that my house was on fire.

KEVIN

21

I THRUST THE CASE OF BEER TO THE FLOOR OF MY TRUCK AND parked, looking toward the congregation of onlookers and first responders in front of my house. Getting out and rushing over, I shouldered my way through the crowd, searching for my mom.

Breaking through the line of people, a police officer stepped in my way.

"You can't go any further. Stay back beyond the sidewalk."

"This is my house. Where's my mom?"

"What is your name, son?"

"Kevin Sloan. Where is my mom?" I was growing more aggravated by the second and being held back only made it worse. My view was only so wide and I couldn't find her anywhere.

"Calm down." The cop pressed one hand to my chest and used the other to hook my shoulder. "Come over this way, please." We walked in front of the crowd over to the ambulance. My heart flip-flopped when I finally spotted her behind a couple of EMTs. None I recognized from the night of the party, my mind noted.

Marie Sloan was strapped down to a gurney in front of the ambulance, wailing incoherently and covered in blood and black soot. Her tears had created defined streaks down her face. She pulled at the straps, begging whoever would listen to let her free. "I need to find my son!"

Tearing from the officer's grip, I ran over to my mom, and when she saw me, she cried out.

"Kevin! My baby!" She tugged at her straps all the harder.

"It's okay, Mom, I'm here. I'm fine. What happened?"

She struggled to control her breathing, choking on her efforts, her breath hitching every few words. "Craig was yelling already because you left, going on and on about that shed. I told him to relax, to trust you to get it done, and he hit me so hard this time, I couldn't —" She coughed, black spit coating her mouth. It was second nature for me to wipe her mouth clean with my hand.

"Mom, it's okay," I tried to assure her, but she couldn't be convinced.

"No," she said forcefully. Though her voice was weaker than before, at least she was calming down. "When I came to, Craig was in the shower. I don't know what happened. I just… Before I knew it, I was standing in front of the shed, holding a can of gasoline, watching the whole thing burn."

"*You* burnt down the shed?"

New tears pooled in her eyes. "If there was no shed, maybe the threats would stop. Maybe he would finally leave if I took away his precious stash. So, I burned up as much as I could."

Unnerved, I staggered back a step and pushed my fingers through my hair, yanking the strands. "Or maybe he would've killed you! That was so stupid!"

"Let him kill me, and they can take him back to prison. As long as he leaves you alone."

"Mom, no! That's not — Hold on. What did you say? You did this for me?"

My mom cried fresh tears and sought to touch me, her bonds making it futile. I reached for her instead. "I'm so sorry you didn't know I would protect you. That's my fault. I haven't done a good job, I know." Her thin body shook with sobs. "My boy. I'm so sorry."

Paramedics cut in and started manipulating the gurney. They asked me to stand back, and I stumbled out of the way. Loss of control had me staggering. Confusion and fear took hold in a way I hadn't felt in a long time. In the past, when suffering abuse, I'd learned quickly I had to deal with it alone. Nobody, least of all my mother, was going to show up and save me. Over time, the sting of her abandonment stung less and less, until I quit hoping to be rescued altogether. Right now, I had the same empty, cold-hearted feeling I always felt when she let me down.

But just then, amidst her broken confession, I wondered if I might've let her down, too. Through the years, I'd become the cold-hearted one, to the point where I'd put as much distance between myself and home as often as I could. Only now did I realize that by protecting myself in this manner, I had left my mom exceedingly vulnerable. She was always there at the mercy of our abuser, even when I wasn't. Marie had her own demons, but that wasn't the whole story. My bitterness had blinded me to the fact that my mother was Craig's victim, too.

The paramedics hoisted her into the back of the ambulance. I headed for the doors, but someone stepped in the way, the doors closing without me.

"I'm sorry. You can't go with her. She'll be taken to Driscoll Emergency for treatment first. But I'm afraid after that, she'll be arrested and transferred to County. You'll have to give your own statement and wait for the next step down at the station. You'll be assigned a social worker who can help you with what comes next."

Before I was ready, the ambulance pulled away into a blinking blur before disappearing. A film of disbelief shrouded my comprehension. I hadn't noticed them before, but the hoses of the fire engine now roared in my ears, and my attention was drawn to the house. The back right side of it was still aflame, a partial casualty of the shed that had caused so much grief and now no longer existed.

Next, the officer from before was standing in front of me, and the EMTs had all gone. "Kevin? I need to ask you a couple questions before we go downtown." He retrieved a small, spiral notepad from his breast pocket and dove right in. "Who all lives inside the home?"

"Just my mom, me, and her husband, Craig Wyatt." I spat the name out as the officer listened, notating as he nodded me along.

"And how old are you?"

"Seventeen."

"Do you have any relatives in the area?"

"No relatives anywhere." My eyes couldn't stop seeking out the chaos. Ash from my charred home singed my nose. A pair of firefighters held fast to the thick, vibrating hose that spewed the strong, extinguishing waters at my house. For a moment, I fought the temptation to be the next victim of the stream, longing to wash away any consequences of this event that would surely come for me next. I may not have known what to expect, but it would've been unrealistic to hope I'd get out of this unscathed. Marie may have freed me from Craig, but in my bones, I knew that monster wouldn't be the worst thing I would have to worry about. Now, the law was involved.

The officer finished scribbling, then flipped his pad closed and pocketed it. "Do you have a vehicle?"

"My truck is back there." I motioned down the road to where it was parked.

"Okay, we'll leave it there. It's best we don't put you behind the wheel tonight. I'll take you down to the station to get your full statement so we can get you sorted out, okay?" His heavy hand was atop my shoulder again, urging me from the house. I stood dumbfounded for a moment before letting myself be pulled away. The flames hadn't been extinguished yet, and the blazing orange flickers left an imprint in my mind I would never dislodge.

SARAH

22

From the moment Kevin left my house Sunday afternoon —
as my official boyfriend, thank you very much — I hadn't been
able to stop thinking about him, more so than usual. I hadn't
been able to reach him since then, either. I held off as long as I
could before texting him. When two messages had spanned from
the afternoon to night with no reply, I resorted to calling. This
morning, I'd sent another text after I tried and failed to find him
before class, and now my small bud of anxiety was in full bloom.

My phone sat open to our conversation atop the table in Bio,
taunting me with its one-sidedness. Dozens of questions spun
around like wildfire in my mind. Where was he? Did he already
regret becoming a couple? Did I say something wrong yesterday?
He'd already explained how important this last credit was, so
why would he skip school? Whatever was going on, I prayed he
was okay.

But, God, it would be really nice if he'd just answer already.

I drummed my fingers on my textbook. There was no way I'd
get through the whole day unscathed with so much wondering
and worrying. And I'd only just then came to the realization that

I did not know where he lived, so there's no way I could check on him after school. The only thing I could do was wait.

Mr. Hallinger was already leaning against the door frame, waiting for the bell to ring. Soon as it did, he closed the door and flipped the latch. My heart sank. Even if Kevin were to show up right this second, he was formally locked out of Bio for the day. And to make matters worse, lessons were always the most robust on the first day of the week. Did his old notes cover today's lesson?

I sighed and pulled out my notebook and pen. If Kevin was going to be absent, then I'd have to pay attention enough for the both of us — just in case. We were partners, after all.

Once class was over, I was distressed that my phone still hadn't buzzed a single time. Birdie said bye to us early, citing a need to do something important at lunch for drama class. Sammy waved her off and then turned in her seat as she packed her bag up.

"Where's Loverboy today?" Her tone was cavalier, and I couldn't discern if it was sarcastic or not. Sammy was my closest friend and, so far, the only one I'd entrusted with my good news. First thing Sunday morning, after Kevin left, I'd called and told her. Naturally, Sammy had been happy that her friend was happy, but I didn't know her real opinion of Kevin.

"I'm not sure," I said transparently.

Sammy raised her naturally and perfectly shaped brows like she might roll her eyes. "He better not be blowing you off already."

There came a slight pinch in my chest. I had feared as much by now, but hearing Sammy come out and say it actually stung. Sammy never let her friends hide behind false hope, and therefore never failed to say something that we were eager not to hear.

Usually, that bold honesty was fair and refreshing, but today, I resented it. "I'm sure it's nothing like that."

"That's what I wanna believe…"

I observed the thoughts swirling in my friend's eyes. "What?"

Sammy leaned down with her palms flat on the edge of the table as I tucked away the last of my things. "It's just, after seeing him ready to pound on Jared and knowing why he wanted to, I was almost impressed."

"And now you're not?"

"It remains to be seen. As does he." She looked up and did a mock sweeping of the room. "It's a bit early in the game to be a no-call-no-show."

At that moment, my phone vibrated, skidding across the table. Sammy snatched it up before I had a chance.

"Not so no-call anymore," she said, glancing at it with a smile before handing it back.

I viewed the screen with abatement. *Finally,* a text. Sammy bounced off, evidently satisfied, but not before I said, "I hate you, brat."

Without turning around, Sammy shouted, "Not as much as I love you."

Chewing my lip, I exited the classroom, everything forgotten except the screen in front of me.

KEVIN

Hey, Sarah. Just woke up. I'm so sorry. I've been dealing with some family junk all night, so I couldn't get to school today. Can we meet up after school?

With speed, I typed.

SARAH

Are you okay? I've been worried.

KEVIN

I'm ok. I am really sorry but I will explain.

SARAH

Where should I meet you after school?

KEVIN

I'll pick you up. I'm ready for you to see where I
live.

KEVIN

23

THERE WERE ONLY A COUPLE HOURS TO GO BEFORE I WENT TO PICK up Sarah, and in the time since our chat, I regretted my plan. I couldn't believe I'd actually invited her over to my house. Never mind the fact that part of it was burnt to a crisp. This would mean going into detail about the things I was most ashamed of. Things nobody, except Russell, really knew about my life at home. But I so badly wanted to prove to the part of myself that believed I wasn't good enough for her that it was wrong.

Regardless of my fears, she expected me to make good on my word after school and I would. Ready or not.

What would she think of my whole life exposed before her? Would she still accept me, still care for me, once she saw just how imperfect my family and I were? My mom was an addict — a felon — for crying out loud. The whole thing felt so daytime-TV-talk-show.

When I first went to Sarah's house and we started talking about our personal lives, she did seem accepting of my plight, or at least the outermost layers of it. I would never forget her small, warmhearted kiss on my hand, and how that had immediately become something big for me. Nobody had ever shown me that sort of compassion before. But today would expose my life to her more than ever before. Seeing my drama would be a lot more to take in than just hearing about it. Hopefully, the rest wouldn't come as too much of a shock.

Then there was the additional issue of money stressing me out. It was now up to me to pay for some expensive rehabilitation program for Marie; otherwise, she'd end up going to prison. Again. No matter how I did the math, it didn't add up. There seemed to be no way I could afford to fix the house so it wasn't condemned *and* keep my mom squared away at rehab. The hospital hadn't even transferred her yet, but based on what the social workers who had spoken to me throughout the night said, I knew I was in over my head. Even if I threw every precious penny of my savings toward her rehab, it wouldn't cover the cost, let alone leave anything to fix the house.

There was only one saving grace from this whole situation. Since I was so close to eighteen, the department didn't think it was pertinent to turn me over to state custody. They'd mercifully agreed my life had been disrupted enough, allowing me more leeway than they usually would in these cases. If I regularly attended meetings with Cynthia Henderson, my new primary caseworker, and stayed with someone over the age of twenty-one while my house was repaired, that was all they'd require.

Luckily, I had somewhere to go. Russell's family said I could stay with them. I figured it would only take a week or two to reinstate the structure of my home with walls and a roof. I'd be able to move back in as soon as that was done. Being under the partial guidance of my caseworker was nonnegotiable and required weekly meetings until my mother was released, or I turned eighteen. Whichever came first.

I was at Russell's now, still trying to wake up completely so I could face Sarah. It had been around 2 a.m. when Cynthia finally dropped me off. Even though Russell's mom, Delia, had gone to great lengths to make me comfortable on the family room pull-out, I had tossed even more than I'd turned and got virtually no sleep. The whole living nightmare had taken every ounce of what I had and then some, but my brain had refused to succumb to blissful exhaustion. Every time my eyes closed, my subconscious kept sending forth the fires.

Once, when I had finally slipped under, the embers in my dream flew up only to fall back down like shooting stars, creeping their way toward me, one sizzling trickle at a time. Repeatedly, flames would flicker up and out from the side of the house. If my mind wasn't enveloped in the fire, it was swallowed by the broken look in my mother's eyes after the incident. As she'd reached out to clutch my hand, her skinny, scarred arm had sort of resembled mine at twelve years old, when the worst of Craig's abuse really kicked in.

I awoke drenched in sweat, my chest tight, as if I'd walked through the fire itself rather than just dreamed about it. If I didn't shove everything to the back of my mind, I wouldn't be able to function. For now, I had to gather myself up and wait for school to let out so I could bite this next bullet.

I was cleaned up and ready to go half an hour ahead of schedule. Nothing had appeased my anxious mind, so I busied myself helping Russell's mom by cleaning up my makeshift bed and fixing a snack for Matthew, his little brother.

"You about ready?" Russ emerged from around the corner at the bottom of the staircase, entering the kitchen nearly undetected.

My head snapped up. "Yeah, in a manner of speaking." I

placed a spoon down in front of Matthew and then pulled a chair out to sit. I bent down to lace up my shoes before leaning back and yawning for the hundredth time that morning. Then, I labored a few bites of instant oatmeal before scooting it to Matthew. His eyes brightened. He was all too happy to reach for it, mouth still eagerly working on his current spoonful.

Russell took a can of something with the word "ENERGY" on it from the fridge before turning back and flicking me a nod. "I'll be out there."

Delia, too, emerged from around the same corner as Russ had, carting a square basket full of laundry. "Not before you eat!"

"I'm covered, Mom. I got breakfast right here."

She hurled the basket onto the counter and pivoted toward him with a snarl, arms crossed over her chest. "Reach back in and grab something of nutritional value before I whoop you, Russell Sprout. Try a banana and you may evade my fury."

He opened the fridge again. "Okay, okay. I'll grab ten bananas. Just quit calling me that."

"Forty-six-point-five hours of labor entitles me to anything I want for the long duration of your life, son. And don't you forget it." Satisfied with herself, Delia victoriously collected all the hand and dish towels in the vicinity and placed them in her basket. She headed out of the kitchen through the far hallway, making a comment to her youngest as she walked by him with a knowing maternal glance. I couldn't help the tendril of envy that flowed through me just then.

Suppressing the unsavory feeling, I popped up to my feet. "I'm ready now."

"Perfect. Let's get outta here."

Once in the car, Russell pulled his little Honda into traffic without his turn signal and with extra jerky movements on the clutch and shifter.

I felt awkward. "You good, man?" I probed.

"Yeah, sorry. Don't mind me."

"'Kay, I won't... Russell Sprout." I snickered and Russell swerved. I could feel his eyes as they alternated between the road and the side of my face.

"You mock me, Sloan!?"

My somewhat stifled reverie burst out of containment, my laughter loud and unrepentant. I didn't realize how nice it felt to not have my own worries on my mind for a second.

"Laugh if you want, dude, but seriously, that woman has no boundaries. She acts like I'm still ten years old."

"Ah, I was only teasing. She was, too. Your mom is kinda cool."

"Umm, my mom is kinda clueless. She doesn't give a flying fig how humiliating she is." Russell shook his head and his hands squeezed the wheel. "I just hate her sometimes."

My cheerfulness died instantly when the image of my mom stumbling from the couch to try and defend me from Craig sprang to mind. It was one of the last times I had thought the very same thing about my own mom. I'd hated Marie then, too. I'd hated her many times throughout my life.

I had been so ignorant.

I'd known Delia for as long as I'd been friends with Russell, but she had been nothing more than Russell's mom. It was normal to embarrass her older children, just like any regular mom would. Now that I was a sudden guest in their home, a pseudo-son of sorts under the care of Mr. And Mrs. Grandy, I had instinctively accepted her as more than just the parent to her children. I thought I might even understand why she acted the way she did and why she felt justified in doing so. Moms were inherently just that way. They teased, they played, they insisted. They *cared.*

Delia had her health, took amazing care of their home and finances, and suffered from no addictions. She didn't have a repugnant man around who used and abused her before moving on to her children. From her mind to her skin, she seemed unmarred by the evils of the world. What I wouldn't give to say all that about Marie, and only a day ago, I would've wanted that simply for my sake alone. So yeah, I understood where my friend was coming from, but Russ had no idea how fortunate he was.

When we pulled up behind my truck, I realized I'd been spacing out. After parking with an abrupt motion, Russell turned in his seat, one arm draped over the wheel and the other on the center console. Then he snapped his fingers beside my face.

"Sloan, you okay in there? You went radio silent on me. Is it because I have mommy issues?"

"Trust me, you do not have mommy issues. Just general ones." I gave a half-hearted smile as I ribbed him. "But for real, it's probably not easy for your family to have me there like this, so maybe just give her a pass for now. If calling you a stupid name once in a while and demanding you eat healthier is the worst she does, then consider yourself lucky."

"Yes, Father. I'll surely try," he said dryly, sticking his thumb up like a good boy. I rolled my eyes and got out, and Russell dropped the act. "Yeah, yeah. Sorry, man, you're right. There are worse things out there. I know you know."

I closed the door and rapped my hand on the open window. "I appreciate the ride, Russ."

"Yep. Oh, I'll be taking an extra shift at Tanner's tonight. Stop by and join me after you meet up with Sarah. I'll be there all day."

Backing out of Russell's way, not allowing the idea to penetrate my fragile thoughts again so soon, I unlocked my door. "I'll see you later," I called.

It was such a relief to be inside my truck again. It was something familiar in my suddenly strange life. It was *mine.* Unlike other things out of my control, nobody could take it away from me. The truck was paid off, insured, and passed inspections with flying colors every year. All on my own dime. This truck was one solid consolation during all that consistently went wrong in my life.

Perhaps Sarah could be added to that short list, and then I would have at least two things in life to be grateful for.

As I sat behind the wheel and looked at the taped-off house at the end of the road, I didn't have the same comforting feeling about it as I did my truck. For most people, their home was a place of refuge, but for some, it was a house of horrors. My home hadn't been very loyal to me as of late. Not for many years. Not since Craig first moved in and started acting like he owned the place, plus Marie and myself.

After consulting my watch, I turned the key, firing up the engine. Without overthinking things a second longer, I drove toward the school.

Twelve minutes later, I was waiting in the school parking lot with the biggest, deepest black pit of a stomach ever. Anxiety danced its uncaring jig across my nerve endings, and I nearly broke and took off, momentarily too afraid to face her. But I sat back firm against the seat and steadied my breathing, telling myself I could do this. If only it were easier...

Things could *be a lot easier,* I thought bitterly. If I had no relationships, for example, then there was no one to disappoint. But I didn't want to be that guy anymore. Sarah had taken a chance by giving me her heart, and I owed it to her to treat it right.

The bell rang and Sarah poured out of the building alongside everyone else, impatient to leave. She was alone with a look of intent on her face when she reached the sidewalk below the stairs and looked out toward the parking lot. "I'm right here," the intrepid thing beating in my chest called out to her. As if hearing it, she immediately turned and found me through the crowd of people. My pulse quickened when she smiled and started walking in my direction. No going back now.

24

After school let out, it took me no time to find Kevin idling in the front lot. His engine was audible over everything else, my mind already attuned to the low rumble of his truck. I searched his face for any sign of his mood or intentions, but he merely watched my approach.

I opened the door and stood tentatively outside the truck. "Hey. How are you?"

"Doin' okay. Come on in."

As I eased into the cab, my feet knocked into something on the floor. I glanced down to adjust and was surprised to see a box of beer. Just looking at it put a foul taste in my mouth. I could go the rest of my life without another drop of alcohol. If ever something wasn't worth the calories, that was it.

"Oh, my favorite," I said sarcastically.

"I'm sorry, you can just kick that aside. Or better yet..." Kevin reached down and I moved my knees to one side. He picked up the beer and reached it around, dropping it onto the floor behind my seat. "Don't worry, it isn't mine."

That was the quintessential response when one was found

with contraband, not that I was judging. Once upon a time, he'd found needles in *my* car and it hadn't been what he thought, either.

Still, I was curious how he'd come by it and for what purpose. "No worries." I readjusted and secured the seat belt. "It wasn't the same without you in class today. I took notes in case you'd need them." Though I was feeling reserved, I reached out and took Kevin's hand. Solace splashed through me as his fingers reciprocated my grip. "Is everything okay?"

"I'm fine."

"Really?"

His hold on my hand tightened. "Let me bring you home and it'll all make sense. We can come back for your car later."

That was no problem. What kept me from focusing on a single thought all day and even now was the unknown. What sort of family drama made a person want to bring their girlfriend home to see it?

To my delight, Kevin didn't let my hand go as he began driving, and we remained like that the whole way, not even talking. I watched the route and then mentally acknowledged when we reached an area of town I wasn't familiar with.

When we came to a stop, he gently withdrew his hand to park the truck, and I looked around. All sorts of vehicles were parked along the curb up and down the narrow street. Some houses had broken chain-link fences while others had grass so tall it looked like where they filmed *The Lost World: Jurassic Park.* The houses were so close together and close to the road, there wasn't much yard space, yet most of them sported clutters of plants, kids' toys, or various equipment. Roofs were falling apart, shingles and Spanish tiles were out of place or hanging on by a thread. I think I even heard a rooster somewhere out there, too.

And this was where Kevin lived. It was nothing like where I did. If I were being objective, most of the homes here had more cons than pros, despite some having a comfortable, cottage-like vibe.

When I looked at Kevin next, he was watching me again.

"Have you ever been to this neighborhood?" I felt my face flush at his question. Why did the question make me feel guilty?

"Not that I can think of."

"I figured as much. I know it's nothing like where you live."

I shrugged and smiled, fighting against my heating cheeks. I didn't want Kevin thinking the condition or location of his house mattered to me, because it didn't. "I don't care. A house is just somewhere you heat your Hot Pockets."

"Well, you're not wrong," he said pleasantly, providing some relief.

"What is this about, Kevin? Are you really okay?"

His face turned serious, and he shifted in his seat to face me square on. "You remember at the beginning of the term when you asked me if I would rather study at my house?"

"Yes, I remember."

"And I said no, and that's why we ended up at yours?"

"Yes. And the next time it was the library, and you refused to let me give you a ride."

Kevin nodded, then opened his door and got out, closing it behind him. I watched him walk around the front to my side and open mine. He offered me a hand down. Again, our hands remained clasped and we started walking.

"Look, Sarah. I know you know that I'm not a glamorous guy. I don't dress or act like Jared or Dan or anyone else you hang with. I don't come from a perfect family and live in a nice neighborhood like you all do. And you, you're so wholesome and I'm —"

"My family, friends, and neighborhoods are not *perfect*, either. And I don't care about any of —"

"It's okay, I know you don't. But that's not my point." He kicked a rock from the curb into the grass ahead, and we walked at a slow pace. "Before, when I acted cagey about all that, it was because I was ashamed of where I lived and who I lived with, and I didn't want you to see any of it. Now that I've gotten to know you better, I feel ashamed I didn't trust you before... *this* happened."

"Before what happened?" I asked.

He'd brought me to a pier-and-beam home coated with gray wooden planks and slate blue shutters, with a front door to match. It was a cute color scheme, but the paint was in bad shape. The house sported a small porch with wooden pillars and, just outside it, a line of lively, albeit unkempt, rose bushes beneath both front windows. The grass was even lush and green, though not mowed recently. On the whole, at least from the outside, this place boasted coziness. There was really no reason I could see for him to feel shame over it, especially when compared to most of the street.

I was confused as I turned, then followed his gaze around the right side of the house. Parting from him, I had to blink against reality when I finally understood. Somehow, I'd failed to notice all the black marring the side of the house. Something in my stomach hardened and I turned to Kevin. His hands were in his pockets and his eyes were downcast in the other direction. I took hold of his arm just to be near, letting him know I was listening.

"Yesterday, after I left your house, I stopped by the corner store to get Craig some beer so he'd be in a *'good'* mood when I got back. After the morning I had with you, I was confident nothing would spoil it, not even Craig. But when I got here, my house was on fire, Craig had run off, and my mom was strapped down beside an ambulance."

"Kevin, oh my…" I wrapped my arms tightly around him. He stepped in and entombed me with his embrace, enrapturing me with his trepidation. "I can't believe it. I'm so sorry. Is your mom okay?"

When he pulled back, I saw the full swirl of emotion in his eyes. "She's okay. Still in the hospital. They'll be sending her to a special rehab facility after that. Thankfully, it won't be prison."

Rehab… So, his mom was an addict. *Addicted to what?* I wondered, but I wouldn't ask. It was obvious he felt embarrassed by it from his tone alone. There was no reason to add insult to injury with my curiosity. Someday he might tell me more, but that was up to him.

"And your stepdad is gone? Did he set the fire?"

"Don't call him that. Craig is no dad whatsoever. But no, he didn't. That's something I would've expected of him, but my mom's actually the one who did it."

"Your mom?"

"She burned down that stupid God-forsaken shed I keep talking about because she didn't want Craig hassling me over it anymore. Hoped to get him off my back because he was threatening to get me kicked out of school so I could work more hours. Apparently, I don't make him enough money." Kevin's emotions changed. His body went rigid. "But then the fire spread, and we almost lost the house, too." Kevin gripped my hand. "Come look."

KEVIN

25

HAND IN HAND, I LED US AROUND THE HOUSE THROUGH A PEELING wooden gate. Just to the left of it was where the house took the damage, and to the right was the offending shed.

Looking around, I tried to see everything the way Sarah might. The backyard was small and made smaller by all the stuff Craig and my mom had collected. An assortment of random junk took focus. A broken-down lawnmower with some sort of flowering ivy growing through it was most notable. Toward the back were the rusted bones of an old swingset I'd been given as a kid by a neighbor who was moving away. It was one of the coolest things I had ever owned. One of the select few means of escape I used to have.

"I wasn't sure if I should go through with bringing you here today."

She stilled, her gaze drawing back to me. "Why?"

"Because I worried that all this crap would scare you away. Maybe it should."

She smiled and stepped closer. "Well, I'm glad you did. It

means a lot to me that you finally opened up some more. And all this *crap* does not scare me. This changes nothing."

"Yeah?"

"Oh, yeah." She linked her arm around my neck and stood on her tiptoes, tracing her nose lightly against mine. "I'm pretty sure I'm going to be into you for a very long time, no matter what you do."

Her words were a tonic I hadn't known I'd needed. I took tight hold of her waist and leaned down to capture her lips, pressing into her until her back was against a tree. Something about her confidence gave me a sense of bliss and righted my incorrect perspective, and it was exactly what I needed to bounce back. Momentarily, I suspected what I felt for Sarah was already something stronger than "like." Whatever it was, my heart was swimming in happiness, which was beyond anything I'd ever hoped for.

Sarah looked up at me with her shiny and bright hazel-greens. "I want to know everything about you, Kevin."

I hurriedly placed one more kiss on her lips before stepping back and spreading my arms. "I'm officially an open book available only to you. What do you wanna know?"

SARAH

26

WHILE ANSWERING ONE OF MY MANY QUESTIONS, IT CAME OUT that Kevin had gone his entire life without going to a single spring carnival. I was floored by this revelation and decided then and there that we simply had to go. What better precursor to Spring Break than greasy food, games, and rides? And if anyone needed a good seasonal reprieve from life's current troubles, it was Kevin. He deserved a fun experience before anything else could threaten his happiness.

When opening day of the carnival finally came on Thursday, I could hardly contain my excitement. The guy inside the ticket booth slid two lime-green wrist bands under the window with a routine "Enjoy!" My family and I had visited this county fair practically every year since I was born but never paid for wrist-bands. I made sure to get them this time. I wanted the experience to surpass all of Kevin's expectations.

I chomped at the bit as Kevin taped them on. With these, we could go on any ride we wanted as many times as we wanted, rather than paying for each ride individually every time we rode it. That equated to extra spending money in our pockets, which meant more games and food. The games were my favorite part of the fair, and for the last four years, I played fish pong until I won a fish. This year would be no different.

"I still can't believe you've never been here before. What a crime."

"Deep down, I think I must have waited so you'd get the special bonus of being the first to show it all to me."

"I can roll with that!"

With his hand on my lower back, Kevin sent me through the line first, down a walkway marked with ropes. Once we were through, I linked my arm through his, and off we went, mixing seamlessly with the buzz of the day. Multitudes of people were walking in every direction, and parents pulled wagons with rosy-cheeked kids. Others went by with roasted corn on the cob, giant turkey legs, and themed water bottles with crazy straws. The smell alone hit us like a tidal wave of sheer deliciousness.

Kevin inhaled deeply. "I know I've been missing out on something important if it smells this good. I'm betting it'll be worth the wait."

"Oh, yes! But we definitely have to do rides first. You don't have a weak stomach, do you?"

"Nope."

"Prove it, then!" I smiled wide and pulled him excitedly along into the very first line I caught sight of.

An hour and a half later, we were burnt out on rides but not quite ready to eat yet. Wandering around the vendors, I did a double-take at a caricature booth. I grabbed Kevin's hand, yanking him to an abrupt halt.

"Oh, we have to," I insisted. We walked up to the table to inquire more, and the artist looked at us apologetically.

"I'm so sorry, kids. I was just fixin' to put out the 'Out to

Lunch' sign. That's where I'm gon' be for the next half hour." As promised, the artist pulled a sign out from inside a small cabinet and placed it on a hanger at the front of his booth. "If y'all wanna wait, yer more than welcome to be first in line when I get back." The artist gave a contrite tip to the brim of his baseball cap and took off.

I deflated. "Oh well, it wouldn't make much sense to wait. We can try to remember to come back later."

I watched Kevin curiously as he walked to the other side of the easel and poked around the artist's things.

"What are you doing?"

Kevin ignored me and instead positioned the stool in front of the easel and made himself comfortable. He pretended to pull his sleeves up and then clipped on a fresh piece of paper. He seemed almost entranced as he brushed his fingertips across the paper's texture.

"Have a seat, ma'am," Kevin said, mimicking the artist's thick drawl.

"You can't be serious. Get up!"

Before I was through protesting, there was a marker in his hand, with the most serious-yet-playful-yet-expectant look on his face.

Hand on my hip, I said, "You're going to get us in trouble."

"Now, don't you worry your purdy lil head, darlin'. You just get yourself cozy on that chair over yonder and let me do the rest."

I wanted to be responsible, really, but Kevin's sense of humor made it so difficult sometimes. With a smile on my face, I had no choice but to do just as he said.

KEVIN

27

Before I forgot, I tucked a folded twenty-dollar-bill under a paint palette where the artist was sure to find it, and then focused my attention on the lovely subject in the chair before me. I'd been admiring her all day long, but the way her nerves caught up in her face and mixed with the warm glow of the golden hour gave her a whole new level of beauty.

It wasn't like me to steal — that was one thing I almost always had going for me, but I couldn't pass up the opportunity to preserve this time together. If Sarah wanted a portrait done, she would get one.

"Just sit naturally," I said, dropping the mock accent. "And try not to move." I traded in the marker, bypassed the paints, and opted for a stick of charcoal instead. I could recall the ridges and curves of her face with my eyes closed, so I started with those. Occasionally, I peeked from under my lashes to compare my curvature of her cheekbones or the slope of her elfin nose to the real thing. A few times, I changed the strokes in order to make subtle adjustments here and there, adding depth to her eyes and definition to her face. All the while, I noticed the edges of Sarah's mouth trying to curl up.

In just a handful of minutes, it was done. I placed the charcoals I had wielded back where I found them and hoped my last twenty would more than cover what I'd used. Unclipping the portrait, I braced myself, considering I'd never done art for anyone other than myself before. "All done." When I handed it to her, I suddenly realized the severity of my nervousness.

Like I guessed it was for most people, my art was a glimpse into the rarest, purest parts of me. And I really wanted her to like what she saw.

I watched as Sarah's expression changed from gleeful anticipation to something else, something more serious. Her cheeks reddened. Mist collected and pooled in the corners of her softened eyes.

"Is this really what I look like?" she asked softly.

Great. She hates it.

I walked out of the booth ahead of her, wiping a flustered hand over my brow. "I'm sorry. I know I'm not Rembrandt or anything, but don't let my terrible art hurt your feelings. I didn't mean —"

Suddenly, her hand was on my shoulder, and I stopped. When I turned to face her, I couldn't decipher her expression.

"Is this how you see me?" She held the portrait up as if it were an exhibit of evidence in a criminal trial. Only I couldn't tell which side of the case she was on.

Carefully, I looked it over and found only one possible answer to her question. "Yes, it is."

Sarah threw herself into my unsuspecting arms, causing me to sway on my feet. With a soft laugh, I took a step back to steady myself and squeezed her tightly.

"So, just a minute. Does this mean you like it?" I couldn't be too sure.

"I *love* it!" Sarah gave me a hard, quick kiss. "After looking at this, I've never felt more beautiful. Kevin, the only terrible thing about your art is how you hide it. If only everyone in the world could see your perspective of them. Your talent is truly something special."

The vast compliment rocked me to my core, and as we walked along together after that, I felt another sliver of the armor around my heart chipping and falling away. How did I have any chance of keeping us at a distance emotionally if she kept doing things like this to destroy my resolve? She was able to bring out the best in me, something no one else had done before, yet somewhere in the far reaches of my mind, imposter syndrome was hard at work trying to convince me it was a bad thing.

Last but not least, we grabbed something to eat and settled down at a bench under a large tree situated just off the main walkway. At this time, the sun was nearly set and the streetlamps and twinkle lights strung up between the trees and poles were in full glow. Sarah gently set her rolled-up portrait, stuffed prize tiger, and new goldfish down on the bench beside her.

"I'm so glad we did this today," she said, while she propped her bag up to keep her loot from falling.

"Mmhmm," I agreed, munching euphorically on my fair food.

Sarah checked her blood sugar app and took care of herself in preparation to eat. I gave her a hearty smile through my food, and she giggled.

"Totally worth it?" she asked of my chili cheese fries and a pickle Chamoy shaved ice. I nodded firmly, chewing away.

"I had a lot of fun with you, Kevin."

I smiled, really liking the sound of my name on her lips. I

tucked away my funnel cake to share on the ride home. Today, I'd had the sort of fun I'd always wanted growing up, so the long-forgotten kid inside me was elated.

"Me too. I didn't know what I was missing out on."

"Well, now that you do, you can take me every year from now on."

Naturally, I relished the thought until the weight of her words hit me. Not only had she implied we'd be together for a very long time — that part I admittedly liked — but she had apparently forgotten I wouldn't be around in a few months. Lately, I'd failed to remember that, too.

When we finished eating, I tossed our trash before settling back in beside her and tugging her close. Truth be told, I had been so distracted that I hadn't given enough consideration to the particulars of my future. Like how current events changed things and the impact the fire would have. How would I pay for my mom's program when my checking ran out, and would it have an effect on my long-term plans? Craig was at least a nonissue. Since the cops had issued a new warrant for his arrest after my and my mom's statements, nobody had seen him. *"Good riddance"* was putting my sentiments too mildly.

I felt Sarah's eyes on me after a while.

"Hey, you. What's the matter?" she probed.

"I'm sorry. I'm just getting lost in my head."

"I can see that. What about?"

"Just life and how I'm going to deal with it."

"Yeah?" she prompted for more.

Reluctantly, I said, "I need to figure out how I'm going to pay for all this stuff going on. I might need to get a second job."

"What about school?"

"I won't do anything to get in the way of school." *As long as I can help it.* "I'll have to take extra shifts with Tanner on the weekends or something."

My savings would only go so far if I wasn't making enough to recover it. And boy, I loathed the idea of losing it all. That money was supposed to get me going in my new life.

I rubbed her shoulder for reassurance, for my own as well as hers. "That will probably mean less time for things like this."

"I understand. You have to prioritize. I'll happily take whatever time you can spare."

"How are you always so positive?"

"I'm not always. But with God's help, I do my best. Without Him, I'd be a gigantic mess."

I was sorry I'd asked. I couldn't relate. There had been no one in my life telling me much about Jesus or God or whatever. My limited impression was that Jesus must not know where I live, just like Santa Claus and the Easter Bunny, because none of them had ever shown up for me.

I'd surprised myself when I prayed for her safety on the way to the hospital, but I wasn't sure how much attention I was willing to give to my girlfriend's God, even if He had maybe been the one to save her life. Who could prove that, anyway?

"How can I help with everything going on?" Sarah asked me.

I was startled by her question, so engrossed in my own mind again. I pondered for a moment before coming up with just the right thing. "More kisses?" I leaned down and nipped her nose, enjoying the joyous grin on her face.

Taking my face with her hand, Sarah turned toward me and found my lips, giving me a full kiss. "Yep, that'll do the trick," I said happily afterward.

"I still want to do something real to help." Sarah snuggled back into my side. "I'm here for you, you know."

"You're doing enough just being around. I can handle the rest."

"You sure?"

"Trust me. I'll be alright."

At once, Sarah came alive with an idea. "What are you doing on Sunday?"

"Hopefully working, but nothing so far. Why?"

"Would you do something for me?"

Uh oh... "I'll try. What is it?"

"Well, I still have to tell my parents about us. And I was thinking…"

"What?" I wondered with reservation. Of course, I knew where this must be going.

"Will you go to church with me and my family? We always go out to brunch afterward, and it would be so nice to have you with us. We could tell them together. My father would really respect that."

"I'm not sure how I feel about church and all that stuff," I said as delicately as I could. That was being generous.

"That's okay. Our church doesn't have expectations of those listening."

The idea really didn't thrill me at all. I was trying hard to avoid telling Sarah the whole truth. I really didn't want to ruin a good day by refuting her beliefs with my lack of them.

However, we did need to tell her parents. The sooner her parents knew the new status of our relationship, the better. So far, Sarah had been waiting for the right time. I supposed I could attend church for her, and for her dad, if that's what it would take to make a good impression. And, considering my one and only prayer to God was technically fulfilled, maybe that meant I owed Him one.

Was this somehow supposed to be my proof?

I'd never gone to a church service before, but how bad could it be? "Yeah, sure," I said.

"Really?" Sarah sat up, the twinkling of the lights above doing nothing to outshine her excitement or beauty. Joy radiated from her, all at the thought of me partaking in something special to her. That and being beside her when she professed our relationship.

I did that.

In awe, I smiled. "Yes, really. Let's do it."

SARAH

28

AT 9:45AM ON SUNDAY MORNING, MY DAD ANNOUNCED, "KEVIN IS late." My dad didn't come by this statement by checking the time, but by already deciding that if Kevin wasn't unnecessarily early, his credibility had already gone out the window.

I rolled my eyes. "No, he's not. I told him to be here by ten."

"Remind me why we're waiting on this Kevin kid?"

"His name isn't *this Kevin kid*. It's Kevin Sloan. And because I invited him to church with us. Jeez, Dad. Where's your Christianly spirit?"

He grumbled and loosened his arms from their constricted fold just enough to glance at his watch. He sported that unimpressed expression all fathers are so good at.

Ignoring him, I bobbed my crossed leg as I lost myself in thought. Kevin still had fifteen minutes until he was actually expected, and I had zero doubts at all that he'd be here by then. I might be insecure and nervous about some things, but I had nothing but confidence about this. And soon, he would know what I'd helped to coordinate on his behalf.

"Trust me," he had said at the fair, and I really wished I could.

As much as he might want me to believe things were okay, I didn't think *he* even believed it. If he didn't want my help then and there, the only thing I could think to do was pray about it and hope a solution came to me soon. No one was impenetrable, no matter how firmly Kevin implied he was. With all the complications Kevin was facing in his life, there was no way he could do it all without support.

It was obvious he didn't have faith, but maybe I could show him what life with it was like. Whatever precisely I decided to do, I'd have to make it count. Kevin deserved my best.

It didn't take long for my prayer to help Kevin to be answered. The most perfect idea for how I could do that came to mind the very next morning, and I'd put that idea immediately into motion. Starting with a phone call to my pastor, I received approval to do a brisket plate sale to earn money for Kevin's expenses. I made more phone calls, and after a few hours, my church family and I had the entire event arranged. Catering details, setup location, petty cash and payments, and volunteer staff. It was an afternoon well spent.

My heart kicked up as the low rumble sounded down the street. "He's here!" I said, giddily jumping past my dad to the front window. Sure enough, Kevin's truck came into view a second later. As I watched him park, I had such a big smile on my face that I had to calm myself down before turning around to collect my bag.

"Wonderful," said Mom warmly as she stood and slung her purse chain over her shoulder. She motioned with her hand, pointing toward her husband. "You be nice."

"I'm always nice," he said definitively as he rose.

Mom raised an eyebrow. "I mean it. Did you forget what he did for our daughter?"

"I certainly haven't, Lynne, but that doesn't mean I know him from Adam."

"You will, and you'll like him," I informed him.

When Kevin got out of the truck, I moved away from the window. "Oh, and he's going to ride *with us* since I also invited him to lunch." I flashed a cheeky grin and off I went to open the door.

KEVIN

29

MY QUAKING HEART HAD GIVEN ME NO REST ALL MORNING, AND IT only got worse the closer I got to the stoop of Sarah's house. I'd parked as close to the curb as I could safely get and made my way up the walkway like the very first time I'd come here. Back then, expectations were low and tensions were high.

Pfft. I now knew all that was nothing compared to this. Nothing sounded so nerve-wracking as spending the afternoon with adults I didn't know, while hiding a relationship they didn't yet know about, and all for the sake of a God that I wasn't really keen on paying attention to.

Can't believe I'm doing this.

Maybe my feelings for her really *were* stronger than I realized.

The front door opened swiftly before I could knock on it, revealing Sarah's dazzling, cheerful self in a flowing, floral-patterned dress. *Oh, wow.* Instantly, my nerves disappeared and my chest swelled with something better.

"Morning," I greeted her.

"Good morning. You're early," she emphasized, playfully side-eyeing someone beside her I couldn't see.

"And you're —" *stunning,* I wanted to say, but when her dad stepped into view I was rendered speechless, swallowing my thought. Suppressing my timidity, I extended my hand right to Mr. Stevenson. "Good morning, sir."

Sarah had told me his name was Jonathan. He accepted my offered hand. Mrs. Stevenson appeared beside him, as bright and shiny as her daughter.

Lynne took my hand in hers next, her grip in tender contrast to her husband's. "Kevin, it is so nice to see you again. You are looking mighty fine this Sunday morning. Don't you think, Sarah?"

Sarah nodded her agreement. "Yep. Mighty fine."

I wanted to look at my feet, feeling sheepish under her parents' scrutiny. With the way Sarah's mom looked at me, I felt as though she might try to pinch my cheek at any moment. She was friendly, and at least I knew she thought well of me. As far as her dad went, I didn't know what to think, but I got the impression it was painfully easy to get off on the wrong foot with him. I didn't know what I would do if, by the end of the day, Sarah's dad tried to forbid us from seeing each other.

Church with Sarah's family was nothing like I expected. My only perceived knowledge of church stemmed from bad horror movies and featured a chorus echoing in the tall ceilings. Old, intricate stained-glass windows everywhere, letting in the barest of light. Cold, wooden pews with melancholy looking patrons, and creepy bleeding statues. You know. *"Church."*

Sarah's church, in contrast to my ignorance, was a well-lit, plain-looking building, with no stained glass or any stiff pews. As far as statues went, it had a large wooden cross draped in white linen at the back of the stage. In front of that, I was surprised to see a full band of happy-looking people playing contemporary-sounding music. It was definitely not the morose, robed choir kind of stuff I was used to hearing on TV.

It was called "Praise and Worship," Sarah whispered to me, as we were all asked to rise for it. Standing up made me feel like even more of a sore thumb, like everyone there knew I didn't belong and didn't believe. Everyone around me was moving, some with just their mouths to sing, some with their arms stretched out, and some only swaying to the melody. Sarah was doing a bit of it all. And from what I could hear, Sarah couldn't carry a tune if she had Gorilla Tape for hands. I suppressed a smile, my mind momentarily preoccupied with something other than my own awkwardness.

She peeked over and saw me watching her. "I know," she said after leaning close so only I could hear. "I'm no Kari Jobe. Can you tell?"

I bit the inside of my cheek, silently pleading the fifth. Laughter tried to tug the corners of my mouth, but I wouldn't give in and risk garnering attention. Plus, I had no earthly clue who Kari Jobe was, anyway, so how could I really judge?

"The Bible says to *make a joyful noise for the Lord.*' It doesn't say it has to be a pretty one," Sarah explained, totally giving herself and her terrible voice an out. She smiled and nudged me lightheartedly before returning her focus to the front.

Leaning further this way than that, I noticed she could brush up against my arm without drawing suspicion, and each insignif-icant point of contact gave me jolts of amusement.

When everyone sat to hear the sermon, I observed Sarah pull a journal and Bible onto her lap. The pastor began speaking, and Sarah was immediately tuned in, her pen scribbling away just like she did in class. "Always taking notes, aren't you?" I quietly commented.

"Always," she agreed.

I wondered if all church sermons were like the one told today. Despite my partiality, I found it interesting. The pastor read from chapter seven in the book of Luke, focusing on a widow woman going to bury her only son. Losing a child was bad enough, naturally. But in Judea of those days, the pastor explained, a widow had only her children to protect her from destitution. If a woman had neither a husband nor children, she had nothing. No income, no home, no protection, no *life*. Without the son she just lost, she would lack all of those things.

The passage described Jesus entering a new town during the funeral procession, and amid all that was going on, Jesus saw this woman. He *saw* her. He saw her pain and her need following her substantial loss, and He comforted her. Then, Jesus touched the boy's coffin and told him to arise, effectively bringing him *and* his mother back to life.

"Now, Jesus was a Jew," the pastor had continued. "And one predominant aspect of Jewish custom was the concept of clean and unclean. Who here knows what those terms mean?"

I balked at all the hands going up around me, Sarah's included.

"If something was unclean, it meant it was not holy, that it was unfit for worshiping God. Touching something unclean would make you unclean, too. There were specific rituals you'd have to go through to make yourself clean again, or you wouldn't be worthy to take part in regular worship to God. As a result, the more unclean you were, the further from God you were.

"All forms of sin, for example, were unclean back then as they still are today. Sin is dirty, and we all sin. All of us have some amount of dirt on us at all times, some more than others. You could say those sins are kind of like coffins of our own. If one sin represents one coffin, then you could imagine how many coffins some of us might be dragging along behind us through our lives. Some people are more heavily burdened than others, holding on to all those coffins full of their past mistakes, because they're unwilling to let Jesus touch and heal them.

"If we could all stop and consider the Word today, what is this passage telling us? It's telling us that Jesus is the Word of God, and Jesus is God — therefore, God *heals*. If Jesus, a lifelong devout Jew, could stoop down and touch a dead boy's coffin and not defile Himself, and instead raise the dead, then what sin of ours can He not also touch? There is no stain His power cannot clean. No one is ever too far gone to reach out and accept help from Him. We need not let the ugliness of our past spoil the beauty of a future with Jesus Christ."

The agreement of the congregation was strong. I considered it; really, I did. It might be true for some, but the more I reflected on the idea for myself, the easier it was to reject it. If clean and unclean, worthy and unworthy, were true today, then I didn't stand a chance. *God would want nothing to do with someone like me.*

Following dismissal from the service, Sarah quickly packed up her things. "Let's go, I want you to meet Pastor Brian." She ushered me out into the aisle, walking toward the front against the current of departing people. The pastor was collecting his Bible and a glass of water from the pulpit. Upon noticing us, he returned his glasses from the top of his head and smiled warmly.

"Hello, Sarah. I'm so happy to have you in the house of God this morning. How are you feeling?" The man settled his items back onto the ledge of the pulpit and straightened up, moving around it to greet her properly.

"I'm good, thank you. That was another great message today."

"Why, thank you. I pray I'm only saying what He wants me

to." He then directed his attention to me. "And you have a guest with you today, I see."

"Yes, this is Kevin Sloan. He's the one I spoke to you about."

I was taken aback. She spoke about me to her pastor? *Is that a good or a bad thing?*

"Oh, yes, Mr. Sloan. Pleasure to finally meet you." He reached out to me. "I'm lead pastor Brian Marsh."

"Good to meet you." I shook his hand.

"We were so sorry to hear about your house, Kevin. We started praying for you right away. But Sarah here was gracious enough to arrange everything for the upcoming fundraiser herself, and so quickly, too. I believe it is to be on Saturday, if I'm not mistaken." He looked at her. "Is that right?"

"Yep. Tyler is just handling a couple of remaining details."

His words went in my ears and got trapped somewhere between my heart and the pit of my stomach. Trepidation brewed within me, manifesting itself in my clenched jaw and ramrod stance. There's no way I heard all that correctly.

Sarah's eyes flicked sideways toward me. "We'd better head out now. My parents are waiting," she said, and it was just as well. The moment she finished talking, a handful of strangers turned up to claim his attention.

Before turning away from us, Pastor Brian smiled with his parting words. "Alrighty, just let me know if y'all need anything else for the fundraiser. God keep you, Sarah. And you, too, Kevin. It was really nice meeting you. I hope I see you again."

On the way out, Sarah reached for my hand, but I remained stiff and unrelenting. "Sorry," I muttered. "Your parents are right there." That might be true, but it wasn't the whole truth.

Wrapped in discomfort, she walked in stride beside me. Her parents were out ahead, already getting into the car.

"Are you okay?" she asked, breaking the silence. I abruptly turned into her path and stopped her just short of plowing into me.

"What exactly was he talking about back there?" My tone was uninhibited, letting her know how okay I wasn't.

"We are hosting a fundraiser to help earn money for your house."

"I'm sorry — what?!" Hearing it again, I still couldn't believe it. "Sarah, what the h—" Realizing what a mistake it would be to say that here, I caught it, looking around as I lowered my voice to continue. "What do you mean, a fundraiser for my house?"

"I told you I wanted to help."

"And I told *you* I could handle it! Just what did you tell these Jesus freaks about me?" As soon as the words left my mouth, I regretted them. Sarah winced, looking on the verge of tears, and I hated it. My guilt slightly overshadowed everything else I was feeling. "Crap, I'm sorry. I shouldn't have said that."

From the moment I was blindsided by whatever exactly this fundraiser thing was, my identity had changed from Church Guest to Charity Case. I couldn't even acknowledge it in front of her pastor, too afraid I might do or say something to embarrass her, but apparently, I hadn't spared her much for long.

"I put together a fundraiser with some of my friends to help with repairing your house. That's all."

"That's all? Sounds like a big deal to me. Why would you do that? Why would you tell your whole church my personal business?"

"It's not like that. I didn't. I wouldn't. All they know is that your house needs repair, nothing else. They respect your privacy and so do I."

"Then I don't understand why you'd do this at all. Springing this on me, not giving me a choice. That doesn't sound much like respect. Do I really have to tell you it's not your problem?"

She turned ashen, wiping fallen tears from her cheeks. "I guess I didn't realize… I'm so sorry, Kevin. All I wanted to do was help. If you want, I can cancel the whole thing. We'll sort it out however you want. But right now, my parents expect us to go and have lunch. Can we just deal with that first, please?"

"Yeah. Sure." I said the words of agreement but my tone betrayed me. It was easy to pretend when I didn't have a choice. I felt that way about both issues, really. Just because she said she could cancel the whole thing, didn't mean it was really a viable idea. How many people were already planning to come through for this? Would scrapping the fundraiser somehow turn into *me* letting *them* down? I didn't want to be responsible for a bunch of strangers.

Sarah brushed past me and continued to the car, composing herself as she settled into the back seat. Sitting beside her, I felt even more like the same screw-up I'd always been.

KEVIN

30

My feelings were zooming around inside me like some sort of baffling, intersecting highway. I hadn't meant to lose my cool, but Sarah's plans to raise money had me completely unbalanced, even though I still felt foolish after reacting so harshly.

The air in the car on the ride to lunch was thick. Sarah and her mother spoke a few light words, but I didn't trust myself to say anything. All I could think about now was getting her alone to hash everything out, but there would be no opportunity for a while.

Once at the restaurant, the hostess seated us at a round table beside large, open windows draped with white curtains. Fresh spring air gently billowed them around, warming up by the minute. As everyone ordered food, Sarah and I were reaching the point of no return, and I worried she might be too upset with me to share our relationship with her parents now.

During all the talking, when nobody was paying attention, I reached under the table for Sarah's hand. She didn't look at me but rubbed her thumb against mine, breaking away when the server returned with our food.

As the server walked away with a cheerful, "Enjoy," Sarah and her parents connected their hands over the table. With an encouraging glance, Sarah held her palm out for me. On my other side, her mom did the same. I didn't have the guts to meet Jonathan's hard stare from across the table, but I could feel it.

Swallowing a hard lump of discontent, I took hold of Sarah and Lynnette's hands. My eyes darted around as theirs all closed, their heads bowing. Though only a few gazes were cast their way from around the restaurant, I felt as if I was part of a side-show act.

"Thank you, God, for this food. Please bless it for the nourishment of our bodies. In Jesus' name we pray. Amen," prayed Jonathan.

"Amen," the women said.

The moment their grips loosened, I hid my hands under the table, wiping away nervous sweat. Sarah gave me a sympathetic look, but this time, she didn't make me feel any better.

"So, Kevin," Lynnette began. With a knife in one hand, fork in the other, and napkin dutifully on her lap, she cut into her lunch. "What did you think of the service today?" Soon as the question was asked, she looked at me with bright, friendly eyes and took a bite of her food. Sarah's father also watched for my response, shattering what little confidence I had.

No, I will not wimp out. I've got this.

With all eyes on me, I cleared my throat and reached for my fork. "It was nice." When it was clear they expected more of an answer, I added, "Thank you for inviting me."

"Of course. We're happy to have you with us."

"What's this I heard about a fundraiser?" Her father joined the conversation, looking between the two of us.

"Oh, uh…" Sarah faltered, shooting me a look of uncertainty.

Unable to let her drown in front of her family, I threw her a lifeline. "It's not for sure yet, but it was Sarah's idea," I said, as if that explained everything. "There was a fire at my house recently. She put something together to help with getting it fixed up."

"A fire?" Her mom's hand flew to her heart in surprise. I had seen Sarah do the very same thing before, and I almost slipped and smiled at it. "I am so sorry to hear that."

"Yeah. It's a really old house."

"Insurance won't cover it?"

I didn't think it wise to explain the details to them, today of all days. "No, I guess not."

Lynne nodded sympathetically enough to look caring without making me want to cringe. Another family trait. "A fundraiser sounds like a great idea, you two. What did you put together? Is there anything we can help with?"

"It's a barbecue plate sale. The food is taken care of. Tables, canopies, and serving stuff, too. We may need more sodas and bottled water." Sarah was still looking apprehensively to me off and on, likely questioning how much she should say. I really didn't know the answer to that myself.

"You got it. We'll bring plenty of both." Lynne gave us both an assuring smile and then dug back into her food.

For now, at least her parents seemed satisfied.

"Thanks, Mom."

Add her parents to the list of people I would feel like I was screwing over if I brought down this effort. *Great.*

Feeling sweaty and stupefied by the topic at hand, I honed all my focus on eating, even though my appetite was nonexistent. All the while, her dad kept his steely eyes on me like a private investigator.

By the time the lunch dishes had been cleared, Sarah and her mom were sharing a slice of strawberry swirl cheesecake. I didn't find an opportunity to converse much, responding only when spoken to, except for the occasional nod or facial expression.

"Guys, I have something to say." Sarah rested her fork on the edge of the dessert plate. "I invited Kevin out with us today because I wanted you both to spend some time with him since… he and I are dating. Officially."

"Oh, Sarah! I just knew it." Her mom reached over to pat Sarah's hand. "I've liked him from the beginning. You two make a sweet couple."

Sarah smiled and welcomed her mother's pleasant reaction, but when she looked at her dad, who suddenly leaned back in his chair and folded his arms, my encouragement waned.

"Dad?" Sarah probed tentatively.

He sat there with his chest puffing up, and I knew for sure this time I was in trouble. I discreetly rubbed my palms dry on my jeans and did my best to ignore the dripping at my temples.

"We still don't know hardly anything about you, Kevin. Granted, what we do know seems favorable." Jonathan Stevenson talked to me directly, whereas Lynne had expressed her feelings to her daughter instead. That had worked out for me just fine, because having fewer eyes on me had alleviated some of the pressure.

Now, however, the pressure wasn't just on, it was tripled, and there was no avoiding it.

"What would you like to know, sir?"

"For starters… What kind of work do you do?"

"I work for Tanner Automotive."

"What do you do there?"

"Anything. Oil changes, detailing… Mostly engine work."

Mr. Stevenson nodded slowly, sizing me up. "What sort of plans do you have for the fall?"

"After graduation, I'm applying to the aviation program at Texas A&M."

Her dad raised an eyebrow. "Aviation, huh?"

"That's right. I want to fly commercial planes."

"Do pilots need a degree now?"

"It's not a hard and fast requirement, but it's highly valued." *So is the part where I get to leave town for school.* "It was either airplanes or art, and I don't think I'm qualified to be the next Bob Ross."

Sarah and her mom both giggled.

"That sounds like a solid career path," Jonathan said approvingly.

Unconsciously, I beamed. "Yes, sir."

Jonathan leaned forward and placed his hands down on the table. "I'll allow you to see my daughter on two conditions. First, I expect you to both mind all of my rules, and I'll ask for your word on it. And second, I want to see you in church with us every Sunday, where God and I can keep a steady and proper eye on you." Mr. Stevenson winked at Sarah as he stood to shake my hand. "Let's get to know you better, Kevin."

I stood, meeting her dad's eyes and shaking his hand. "Of course. I'll be there."

"You seem like a good kid. And my daughter is very smart. If she believes in you, then I will do my eagle-eyed best to give you a fair chance."

"Thank you, sir." I had never been so relieved. Rules were always a given, though I never thought I'd be expected at church every week. It was a small price to pay to be with Sarah, and one, I decided, I didn't mind paying. Even during our tiff earlier, I knew my heart couldn't do without her. By now, I was already too invested in her to refuse anything that meant keeping her as long as I could.

One issue was resolved, but one was still lying in wait for its turn to pounce on my momentary triumph.

31

After returning home that afternoon, Mom and Dad gave me and Kevin permission to go for a drive. Now we would be able to clear the air about the looming fundraiser, but that wasn't the only thing on my mind. My parents knew now, and they approved. My heart warmed.

We pulled away from the house and hit the main road, and I squealed before leaning over and kissing his cheek. Giddiness got to me like a Christmas morning. "That went better than I could've imagined!"

"Is he always so… inquisitive?"

"Oh, yes, more so usually. It's never this easy. I think he might already like you."

"I'd hate to be hated."

"That could never happen. But yeah, it's a blessing to be on his good side."

Onward we drove. Once clearing my neighborhood, he continued past the wetlands toward the open country roads. I could feel Kevin's tension building but wanted him to open up when he was ready.

A few turns later, Kevin released a hard breath. "Okay, Sarah… about this fundraiser," he said, his tone even. "I don't want to fight, but we really need to talk about it."

"I know."

"Remember when I asked you to trust me? I said I could handle my own issues."

"I believe you're capable, Kevin. But it's okay to accept help sometimes. We can't do everything on our own."

It didn't take much for his nerves to slip after that. He pulled the truck far off the road and got out, leaving the door open, which I surmised was his way of not slamming it in my face.

The wind waved through my hair as Kevin paced back and forth in the grass against the farming backdrop of large, round haybales. "Kevin," I urged gently. "Come back in the truck."

He turned, and the conflict on his face pierced me like an arrow. "Tell me why you did this if you believe what I said. Make me understand because I really don't want to be mad at you."

I let myself out of the truck and joined him beside the field. "Just because you *can* handle things on your own doesn't mean you should have to. There are always options; people who care, if you're willing to give them a chance. Listen, Kevin. Hey —" I grabbed his jaw, forcing him to face me. "—please. Trust *me* with this one, okay? I promise I won't let you down." He took hold of my wrists as my hands held his face.

"Handouts make me uncomfortable. People who say they care about me always have an agenda. And I don't want anyone invading my personal life. It's not pretty. Look at everything you've seen so far."

"These people aren't giving you handouts, Kevin. They're sharing their time, energy, and money with you because they want to."

"They don't even know me," he protested.

"That isn't the point," I countered. "They don't even need to know your situation to be called to help you. It's just that simple. And nobody knows any of the details. Nobody's going to be gossiping about you. That's not a thing we do."

His arms dropped and I wound my fingers tightly through his. He rested his forehead against mine with a sigh. "This kinda stuff feels weird to me. It's my problem, and this feels like begging total strangers to fix it."

"Well, I can assure you, that is not true. And if it were me, I would give those worries to God first thing, so I wouldn't ever have to deal with them all by myself."

"That's just it. I don't…" He paused, looking conflicted.

"What is it?"

"Never mind."

"You can tell me anything. It'll be okay." I glanced up at him, trying to ensure he saw that I meant what I said.

Before he responded, he turned away from me. "I don't actually believe in God. Especially not like you guys do."

"I already know that."

"How?" he questioned, facing me again.

"Well, when you have a heart for Jesus, you want everyone to know." I smiled, winding my arms around his middle, and resting my cheek on his chest. He stayed still. "Have I ever made you feel bad about what you do or don't believe?"

"No. You haven't."

"So, why do you judge yourself on my behalf?"

"I'm just… scared." There it was. The admission he clearly didn't want to make.

"Scared of what?"

"Losing you." He wound his arms tight around me like it might still happen.

"Don't be. I'm right here. Even if you don't have or want God in your life, I believe He brought us together for a reason."

"What reason?"

"I don't know, but He does, and I'm glad He did it." I rose on my toes and planted one, two, three delicate kisses on his lips, feeling him smile.

"I will admit, I wonder what it would be like to have your freakishly contagious confidence for a day. It must be nice."

"Who knows? Maybe someday you'll have it. It can last a whole lot longer than one day."

"Just don't expect to make a miracle out of me, okay? Because I can't stand the thought of disappointing you."

After we made our way back to the truck, Kevin sat with his hands in his lap. The sound of passing vehicles blew in around us as I watched and waited. "So, how many people are already involved in this fundraiser thing?"

"Around a dozen. There were different volunteers for different things. Some provided food, some forks, some drinks, and all the rest. Some people will be there on the day to serve the food, myself included. I mean, if you want to go through with it. It's completely your call now."

His head fell back against the headrest. "Would *I* have to do anything?"

"Not necessarily, but I thought it might be nice if you went. I know I'd like to have you there."

He obviously heard the smile in my voice because he lifted his head, looked at me with a smirk, then turned the key in the ignition. Then, taking hold of his steering wheel, "Alright, Sarah. Go ahead with the fundraiser. Tell me when, and I'll be there."

KEVIN

32

The morning of the fundraiser, I still wasn't sure about it.
Sarah and the other coordinators moved it up to ten in the morning, and by half past nine, they had finished setting up. I watched from concealment inside my truck, trying to talk myself into going up early, but sitting back and watching the bustle was momentarily the best I could do. Sarah and the others stood around, hands linked, and prayed. They were too far away for me to hear, but I felt awkward that I was the reason behind it.

There were already half a dozen cars parked with people waiting. The generators were humming loudly, giving life to the electric grills and heating containers. Volunteers bustled around the canopies, and the smells of sizzling chicken thighs, fajitas, and buttery parmesan corn on the cob teased the senses. Someone lifted a hot lid and stirred a batch of fresh, cheesy macaroni, the plumes of steam fragrantly mouthwatering.

When I summoned the courage to step out and join them, it was ten minutes 'til. Sarah was busy with her back turned, shaking bags of ice into various coolers and stuffing them full of beverages, and didn't see me.

A guy looking to be in his early to mid-twenties jogged over to me, and though I had never met him, I recognized him from Sarah's church.

"Hey, there. Are you a volunteer or are you buyin'?"

"Guess I'm a volunteer."

"*Órale!* I'm Tyler Cortez. I'm helping facilitate today." He reached his hand out and shook vigorously when I took hold. The guy was insanely chipper.

"Kevin."

"Do you have a last name, Kevin?"

"Sloan."

"Nice to meet you, Kevin Sloan." He dropped his hand and eyed me. Then he held up a finger like he'd touched on reality. "Ah, you're *thee* Kevin."

I turned out my hands and shrugged. "I guess so."

"It's nice to meet you, bro. I've heard great things about you already. I'm glad we could come together and do this today."

I gritted my teeth and forced a meager smile. "Yeah, me too." Tyler returned my fake smile with a real one.

"So, would you rather take payments or be on sign duty?"

"I thought I'd just do whatever Sarah was doing." We turned toward the aforementioned. Sarah was throwing empty soda boxes and water cases into a large trash bag and handing it over to someone else who hauled it to the back of a car. People began lining up in front of the booth, ready to buy food.

Ready to spend money on my extreme disaster of a life.

As humbling as it was humiliating, I focused my attention on the guy standing in front of me.

"I'm sure she'll be far too busy to be making goo-goo eyes with you this afternoon, Prince Charming." He made an easy sort of laugh at his own joke. "It looks like she's got all the hands she needs over there. We'll find somewhere else to put you."

Tyler's boldness made me do a mental double-take. I pretended to laugh, but it came out badly, compounding his humiliation.

"Perdón, amigo. I always forget to remind myself that I need to get to know someone before I tease them." He patted my shoulder, then indicated with a tilt of his chin. "Follow me this way." We ended up down the way from Sarah, at the very last table. "You can help me with this part. I'll take the money, and you write out one of these slips."

Tyler gave me a small notepad with pages of three colors, then scooted a chair out for me before taking up his own. "It's just a receipt book. Some people will want one and some won't, but the church collects detailed records for their own books. Everyone who comes down here with money gets offered one. You with me so far?"

"Yeah, I got it."

"Great!" Tyler then leaned over the table and looked toward Sarah and the volunteers who were working the first table of food. "We're ready!" he called out, and Sarah's attention was drawn our way. She seemed to radiate excitement when she saw me, waving with her gloved hand. Forgetting my unease, I gave a reluctant smile, her glee infectious, and waved back.

Tyler situated himself and turned to me. "They'll start coming down to us shortly. Just let me know if you get confused about anything."

"Sure."

"So," Tyler drummed his fingers on the table. We had a little time to wait before the first person reached us. "How did you meet Sarah? School?"

"Yeah. We're lab partners."

"*Ah, claro que sí.* What a timeless beginning, is it not?"

What does that even mean? Shrugging, I readied the notepad and found a pen beside the small, black till box. "Where did all this food come from?" I changed the subject, not wanting to discuss my relationship with Sarah. Even if this Tyler guy had a decent vibe, I didn't know him like that.

"The BBQ restaurant downtown donated it."

Wow. I wished I hadn't asked. Seriously, all these people and an actual restaurant had done all this for me? It still didn't compute. "Oh."

"They have sponsored our fundraisers before," he said, "and it's always been a good experience. Sarah approached them herself this time."

Just, wow...

"They have *reeaaallly* good food. You should grab a plate before the rush comes in. I'll handle the receipts for a minute. In fact, grab me one, too, will ya? I'll take a Sprite if there are any. If not, just plain water is fine."

Tyler spoke gently yet assertively, lacking no confidence that I would accept the task. "Yeah, sure." Feeling strained, I procured a ten-dollar bill from my wallet and waited to hand it to Tyler, who was just finishing up with the first person in line. A woman set her Styrofoam tray down on the table, and the smells wafted over. I did have to admit it smelled delicious.

"Thank you for your kindness, ma'am. You have a blessed day," Tyler told the woman as she refused her change. Watching the exchange made the annoying cloud settle back on my mind, and I wanted it gone.

"Here," I said, jabbing my payment at Tyler.

"What's this for?"

"My plate." *Remember the one you're forcing me to get?*

"Ohh. No, *amigo*. Volunteers get one on the house. My fault. I forgot to tell you that part."

You've gotta be kidding me. I shoved the money into my pocket, scooted away from the table, and walked over to get in line.

When Sarah noticed me approaching, she flashed her best smile. "Well, hello, good sir. Welcome to our hearty BBQ stand. What can I get for you today?"

I shook my head, grinning at her good humor. I wanted to tell her she could get me out of there, but that would only hurt her feelings. She still didn't understand the gravity of how this all made me feel, but I ate my feelings on the matter. At least outwardly, I would try to be appreciative and not so bitter.

And as for my house, I simply could not do it alone. It sucked to admit that, even to myself. As begrudging as I may have felt, I could not walk away from Sarah's efforts. So, I would order food like anyone else. "Two plates, please."

"One for you and one for Tyler?"

"Yep," I affirmed.

"With the works?"

"However it comes."

"Good choice, sir! Your taste buds will thank you endlessly."

Sarah must have really been enjoying the opportunity to tease me, and I can't say my mood wasn't slightly lightened. "Tyler is pretty cool, huh?" she asked.

I briefly glanced in Tyler's direction. "I haven't quite figured that out yet," I said, chuckling.

"He is not your average youth pastor, is he?"

Startled by the information, my eyes widened. "You're telling me that guy is a pastor?"

"He sure is. Probably the best one ever." Sarah loaded the first plate up with one of each kind of meat and then collected a heaping scoop of mashed potatoes to go beside it. "Tell me, Kevin… Are you a gravy guy?"

"But, of course," I said, matching Sarah's fancy dialect.

"Excellent." Then, taking a ladle out of a metal-lidded pot, she drizzled some of the brown gravy atop the potatoes. "Stacy, here to my left, will take care of your veggies, and I will see you later." Sarah winked, handing off the plate to where it was added to as promised. To the last person in the lineup, hovering over an ice chest, I requested two Sprites.

As I sat down, I slid one tray over to Tyler. Having made up the end of the line myself, there was now a lull in the activity.

"Mmm, mmm, mm!" Tyler rubbed his hands together. "Thanks for getting this for me, Kev. Let's enjoy before it gets busy again!"

"I'll try," I said dryly, the words unconsciously seeping out.

"Have you ever eaten at this place before?" Tyler asked, casually breezing over my revealing slip.

"Nope. Don't eat out much."

"Oh, boy. You'll be a fan after the first bite."

I finally put the man out of his misery and tried some. Right away, I was swayed by the flavor alone. Perfect texture, just right tenderness. "Alright," I willingly conceded. "I get it."

Tyler laughed. "See, I told ya. You're a fan for life now."

"It's pretty solid stuff."

Each of us ate, taking hearty forkfuls between accepting payments. Over an hour had already gone by, and according to my mental math as I'd scribbled out receipts, we'd already reached an insane profit. Not enough to rebuild my entire house or relocate me to an island bungalow or anything, but it was much more than I had come into this expecting.

To top it off, food stock was already running on E. From what I'd heard through the grapevine, someone was going to get a brand new batch.

Truthfully, I was beside myself, reeling from the generosity of others — all the people who spent their time doing this today and those who drove by and stopped in to give. They could've eaten anywhere else. It was incredibly humbling. As uncomfortable as I was with it, I had no other choice but to feel grateful. Because of this fundraiser, there was a solution to my most pressing problem. My home would be fixed, or at least as near to fixed as it could be for now.

And it was thanks to Sarah for seeing to it despite the pushback from me. I'd said ugly things to her and rejected her offer of help. How much I'd missed the mark of gratitude for the person who deserved it most. I decided, once all the chaos was dealt with, I'd make up for it somehow.

At some point, Sarah's friends had come through the line. If any of them wanted to give me grief for my behavior at the hospital, they all mercifully decided not to. Interacting with them for the first time since then actually wasn't all that difficult, and I thought I saw a glimpse of why Sarah cared about them so much. They seemed pretty cool.

It made sense they had come. They cared an awful lot about Sarah and had shown up to support what she was doing. That's the only reason they were there, I was certain. Surely, they didn't care any about me, but that didn't matter.

By the end of the afternoon, when the food containers were nearly depleted for a second time, I saw someone else I knew stop by.

Merrick Serrano's face lit up when he saw me.

"Well, well, well. So you are here," Merrick referred to me as he handed his money to Tyler, balancing his tray and sweating bottle of water with one hand.

"Merrick, hey. Long time no see." That was because when I began my downward descent into hooliganism, as Mr. Hallinger would call it, I stopped hanging out with Merrick and the others.

"No kidding. How've you been?" Merrick shook his head when Tyler tried to give him his change. Tyler nodded and thanked him, and I ignored it.

"Fine enough. Until, well…" *Half my house burnt to a crisp, hence the reason we're all here right now.*

Yeah, that.

"Right. I was so shocked to hear about what happened. Sorry, man."

"Thanks. I'll work it out."

"For sure, for sure. Hey, we still get together at the skatepark on Fridays if you ever want to come hang."

"Thanks, Merrick."

"Catch you later."

Merrick's appearance left me mystified long after he'd gone. Come to think of it, I couldn't remember the last time I'd even ridden my skateboard. That phase of my life hadn't lasted too long after I'd gotten my license. I had enjoyed it, and the guys were cool, but my truck offered more opportunities. Not all of them were great, I accepted now. Maybe if I'd stuck with Merrick and them more, I wouldn't have struggled to pass my classes last semester.

Who knows? Clearly not me. And now was no time to dwell on it.

Tyler, thankfully, said nothing about anything after Merrick was gone. Left to my own thoughts, I toyed with the idea of going back to hanging out with them, but deep down, I knew I wouldn't. Not because anything was wrong with them, I just knew better. There was no going backward in time. Things just couldn't be like they used to. I, myself, was turning into living proof of that.

And as I glanced up to Sarah, wiping the heat of high noon off her forehead with her arm, I knew I didn't want to be anything like I was. Whatever that meant for my future remained to be seen, but at least I was making an effort.

SARAH

33

Friday night, after a long three and a half weeks spent working on his home repairs, Kevin and I were finally able to relax. Together, he and I tackled the small stuff on our own. Before that, a contractor had come in to tear down the outside wall and all the damaged bits around it. Not wanting to feel like a burden at his friend Russell's house, when he wasn't working or at school, Kevin came to the house to watch the progress and clean up.

He kept telling me what an incredible help I was, and it made me happy to see the small change in him. Before, he might not have wanted me there, but we'd already come so far together that he accepted from me what he normally wouldn't from anyone else, and that made my heart happy.

Before it was time to take me home, Kevin collapsed onto his bed in a tired heap and I followed suit beside him. Turning toward one another, Kevin put his hand on my hip. I bent over to kiss his cheek, but Kevin turned and caught my lips instead. His fingers dug in as I felt him resist pulling me closer. I pushed

181

forward, deepening the kiss, snaking my foot around his ankle as my heartbeat became feral.

Kevin withdrew and gripped my chin, swiping his thumb down over the thrumming pulse in my neck, which gave away exactly how I was feeling. I didn't know what, if anything, he wanted out of a physical relationship. We hadn't discussed anything of that nature yet, but it was probably fair to assume he was a lot more experienced than I was.

"Should we do something else?" he asked.

Kevin's question brought me to my senses. I untangled myself and rolled onto my back. "I'm sorry. I didn't expect to get carried away like that." My toes still tingled from the lightning coursing through me. How was it every new kiss we shared was better than the last, gripping me a little more each time?

"It wasn't just you." Kevin toyed with a bit of my hair. "You know what I wonder all the time?"

I lifted to my elbow and turned to face him. "What?"

"Why you like me."

"What's not to like?"

"Plenty."

"That's your own incorrect opinion."

"I'm just not —"

My hand shot out and pinched his lips together like a duck. "Don't go down this road again, dude. There's no reason to disrespect yourself, or disrespect me by insinuating I have terrible taste in company."

"But my past is —"

"In the *past*. Leave it there. I'm perfectly happy with my Kevin the way he is today, and that's all there is to it."

Kevin smiled incredulously. "I don't deserve you."

"Not true at all. You keep yourself together a lot better than you must think. You're obviously doing something right to stay so level-headed and driven."

"I didn't always care about stuff. Things used to be very different, and my method of relieving stress usually wasn't anything good. Now, I just stay focused because I've tried it the other way. Accountability is hard work, but it's my ticket out of here."

I scooted back over and rested against Kevin's open arm. He adjusted until he was on his back, too, and I naturally nestled onto his shoulder. His heartbeat was lashing against my cheek, and it made me smile. "Your heart is making your shirt bounce. I can see it." I took a deep breath and let it out slowly to help regulate my own, which was still going wild after our kiss. "Can I ask you a personal question?"

"You can ask me anything you want."

The assurance was nice but didn't help me feel any less nervous. I'd never probed a guy for intimate details before. There were still so many things to learn about him. All aspects of him. Especially now, I thought there were important details we should know about one another.

"Have you had a lot of girlfriends?"

"Seriously? You mean my off-putting exterior doesn't speak for itself?"

"Not to me."

"Well, you're different from everyone else." He turned and kissed my forehead, then returned to how he was. "No, I haven't. Just a few and none were ever serious. What about you? How many boyfriends have you had?"

"Besides you, only one. And it wasn't serious either."

"Who was it?"

"Just a guy. It was only for a couple of months before he

moved away."

"Is that why you guys broke up?"

"That would've been a good enough reason, but no. He broke up with me right after our two-month anniversary because he met some girl at soccer camp who said yes to the things I said no to." I inspected my fingernails, indifferent. "I didn't like him that much, anyway. He gave me jerk vibes from the very beginning, but he was the only guy my parents would let me go out with at the time. They used to play canasta with his parents once a week, so it was just a relationship of convenience, and mostly for them."

"He sounds like an idiot."

I laughed. "You said it, not me."

"No wonder your dad wants to keep his 'eagle eyes' on me."

"Yep. So, what about these old girlfriends of yours? Anyone I know?"

"Probably not. Only one of them goes to our school and I rarely ever see her. Mostly, they were just girls I'd hang out with at parties."

"And kiss?"

He rolled his shoulder, skirting the answer, but it was answer enough. The thought of him making someone else feel the way I did was discontenting, even if it was a stupid. Of course, I wasn't his first kiss. Kevin wasn't mine either, but he could be my last, as far as I was concerned.

I took a deep breath and summoned all my courage. I was going for the big one. "Are you a virgin?" Right away, shame coated me, and I regretted asking. "I'm sorry, you don't have to answer that."

"I said you could ask me anything." He laughed softly, then went quiet. "Is it a deal breaker if I say no?"

"I kinda figured you weren't."

"Well, I hope it doesn't bother you to be wrong."

"Are you saying you *are?*"

"Yeah. I am."

I could sense some unrest in him. "I'm sorry, Kevin. I hope I didn't offend you. If you'd said no, it wouldn't have changed anything. Like I said, the past is in the past, and I would still feel the way I do about you. But I admit, I'm surprised by your answer based on the way you kiss."

He tilted his head in amused confusion. "What's that mean?"

"Let's just say you're really good at it. I wouldn't have been surprised at all if you were, uh, way more experienced."

"Ha. Sounds like an interesting compliment. I assure you, though, nobody has climbed this tree."

I barked out laughter. "I can't believe you just said that."

"I can't believe how much I like hearing you laugh."

"So, is it a deal breaker if I say I'm actually happy about your answer?"

"No, but it shouldn't be a big deal. Should it?"

"Depends who you ask, I guess. It always has been to me."

"Because of God?"

"That's how it started, but it's because of my own conviction. I want what God has promised us all in marriage, and I'm willing to wait for it. If teenagers aren't old enough to get married, how can they be old enough to have sex?"

"I guess it depends on who you ask."

I was surprised and slightly humored to hear my words parroted back at me, similar to how I just did to him. Kevin was paying attention, hearing me out, and that spoke volumes.

"Teenagers can get married, though. They do all the time with parental consent. Plus, eighteen and nineteen-year-olds are both teenagers *and* legal adults."

I buried my head in my hands. "Fine then, technically, some teenagers *can* get married, but that doesn't mean it's a good or ethical idea. You can't even rent a car until you're like twenty-five! I mean, consider the maturity level of some of the kids in our grade. Yikes."

"I think I'm losing you now."

Shaking my head, I said, "My point is, that kind of love shouldn't be casual, and I don't believe it's meant for people our age. Everyone throws it around like it's nothing, sharing themselves with anyone who's interested."

"Not everyone. You make high school sound like a brothel or something."

"Exactly. Not everyone. But for some, high school *is* very much like a brothel. Maybe on some level, you felt there was something more to it, too, since you've abstained so far. Many of those around us haven't."

"It's not always so easy to say no." Kevin sat up, stretching. "Do you know what it's like to get completely caught up? Have you ever gotten close enough to stand on the decision to abstain for yourself?"

I do believe I blushed. "Not really..."

"Then you can't really know. You might change your mind if or when it were to happen."

I sincerely hope not, I reflected. I slid off the bed to my feet, needing something stronger than a change of mind. "Well, anyway... Now that your house is basically done, what do you think about taking me out on a date?"

He stood to meet me. "Aren't you supposed to let me ask first?"

I put my hands behind my back and rocked on the balls of my feet. "Well, then, go ahead."

Smiling, he cleared his throat in preparation for a grand request. "Sarah Something Stevenson —"

Interrupting him, I covertly cupped a hand over my mouth and leaned up, him bending to listen. "Lucille," I whispered.

"Got it," was his hushed reply. He straightened up to start again, all proper-like. "Sarah Lucille Stevenson... Will you go out with me this weekend?"

I puckered my mouth in thought, teasing him with mock suspense. I tapped a finger on my chin as though I might have a pedicure scheduled that day. "Yeah, sure. Why not?" I finally said in a blasé tone.

He laughed again as something that looked like a brilliant idea came to life in his eyes. "Actually, there is somewhere special I've been wanting to take you."

SARAH

34

"Are you sure this is a good idea?" I wove my arm through Kevin's as we walked through the parking lot. The extensive building with reflective glass windows loomed ahead of us, and my second thoughts rang through my mind for the billionth time. "Maybe it's too soon."

Kevin rubbed my arm. When we'd made our plans to come here, he'd told me I was the most important person in his life other than his mother, and was consumed with excitement that finally, the two of us would be meeting.

"It's not," he said, sounding certain enough for both of us.

"Did you tell her I was coming?"

He didn't answer me. The electric doors opened for us and we approached the check-in counter, my curiosity increasing. Through the glass wall behind the front desk, I could see all sorts of people in robes and casual wear, and others wearing scrubs. I surveyed them, seeking a woman who might resemble Kevin, but none matched my imagination.

"Hi, how can I help you?" A blonde woman tilted her face up, her hand still on the mouse and eyes glued to the screen. She click-clacked on the keyboard. The pin on her shirt said her name was Raegan.

"We're here to see Marie Sloan."

"Alrighty, hun, gimme just one moment." Mouse, eyes, screen. "Can I see both y'all's identification, please?" We handed them over. Raegan peeked at our IDs, tapped at the keys and mouse until the printer roared to life, and slid them back along the counter. She grabbed a form and placed it in front of Kevin, along with a pen. "Y'all both need to sign at the bottom, please."

Keeping quiet, I thought to myself how complicated of a process it was to visit someone here. I recalled seeing my grandpa at a nursing home before he passed. The only thing required of the visitors there was a name and time scribbled on a sign-in sheet. Then again, I supposed a rehab facility was nothing like a retirement community where the inhabitants were there by choice.

Or more of a choice, at least.

From what I remembered, Kevin's mom was forced to either come here or go to jail. After her detox, she elected to stay. Kevin said she was in such a good place now that it was the perfect time to meet her. I'd been excited at the prospect, but now, the reality gave me reservations.

What if Marie didn't like me?

This must've been how Kevin felt meeting my dad...

I followed Kevin past an orderly pushing a cart into the hall from one of the rooms. He nodded a greeting as he continued by with his toils. Soon, we reached his mom's room, and Kevin gave my hand a squeeze and smiled. "Here we are." He reached out and knocked. Without delay, Marie replied, "Come in!"

When he opened the door, my heart felt like it was running its own marathon. I couldn't figure out why I was so nervous to meet this woman. The first I saw of her, she was seated in a brown suede recliner, turned slightly toward the window. Her feet were up, knees to her chest, with a book in her hands. A strong beam of sunlight cast over her. It wasn't until the door closed behind us that she looked up, and right away, her countenance dropped.

"Well, hello," she replied in a questioning tone.

Apparently, Kevin had *not* told his mom to expect a plus-one at his visit today.

I became overwhelmed with feeling like an intruder and wished it wasn't too late to turn tail and run.

"Hey, Mom." Kevin looked between us. "I thought you'd like to finally meet Sarah." He was still smiling, but his mom's obvious lack of enthusiasm quickly curbed his hopeful anticipation. He pushed through it. "Sarah, this is my mom, Marie Sloan." Kevin nudged me forward a little, and I had no choice but to extend my hand.

"It's so nice to meet you, Mrs. Sloan."

Marie snorted, ignoring my hand completely. "I'm sure it is." Then she turned to her son. "I wasn't expecting extra company. They only brought me enough for two, as is custom." She inclined her head toward the dresser. There sat a tray with two cups, two sandwiches, and a plastic decanter of orange juice.

I thought I might truly die of embarrassment.

"That's okay, I'll share mine with Sarah." Kevin was determined to make this work. The sweet boy.

"You do you, baby," his mom said. "Now, then, tell me what's been happening at the house. How much more is there to do?"

With his hand on my lower back, Kevin directed me to take the only other available chair, then he sat down on the edge of his mom's bed. "Actually, it's all done," he said, smiling. "Just about, anyway."

Her impressed expression pleased him all the more. "You're kidding! All that damage probably cost a fortune to fix so quickly. What'd you do, rob a bank?"

"It wasn't that bad. We managed."

She looked sternly at him. "We who?"

I stepped in, hoping to take some pressure off Kevin. "We held a fundraiser with our church and earned enough to cover the repairs and then some in just a few hours. The community is really amazing."

Marie's eyebrows went up in displeasure as she listened, but then she turned her vexed expression to Kevin. "Didn't I teach you better than to take charity from the church?"

"It wasn't charity, Mom. We sold lunch plates."

"Uh huh. And walked away with a stack of cash that the church officials gave you? And what're you even doing at church?"

"It's a long story." Kevin tried to brush it off, but his mother wasn't having it.

"We've got an hour. I'm listening."

"It's not that serious. I've been going to church with Sarah."

"Wow. Did you guys bring Bibles with you today to pass out to me and my fellow addicts? Are you going to ask me if Jesus Christ is my Lord and Savior and hold a prayer circle in the padded room?" She laughed humorlessly. "My son. I never would've thought."

Marie took a pack of cigarettes from her nightstand drawer along with a lighter and walked over to the window, pushing it open. Kevin turned to meet my eyes, but I couldn't stop looking at a random diamond-shape in the pattern of her carpet.

"Mom, what is this? What are you doing?"

She looked at him with such uncaring eyes, it rocked me. "I'm sorry, hun. Am I embarrassing you? Maybe you shouldn't have brought your little girlfriend to meet your messed-up mom after all." She spoke through her cigarette and then withdrew it to exhale out the window before taking another long puff. "What did you expect would happen? Look around you. This isn't the Ritz-Carlton, son." Then, she turned her sights on me. "Honey, do you even know what I'm doing in here?"

I looked up when she spoke to me, but I was at a loss as to how to respond. Not knowing what else to do, I thought I'd better get out of there. "I'm really sorry to have upset you." I stood and looked at Kevin, who was already rising to his feet, ready to protest. "I'll just wait outside, okay? Take your time. It's alright."

The moment a closed door separated us, I broke into tears, sliding down the wall and hugging my knees. I had suspected all along that showing up with Kevin might be a mistake, but I couldn't have guessed it would go *that* badly. Why would Kevin's mother treat me that way? What if she *never* accepted me? What kind of impact would that have on my relationship with Kevin?

KEVIN

35

I FELT GUT-PUNCHED. MY MOM HAD DONE SOME MESSED-UP things before. Accidentally putting one of her cigarettes out on my arm rather than in the little built-in ashtray of her old beat up Cougar. Leaving me in the shopping cart in the H-E-B parking lot. Forgetting me in a Stripes bathroom across town. Passing out in a swing after taking me to the park…

But those things had all been done unconsciously, under the influence of something or someone else. None of those things had been direct and intentional, like what she was doing right now to Sarah.

Furious with my mother, I started after Sarah. Guilt wracked me as I thought back to how nervous Sarah had been when we arrived, and I mentally prepared a major apology for dragging her here. But I stopped short of reaching for the door and turned around rather than leaving. Marie didn't deserve to get away with what she'd done.

"What is wrong with you?" I demanded. I asked for answers that I knew wouldn't fix anything. Shame had already vanquished all the hope I had before walking into her room.

"Is that any way to talk to your mother?"

"Is that any way to talk to my girlfriend? You were so rude. She couldn't get out of here fast enough."

"That's exactly right." Immediately, her tone was low and mild, devoid of the shade from before.

I waited for her to elaborate, standing eager for the explanation that would make sense of her madness and soften my mood. She pressed the end of her cigarette into a glass ashtray on the windowsill and then flicked the butt out the window. When Marie turned around, her face had changed completely. She no longer looked aggressive or on the offensive. Now she looked sullen and on the verge of tears.

"I'm sorry, baby. You just don't get it, do you?"

"No, I really don't. Explain it to me."

"Come and sit." She sat down on the edge of the bed and tapped the space beside her. Upon closer inspection, her weathered eyes beheld me the same way as they had the night of the fire, when she'd been determined beyond everything else to protect me from Craig.

"What is it?"

"Kevin, how serious are you with that girl?"

"What's the point of this question?"

"Pretty serious then, I assume."

I hesitated a moment, just long enough to wonder again why it mattered. What was she getting at? "Yes," I said. The truth. "So what?"

"And you stayed here to give me a piece of your mind, no doubt."

"Maybe."

"And where is she?" Marie opened her hand to the room.

"You scared her off!"

She reached out and grabbed my hand. "I was trying to. Look here. There are two problems with you and her being in a serious relationship, and it all boils down to hurting each other."

"You're not making any sense."

"She didn't stay for you, did she? At the first sign of a little heat, she left to save herself. You stayed behind to fight for her, but she didn't do the same for you."

"You don't understand her. She was giving us space. She was already nervous about coming here, but I insisted it would be okay. Your behavior made her think she was right to be worried."

"Son, that's only one reason. The second one is she's too good for you."

I couldn't believe the belittling. My own mother didn't support me. "Wow, that's great. Thanks."

Marie's eyes glossed over like crystalline pools. "You still don't understand. People like you and me... people like Craig... we take good people and twist them up until they're just like us. Disease breeds disease, son. Being with her will have you doing things you won't even recognize yourself for. And sooner or later, when you've screwed up so badly you don't know who you are anymore, she'll break your heart over it."

"This is ridiculous." I stood briskly. "I thought we were finally making progress, Mom, but you really don't know anything if you think you can compare me to a demon like Craig. I'd never do *anything* to hurt Sarah."

"Emotions make people do crazy things. Once upon a time, even I was normal and innocent like her."

"So, what, if you don't hurry up and traumatize her, you think I eventually will? What kind of crazy logic is that?"

"I know you may not appreciate my methods, but I've always tried my best to love and protect you. I know I have rarely ever done a good job, and I'm sorry for that. Hopefully, this huge favor I've just done you will make up for it. I wish there had been someone around when I was her age to do that for me."

"You had me when you were her age. Are you wishing me away, too?"

"That's not what I mean, and you know it."

"No, I *don't* know it! I don't even know what to think right now. I can't believe I spent all this time bragging about your progress, relishing because I might actually have a mother again, a real one for the first time ever, and here you are, making a mockery of my faith in you."

At last, her eyes overflowed, and the tears spilled out as she turned away. "I'm sorry, son. I only want the best for you."

"If that's true, then you want Sarah for me because she *is* the best. I love her. And despite your little freak-show effort, I'm never giving her up. I hope, in the interest of our new relationship," I waved my finger between us, "that you can simply accept what I'm saying and learn to support me like you should. Whatever this was today, I'm not putting up with it."

"Kevin…" Marie tried.

"I'll see you later, Mom." Finally, I left, slamming the door behind me without another word, and found myself face-to-face with Sarah in the hallway. She had tears that rivaled my mom's, except hers were accompanied by an unrepentant grin.

"Did you mean what I just heard you say?" came Sarah's timid question.

"All of it."

"Even the part where —"

"Yes." *Even the part where I said I love you.*

Arms embracing, I held her like we were the only two people in the world. Sarah rested her head on my shoulder, and I grappled with the distinct and immutable feeling inside me. I hadn't meant for Sarah to hear it, but now that it was out, I felt a dozen times lighter and more full at the same time. However that worked.

"I wanted to compose myself and go back inside, but it sounded like I should leave you two alone. I didn't mean to overhear everything. But it didn't feel right to just leave you."

I held her tighter. "I knew you wouldn't. My mom was talking all that crap, but I told her she was wrong."

"I'm so sorry I caused you issues with your mom, Kevin."

"Don't be. She caused the issues all by herself."

"Do you think we should go back in and start over?" Sarah offered apprehensively.

"Maybe another time, but I think that's enough for today. She needs to chill out and so do I."

"Are you sure?"

"Absolutely," I said, resolute. It was nice of Sarah to offer to go back and try to smooth things over with my mom, but that just wouldn't be happening today. Sarah had gotten more exposure than necessary to the insanity that was Marie Sloan. I'd had enough of her antics for one day. Even after all that, I still wasn't giving up hope that Sarah and my mom would one day get along.

Because of Marie's crisis, she and I had spent a lot of time at the facility together, reaching a new pinnacle as mother and son. We'd spent more quality time together than ever before, indulging in a lot of sober opportunities to learn about one another. Come to find out, we actually had a lot in common.

Before reaching the exit, a man in a suit waved us down. The man introduced himself as Jackson Ruger and asked for a moment with "Mr. Sloan." I asked Sarah to go ahead to the car and wait for me, then followed the guy to an office behind reception, beyond the glass walls.

"I'm glad I caught you. Go ahead and have a seat." He indicated to a chair in front of his desk while he held his tie to his barreled chest as he sat.

"Is everything okay with my mom?"

"Everything is fine with her, going great actually, from what I hear. And I'm sure glad to hear it."

"Me too. So then, what's the problem?"

Mr. Ruger shuffled through a stack of papers on his desk. He pulled one out and read it before setting it in front of me. "This is your mother's bill."

My stomach dropped. I grabbed the invoice and cringed at all the itemized reports, but especially the grand, past-due total at the bottom.

"Past-due? But I've made a payment every week."

He nodded. "Yes, I see that you have, but unfortunately, the payments you've been making have not been enough. I'm real sorry."

I was at a loss. What did this mean for my mom's future here? "What happens now?"

"I can give you one thirty-day extension to bring her bill up to date."

"If I can't pay it all, what happens to my mom?"

He shifted in his seat, clearly not wanting to answer. "We would have to discharge her from the program."

Great. So if I didn't cough up all this money within a month, my mom would be back at square one. I knew she was not ready to leave yet. Every Sunday, for the last few weeks, after brunch with Sarah's family, I'd come to visit her. Even the nurses said she was a shining example of the program gone right. Seeing my mom bright-eyed and clear-headed for just an hour once a week was worth nearly anything. "My mom needs to stay. She's not ready to be sober on her own."

He nodded sympathetically. "That's a real concern, which is why our program is so unique. We don't send people on their way after their court-appointed treatment. If they need more time, we welcome them. We are here to help, but that help just doesn't come cheap."

There goes my savings. "Thank you, Mr. Ruger. I'll make it happen." I folded the bill and slid it into my pocket as I rose, then shook Mr. Ruger's hand before leaving. Sarah was waiting for me, and I could do nothing more right now.

When I got back to the truck, Sarah asked what the man wanted. All I told her was that he needed to discuss the bill, and I did so in an even tone so she wouldn't probe further. I was grateful it worked because the last thing I wanted to do was burden either of us with more of the bitter truth. I only had one month to confront the fact that I was more broke than I needed to be. Sharing those details with her now would only take away from Sarah's help with the fundraiser. It wasn't her fault it ended up not being enough to fix everything.

Our hands met on top of the gearshift. Sarah scooted closer and rested her head against my bicep, winding her arm around mine. I never wanted to bring her into my money problems again, vowing in my heart to keep her in the dark from now on. If I was ever going to prove to myself or anyone else that I could do life on my own, I had to start right now.

I drove us home in silence. Today, I just wanted to enjoy her company and forget the fact that bills and graduation were both just around the corner. Tomorrow, I would go to the bank. But after that...

KEVIN

36

"I'M REALLY GLAD WE CAME OUT TODAY, BUT I'M NOT GONNA LIE. That movie was pretty boring." Sarah's comment reflected my feelings exactly. We saw some cheesy rom-com I wasn't jazzed about, either.

"Yeah, it was. Good thing the company more than made up for it."

I spent the first hour doing my best to pay attention, even though my arm was around her neck and she was stealing constant glances at me. I had to fight the constant desire to lean over and kiss her. It seemed to be all I could think about lately.

When we exited the theater, daylight was saying its last goodbye to the world, and the last of its warmth was going fast with it. Deep glows of red and orange stretched across the sky.

"Where to now?" I asked as we stepped off the curb linked at the elbow, heading toward my truck.

"I don't know. But I don't want to go home yet."

I opened the door for her and she climbed in. "Neither do I. What sounds good?" I lingered there while she buckled her seatbelt.

She turned to me and lifted her shoulders indecisively. "Anything. You pick."

"You got it. I know a cool place we can go." I closed her door and headed to the driver's seat. The truck hummed to life around us as we made our way across town to the Island.

By the time we reached Padre Balli Park beach, most of the day was gone, and most of the daily visitors with it. The farewell colors of sunset were in full bloom, with the sun having already disappeared beyond the horizon. Toward the entrance of the driving path, there were a handful of bonfires lighting up and even a few pitched tents. Now that the parking lot and gazebos were gone, beach parking permits were the way to go.

I drove further down the beach, following the skyline to nowhere in particular. When I came to an acceptable section, I maneuvered the truck around and backed it up as close to the water's edge as I dared get. Even with four-wheel-drive, I didn't want to risk any mishaps that could break Sarah's curfew.

Going around, I opened the door for her. Sarah slipped her sandals off and stashed them on the dash, then hopped down into the sand and wiggled her toes. She looked out over the gold and white ripples of the ocean. "Wow, it's beautiful here. I always forget."

"Don't get down here often?"

"Hardly ever. I've probably only been to the beach once since I was super little. My family and I ate at the pier restaurant. I can't believe it's all gone now."

"Me neither." Such a contrast to my childhood. The beach was free, so that's one of the only happy memories I had growing up. But things had changed.

In 2020, Hurricane Hanna did what Harvey had failed to do and completely took the Bob Hall Pier and Mikel May's restaurant out of commission. I'd fished off the T-end of the pier a couple times, but mostly I just liked it because it was part of the beach itself. It looked eerie and empty down there now. Just like any other straight stretch of sand and water.

Still, this place *was* beautiful.

"Any time you wanna go, just say the word."

"I will. Thank you." Sarah leaned up on her toes to kiss me, but she sank into the sand and only caught my chin. We shared a laugh and I bent down for a second try. "That's better," she said.

I pulled her close, angling her head with one hand. Moving her hair aside, I exposed the curvature of her neck, dusting light kisses all the way to her jawline. After one last, languid kiss, I forced myself away from her.

Need a distraction.

Ignoring the aching that gripped me from head to toe, I redirected my focus to the truck. I opened the back door and moved stuff aside, then bent the back seats forward and revealed a small storage compartment. From there, I retrieved a wad of blankets and a pillow. "Good thing these were still in here." I felt Sarah's questioning gaze on me as I handed her the bundle. "The social worker gave them to me the night of the fire. Anyway, luckily, we can now benefit from my forgetfulness. The truck bed isn't a deluxe resort chair or anything, but at least we'll be warm. It gets cold here real fast without the sun."

"That'll be just fine." Sarah dropped the blankets and pillow into the bed of the truck. "I'll lay them out in a bit. I want to get my feet in the water while there's still enough light left to see what I'm stepping on."

Jumping into the truck bed, I cleared it as best I could before taking over blanket duty. While spreading out the first layer, I heard a squeal coming from the water and jerked my head around to see her hopping from one foot to the other, murmuring something about the temperature. Chuckling to myself, I turned back to my task and finished our makeshift stargazing lounge for the evening.

A cluster of driftwood caught my eye from amongst a collection of debris the tide had washed ashore. I smiled to myself, an idea brewing, then jumped from the truck and went over, inspecting the pieces. I plucked them out, shaking off bits of seaweed, and cleared an area to lay them out in. Arranging them just so, I formed a heart, packing the pieces firmly into the sand with a rock, and then left it there for her to discover on her own. Then I just watched her.

Sarah walked up and down a small section of the beach until all the color was drained from the sky, and the first twinkle of stars shone brightly against their satin backdrop. Her gaze tilted up, and she looked in a state of awe.

I saw her shake from the fresh sea breeze and came up behind her, rubbing my hands over her arms. "You ready to get under a blanket?"

Teeth chattering, she said, "Yes." Walking over, I saw from the corner of my eye when she saw my clever arrangement of wood. "Did you do that?"

"Maybe I did. Or maybe a mermaid crawled up onto the shore while you weren't looking and made it for us." I luxuriated in the sweet melody of Sarah's laughter.

When we were settled into the truck bed, looking skyward, each of us lying on our own piece of the pillow and warm beneath the blankets, Sarah broke the silence first. "This sky is wild."

I looked up, taking in it all in. "You like it?"

"I love it. How could I not?"

The complete lack of earthly-light around us aided in the stars' splendor. I'd never seen the sky so lit up by its own stars before. She reached for my hand.

"Thank you for bringing me here. This was perfect."

I drew her hand up to my mouth for a soft kiss. "You're welcome."

Though her touch was still doing things to me I had to ignore, my eyes stayed fixed on the scene above us. Countless stars were sprinkling their light, coating the heavens with their awesomeness.

She sighed dreamily. "How can anyone look at beauty like this and not believe in God's existence? Where else would it come from?"

"It's only rocks and atmosphere."

"Without God's purposeful touch, it would only be rocks and atmosphere, but because He made them, they're wondrous. Marvelous. Inspiring."

"Well, I think *you're* pretty wondrous, marvelous, and inspiring. If the same God made you who also made those stars, then I might have to believe it's all true."

Sarah let go of my hand so she could wrap her arm around mine, hugging it tight like she would fall into the sky if she didn't anchor herself to me.

"God made you, too, Kevin. And you wanna know something?"

"Hm?"

"I've never believed in such a thing as soulmates, but I wouldn't be surprised if you were made just for me."

"Why do you say that?"

"Because I never imagined that I would love someone this much. To think that a couple of months ago you weren't in my life at all is unbelievable. I can't picture it without you again. I want nothing more than to see you thriving and happy, and I want to take part in making those things happen. That must be love, right?"

My heart was in my throat, beating so wildly I thought I might choke. How did she always have that way of articulating things I could barely even comprehend? Every moment we spent together, I was struck by her more and more.

It was crazy how quickly I'd come to the conclusion that I loved Sarah, even long before it finally slipped. I had fallen for her after my first visit to her house, when she kissed the ugly scar on my hand like I was worthy of more than pain and suffering. She made everything more beautiful without even trying. The stars, the ocean… even me. Maybe that meant I could learn to be as good as she believed I was. If that were possible, I wouldn't mind being her soulmate.

I bent up on my elbow and leaned down, kissing her gently. She eagerly accepted and gave more than I asked for, shaking up my mettle. Her hands fisted my shirt, and as the seconds passed, the more intertwined we became. When her trembling hand reached under the hem of my shirt, my heart rate was already sky high. Sarah pulled the material up higher, peeling it off of me, before letting it fall away.

I towered over her, framed by the dotted blanket in the sky. In a mesmerized motion, Sarah touched my toned olive skin, following a path from my sternum to my abs, seeming perplexed by the hard softness of my muscles.

As I ran my own hand up Sarah's side, I hooked the material of her shirt and began lifting it. On the way, I bumped into the glucose monitor adhered to the side of her abdomen. "Oh, sorry," I said, abandoning my effort.

"It's okay. It's just another part of me. As much as you are," Sarah told me.

"As much as I am?"

"For your quick and caring actions," she said, and I understood.

"I didn't hurt you, knocking into it like that?"

"Not at all." Intensity was etched into her gaze and in every bead of sweat on her exposed skin. Her expression seemed to make more demands than I first realized. *She couldn't possibly mean...*

Could she?

"Sarah?" My question hung in the air, suspended like the stars above.

A beaming set of headlights turned down the beach, capturing our attention. I drew the blanket over us and crouched, shielding Sarah from whatever was approaching. A Jeep full of people and surfboards loudly sailed by, leaving only sand for the wind to blow around. Their laughter and the vibrating hum of the engine soon faded down the shoreline, disappearing beyond the dunes.

My lungs felt on the verge of exploding. I released a deep breath of relief and hung my head. If I wasn't so freaked, I might've laughed. How I didn't notice that vehicle before it was right in my face, I'll never understand.

But beneath me, exposed in more ways than one, Sarah wasn't laughing at all.

SARAH

37

It wasn't until the threat of being seen had passed that I realized I was more vulnerable, both physically and emotionally, than I had ever been in my life. As the comprehension hit me, panic set in.

"Kevin, get up."

He zeroed in on me, noting the sound of my voice. "Are you okay?"

"No. Please, get up." I wasn't okay, and neither was this. The moment his weight was lifted, I fled from under him and righted my shirt. I bit my tongue as I tried not to break down and cry.

God, I am so mortified. What am I doing?

Not very long ago, Kevin had warned me I might change my mind about refusing sex when I was finally faced with the chance to have it. At the time, I had been so sure of myself, but just look at me now. At the first opportunity to stay true to my own convictions, I had all but thrown them away.

Mortified, I leapt from the truck. "I'm so sorry, Kevin. I just need to go home."

"It's okay, we'll go right now." Kevin's bewildered gaze followed me as I scurried into the passenger seat and closed myself in. I listened to his movements — pulling on his shirt, balling up the bedding, and hoisting up the tailgate. By the time he got back into the truck, my mind was a colossal mess. And he didn't seem much better off, which of course only made me feel worse.

"Sarah, talk to me."

He reached over and sought my hand, but I yanked it away and shrank myself against the window.

"I'm sorry. I feel like such an idiot," I said, keeping my sights on the dark, sandy void.

"Why?"

"Tonight was so perfect. You make me so happy, Kevin. But I can't believe I almost —"

"*We* almost. And that doesn't make you an idiot."

He could say that all he wanted, but it didn't change how I felt. Even if I was overreacting — and who gets to decide that? — the shame I felt was real.

When we pulled up to my house, I wanted to take a minute and try to explain the way I felt, but I didn't think I could face him. So, instead, I opened the door and bolted without a word.

"Sarah, hold up," he tried, but I was already halfway up the drive. He ran around the front and caught me by the wrist. "Please, talk to me. It's okay."

I looked down and away. "I should just go in."

"You're not running away from me. We do things as a team now, remember?" He took my chin and tilted my face up, forcing me to make eye contact. Tears formed and spilled before I could blink them away, but he didn't back down. "Did you mean what you said at the beach?"

"Yes, I did."

"Then don't shut me out now."

"Talking isn't going to help. When we talked about this before, I was so confident in my beliefs. And now…" I shook my head, the shame building up inside me like a dying star about to go supernova. "This is my fault. I started it. I teased you. And now I feel terrible."

"Is this all because of your faith?"

"Not all, but yes."

"Isn't faith supposed to make people feel better, not worse?"

He couldn't possibly understand… "Things aren't that simple."

"It doesn't even matter. There's nothing to feel bad about because nothing happened."

"That's not because I was strong enough to say no. If that car hadn't gone by…" Overcome, I buried my face in his chest. His arms engulfed me, and despite my personal discord, I felt marginal comfort.

"You practically faced your own death not too long ago, and simply feeling good upsets you this much?"

"It's so much more than that, and once it happens, it can't be undone."

"I get it. But everything's okay." Kevin ran his hand over my head, smoothing back my hair. "I love you."

"You're only saying it because you feel bad."

"That is not true."

I hadn't meant to voice my doubt out loud, and it made me cringe to hear the hurt in his voice.

A light turned on inside the house, drawing our attention. "I have to go inside now. It's probably curfew time, anyway." I sniffed and wiped my eyes dry, trying to make my face look presentable in case I ran into anyone inside.

"I'll only let you go if you promise we can finish this conversation. Tonight."

I exhaled in defeat. "Okay. We will."

"Promise me."

"I promise."

Luckily, nobody stopped me on my way in. Upstairs in my room, I waited in the dark until I heard Kevin's truck leave, then proceeded to get ready for bed. After a shower and a change into comfy clothes, I texted him.

SARAH

I hope you don't hate me.

Then, I waited in knots for his reply.

KEVIN

Do you really think I would? Have I ever pressured you in any way?

SARAH

Of course not. I didn't mean to imply anything like that. I just feel so bad. Like I led you on.

KEVIN

You didn't, so don't be pulling away.

But I was, and I couldn't help it. Swept up in the moment, I had been willing to do something I could never take back. The fear that it almost happened didn't want to leave me. I loved him wholeheartedly, and something inside me believed he was the one for me, but that didn't excuse anything.

So tired of crying, I growled and wiped away new tears. It didn't matter if we loved each other. We were too young for the next level. Maybe Kevin didn't think so, but we weren't raised with the same values. If I ended up not waiting until marriage, I would never forgive myself. Pleasures of the flesh were great but temporary, and if I felt this bad after barely a hint of it, there's no way I could handle anything more.

KEVIN

Is that what's happening? Are you pulling away?

SARAH

I'm not trying to, I just don't know what to think right now. I'm confused.

KEVIN

Confused about what? You're not sure how you feel about me?

SARAH

Oh, no. I know how I feel about you, Kevin. I just don't know how to deal with myself.

KEVIN

You're always talking about forgiveness. Why don't you start with that?

To that, I didn't know what to say. He had a point, but such a thing felt impossible right now. Thankfully, we hadn't crossed that line, but it didn't take away my personal responsibility to my beliefs. If we had any hope of staying together, I had to get a handle on my emotions.

I typed my reply.

SARAH

I think those lights were divine intervention, saving me from making a bad decision. Does that sound stupid?

KEVIN

If that's how you feel, then it can't be stupid.

KEVIN

It doesn't matter what stopped us. The bottom
line is we didn't do it. And we don't have to.

SARAH

Thanks, Kevin. Let's both get some sleep.

KEVIN

Are we okay?

SARAH

We're okay.

I replied, not all that convinced myself.

SARAH

38

I DIDN'T FEEL READY FOR THE DAY WHEN I WENT DOWNSTAIRS, BUT I had no choice. I had to make an appearance at breakfast if I hoped to act normal. "Morning," I told my parents as I slid into my seat at the dining table. Dad was seated already, but his mind was engrossed in the newspaper he held out in front of him.

"Good morning, honey," Mom reciprocated from the other side of the kitchen island. She had a pan of eggs finishing up on the stove. "I didn't catch you when you came in last night. How was the movie?"

I looked at the spread before me and nearly groaned. Typically, I looked forward to one of my mom's big breakfasts, making glucose adjustments accordingly, but not today. Just my daily injection would do for now. It was hard to indulge without an appetite. "Not that great," I told her.

"That's too bad. What'd y'all do after?"

They hadn't given thanks yet, but I took a forced bite of food, trying it out. The savory morsel turned to rubbery cardboard in my mouth, my will to eat leaving completely. "We went to the beach," and I offered no more.

"Really?" My mom perked up. "Oh, now that is fun. We haven't had a beach day in far too long. How was it?"

"It was really nice." *At first.* "I'd forgotten how pretty the water is." *And how amazing the sky was out there when you could look out and feel like the only two people alive.*

Mom came around with the scrambled eggs and seated herself. Dad folded up his paper and set it on the end table beside his chair, arranging himself to say grace.

Now that my parents weren't distracted, I felt unable to face them. "I actually need to go look at my numbers. Get started without me."

"Sure thing," Mom said casually, watching me leave.

By the time I was out of the bathroom, eyes swollen and red again, my mom was waiting on my bed. She was looking at me like I knew something was wrong, just as I suspected she would.

"Come sit, honey." When I did, she put her arms around me and squeezed. When we separated, she said, "Tell me."

I looked away. "Tell you what?"

"Whatever is bothering you."

"There's nothing. I'm just tired."

"I'm your mother. Look me in the eye and tell me there's nothing wrong if that's what you want me to believe."

I looked at her but couldn't say the words. I already knew that she knew.

"Did something happen last night? Between you and Kevin? You can tell me."

"No, but…" *Well, out with it.* "Almost."

"Okay. I'm listening. Tell me what happened."

"The beach really was wonderful, Mom. Kevin is the best."

"I know, honey. I've seen the way he is with you."

My melodramatic eyes watered again and I had to look away.

"We were looking at the stars, talking about God actually, and we got… distracted. Nothing happened, but it could've."

My mom was quiet for a minute, and I summoned the courage to look at her. I was surprised to see big tears in her eyes and the saddest of concerned smiles on her face.

"I feel so bad. I know I messed up."

"Oh, my girl." She put her arm around my shoulders. "It goes without saying that I'm happy nothing happened, but I know what the struggle is like. I know you've heard me say that I was your age once, and that is absolutely true. When I say I know, I know. It's not always easy to do God's will in this life. You have to choose to want it every single day."

"I do, but… I still feel so much for Kevin."

"And that's probably not going to go away. But you were tested, and you learned a tough lesson. You will be stronger for it. Don't you think so? You know the difference between right and wrong."

"I don't know if I could choose the right thing if it were to happen again." Heating with embarrassment, I couldn't believe I admitted that to my mother.

"Well, maybe you could do with a time out until you do."

"You mean like dump him?" I was horrified by the idea.

"No, honey. Allow yourself some time to realign your heart and mind. Regain your composure."

I shook my head, shoulders slumped. "He wouldn't understand."

"It's not your fault if he doesn't. But even the blind could see how he feels about you, so I think it'll be okay."

I turned the advice over in my mind. I woke up hoping to keep any hints of this mess from my parents, but talking to my mom had actually given me a bit of peace. Then, giving her a side-eye, I had a question for her in return. "How do you always know what's going on, anyway?"

"It's a gift we mothers get. Plus, I track your app like a hawk. I knew you already took your insulin this morning." My mom laughed and pulled me in close again, rubbing my shoulder. "Pray about it. It'll all be okay, my girl. Just be honest with him. And for what it's worth, thank you for being honest with me, too."

"You're not going to tell Dad, are you?"

"No, baby, I think we will keep this one between us."

As soon as Mom left, I let myself fall back onto my bed. It didn't take me long to realize I had to follow her advice.

God, I really love him. Please, make him understand.

KEVIN

39

Last night, I had the most fitful sleep I'd had in a while. I tossed and turned, and every time I woke up and looked at the clock, hardly any time had gone by. When I did finally fall into sleep's clutches, I was held captive by the craziest dreams.

In the first one, Sarah and I were back in the truck bed watching the stars, until suddenly they all fell from the sky and came after us. We hid under the truck as each one came crashing down, burning tiny holes through the metal. Sarah was so scared she couldn't be comforted, no matter what I said or how closely I held her.

There was another dream where we were on the couch in my living room. Sarah disappeared, and I was standing alone outside my house, clothed as I was on the day of the fire, watching it burn all over again. Instead of just one side of the house being destroyed, it spread higher and faster and consumed the entire thing. As I looked on, I saw my mom through the window, screaming and crying while trying to get out. I tried to run toward the house, but I didn't move. I looked down, and yellow caution tape was wrapped tightly around my feet and legs, constricting me tighter as if it were alive. The more I struggled, the higher up it climbed until it had taken me over completely. I was rendered voiceless, unable to scream. My mother couldn't be saved, I could do nothing about the fire, and Sarah was nowhere to be seen. "God, help me!" I cried out, the voice coming from me somehow, even though my mouth didn't move. Then there came a sonic boom, resulting in a too-bright white light just above my house. In the blink of an eye, I was free of the tape, my house was standing perfectly with no fire, and my mom wasn't trapped. The white light dissipated into the middle of the sky and twinkled out, becoming integrated with the stars in the sky. It was the same sky we saw at the beach, but that view was impossible from my house on the southeast side of town. The city was too lit up, its atmosphere too cloudy. I knew something was amiss, and yet, I felt oddly calm.

When I woke up the last time, it was 9:28 a.m. It was way later than I needed to be up, but I still had time to make it to my morning shift at Tanner's if I got up now.

I checked my phone, hoping to have missed a text from Sarah, but there was nothing. Plugging it in to get some juice while I got ready, I left my bed and showered. I dressed in my gray "Tanner Automotive" t-shirt and black Dickies shorts, fastened my belt, and pulled on socks and shoes. All the while, my bad dreams were front and center in my mind.

Finally, a text arrived.

SARAH

Good morning.

KEVIN

Morning. How are you?

SARAH

I'm okay. You getting ready for work?

KEVIN

Yeah. Going in at 10. How are you really?

There was a pause between responses. I watched with anticipation as her typing dots appeared. I'd made it all the way to the truck before she sent an actual reply.

SARAH

Better, I guess. Can I call you after work so we can talk?

A black hole formed in my gut. She didn't have to explain herself for me to know what she intended to say. I really didn't want to hear it, but I didn't think I could wait all day for it, either.

KEVIN

Why did you message me now if you didn't want to explain until later?

SARAH

Sorry. We'll talk later, k?

I couldn't deal. I squeezed the steering wheel with my free hand and dialed her number with the other.

She picked up just before her voicemail took over. "Hi."

"Sarah, please, just put me out of my misery."

I heard her sigh into the receiver. "It's not like that. I love you —"

"You love me '*but*,' right?"

"There is no 'but.' I love you and because of that, I recognize I need some time."

Time? What does "time" even mean? "We both slipped up for a minute. It's not going to happen again."

"But it easily could, especially with how strongly I feel for you."

"What about how I feel? Doesn't it count?"

She didn't say anything.

"I love you, too, Sarah. I haven't had a good example of love put in front of me until you." I could tell by the soft sounds she made that she was crying. It's not what I wanted at all.

"I'm so sorry, Kevin. My feelings for you won't change, but I need to make sure I can handle how big this is. The next time we encounter temptation, I need to know that I'll resist. This is on me."

My reiteration of love had zero impact, and I felt on the verge of desperation. She was still going to drive a wedge between us, even if that wasn't her intention. "Don't do this. You said we were okay."

"Let's just take some space for the rest of the break and then we'll forget any of this ever happened, okay? We'll put it all behind us."

"It's *already* behind us *right now*," I insisted.

"It's just a little breather until Monday. We can still talk. I just think it'd be best if we didn't hang out for a little while. That's all."

Now, it was my turn to be silent. What could I possibly say at this point? She'd clearly made this decision without me, and nothing I could say would change her mind if it hadn't already.

"I'm not upset with you over anything, you know," Sarah told me. "This isn't a punishment."

"Then why does it feel like one?"

"I wish it didn't."

"Are you sure this isn't some excuse? Because if you're going to just break up with me later, I'd rather get it over with now."

"Kevin, no. When I say I love you, I mean it. That's why I think this makes sense. Can't you just give me this and know we'll be fine?"

Since when was it "fine" for a relationship to cut it off abruptly, without proper discussion or agreement? If all she really wanted was to forget that *nothing* happened last night, then why couldn't she just do that? It felt like something more. And then to say it's not a break-up? I didn't know what to think anymore, but I didn't have the time to figure it out.

"This isn't okay with me, but it really doesn't sound like I can change your mind." Once again, she said nothing. *Whatever.* "I gotta get to work. I'm already late."

"Okay. Why don't you call me after?"

What's the point, I wondered sardonically. So we could chit chat like awkward strangers all over again? It was so nice to be past that awkward point with her, and I didn't want to backtrack. She was the first great thing life had ever given me, but it was clear she either didn't feel the same or I had no clue how to handle a relationship with someone so pure. No matter how I sliced it, I felt like I would lose her.

Maybe after a hard day's work, and some of her *"distance,"* I would have a different perspective. Maybe *"some time"* of my own would help explain why my girlfriend suddenly wanted nothing to do with me.

"Will you call me after work?" she probed again.

"Yeah, sure," I finally said.

"Okay. Bye, Kevin. I love you."

"Bye." Without a more graceful goodbye, I hung up the phone

and drove to work, doubt clinging to every corner of my mind. At least I wasn't dwelling on my dreams anymore.

That night, I didn't call Sarah back after all. Between our issues and my finances, I felt all but defeated by the end of the day. So, when Tanner himself cornered me about one of those side jobs, I wasn't prepared to refuse.

KEVIN

40

NEAR THE END OF MY SHIFT, TANNER APPROACHED ME ABOUT making one of the special deliveries Russ was always talking about. One of Russ's regular clients needed packages delivered tonight, but Russell was out sick. He knew I wanted extra hours, and there was no one else Tanner trusted enough to ask. To my credit, I really wanted to turn him down. But when Tanner handed me an envelope with that night's pay in cold, hard cash, I pictured my mom's past-due bill.

Following the route I'd scouted on my phone prior to leaving the garage that night, I was engaged in my first *job*. The twists and turns led me to county roads outside the city, where the only things I could see were directly in sight of my headlights. There were no street lamps of any kind, and the roads weren't maintained by the city. It was just me, the moon-less night, and my conscience.

And a back seat full of illicit paraphernalia.

The house I came upon was nestled behind a cluster of mature, live oaks and crepe myrtles. I entered the property over a cattle guard and followed the driveway toward the only other light source around for miles. There was a large industrial garage around the back of a ranch-style house with a wraparound porch and a single floodlight in the topmost arch of the building. It kicked on when I got closer.

I parked and waited, double-checking the destination on my phone, until someone coming out of the garage caught my attention. I tossed my phone into the passenger seat and got out, closing the door with extra care so as to not alert the countryside I was there. "Miguel Arias?"

"Yes, sir," the man confirmed.

As I inspected Tanner's client more closely, I noticed his hands were the only filthy looking thing about him, aside from his business dealings. He was an older looking gentleman with a kind face, dressed like one of those slick *vaqueros* at Sarah's church on Sundays. He had shiny black snakeskin boots, closely cropped hair beneath his western hat, a bolo tie cinched up neatly, and his shirt buttoned all the way to the collar. His voice was thickly accented. If I'd seen him on the street in the daylight, I would never have guessed he was into illegal activity.

As now I was, too.

In order to get through this, I had to quiet my negative thoughts.

"You brought the six?" Miguel asked.

"Yep. All here."

He clapped his hands together, looking pleased. "Great. Let me help."

Not knowing the proper etiquette for things like this, I simply opened the back door and allowed the cowboy to grab half of his purchase. I toted the other half behind him. We walked through the giant dome of a garage, past tractors and plows and large grain cans and stacked bags and hay, into a little office in the back. He placed the packages on a desk and I followed suit. All stacked up together like a collection of meats directly from the butcher. If I thought of it that way, I felt slightly less guilty.

But not really.

"Thank you very much, sir." The polite criminal extended his hand and I shook it, nodding my welcome.

While heading slowly down the driveway to leave, I questioned how a normal-looking guy with such pleasant manners, who had a portrait of his family hanging on the wall in his office, got caught up in what Tanner was doing. Was it the only way Miguel could maintain his blue-collar lifestyle with all this expensive machinery? Or maybe he had a despondent mother in a nursing home with an exorbitantly high bill or something...

Pulling off the hard-packed caliche and back onto the county road, I didn't notice myself praying the money was worth it.

41

I woke up just after eight in the morning, upset with myself for falling asleep before Kevin got off work, only to find out I had no missed calls or texts from him. He hadn't reached out at all.

Was he really so angry that ignoring me was his best option? More than hearing my voice, he wanted to distance himself? Punish *me* for asking for space? I didn't want to believe he would do that, but was it a possibility?

I ditched my phone and rolled over, folding my hands together. Squeezing my eyes shut, I said my morning prayers.

Before the end, I took a cleansing breath and let it go slowly. "And, God... please be with Kevin and give him a desire to know You. Bless him with Your presence and keep him safe. In Jesus' name I pray, Amen."

Feeling renewed for the day ahead, I listened to the sounds of morning as they crept into my room. The weather had been so perfect lately that I'd been sleeping with the window cracked at night. Nestling under a nice, heavy quilt with a pleasant chill in the air was the best feeling. I wouldn't mind staying in bed like that all day.

Talking myself out of texting Kevin for the hundredth time, I opened my group chat with the girls.

SARAH

Good morning, ladies.

BIRDIE JO

Morning!

SAMMY

Whazzaaaaappp

Jenna probably wouldn't respond because she was camping out at the beach with Dan and some others for the weekend.

In the back of my mind, I felt a twinge of jealousy that Jenna and Dan seemed to have it so much easier than me and Kevin. How nice it must be for them to spend all their time together without apprehension and self-reproach. For one dark second, I failed to remember that things were only easy for them on the surface, as was the case for anyone. Besides, it wasn't a fair comparison. No two couples were exactly alike.

I sent a reply to the group:

SARAH

How've you guys been? Doing anything fun?

BIRDIE JO

We were just packing to go meet the others at the beach. You should totally come with us.

SAMMY

No, you totally HAVE to come w/ us!

Immediately, strange feelings took me back to two nights

prior. After my close call with Kevin, I wondered if I would ever view the beach the same way again.

Jesus says our sins are under his blood. The least I could do is act like I believe it.

I couldn't let the location be forever altered.

SARAH

I'd love to!

BIRDIE JO

That's the spirit! We'll pick you up in about an hour. Don't forget your insulin!

That was the first time one of my friends had brought up my condition since they all found out at the party. It struck me that it didn't bother me like I always expected it would, and I felt comforted by my choice to spend time with them today.

SAMMY

Yes, did we mention we're also staying overnight?

Well, crap. At least, I would be plenty occupied while Kevin was busy working, or whatever it was he ended up doing. A pang of curious sadness sprang up, but I couldn't dwell. I owed it to my friends to be present.

SARAH

Sounds good. I'll be ready.

Getting my parents to let me go hadn't been difficult. "As long as you'll actually eat breakfast this time," Mom said. Then afterward, up in my bedroom as I packed, my mom came up.

"You know I have to ask. Will Kevin be there?"

"No. No Kevin. I actually took your advice and asked him for some space for a few days."

"Oh, you did? How'd it go?"

Movements slowing, my mind grew heavy. "He wasn't thrilled."

"I wouldn't be too happy, either, if you asked me to stay away from you." Mom tweaked my nose and then fixed loose strands of hair behind my ear.

I smiled. "You don't count."

"Now, that hurts."

"Pfft." A few degrees happier than before, I stuffed the rest of my belongings into a duffel bag. When I was away for anything overnight, I swapped my regular insulin pack with a larger one, just in case. Besides that, I always had an emergency travel pack and a brand new Glucagon pen in my purse at all times. Aside from a change of clothes and my favorite pjs, phone charger, and a few other random things, I didn't have too much to pack.

My mom peeked into my bag. "Do you really think you'll be doing any swimming? It's not supposed to get much over seventy degrees until next weekend, and the water stays much cooler."

"I'm sure I won't, but I'd rather bring it and not need it than have to swim in my pjs, just in case."

"Fair enough," she said, stretching as she rose from the bed's edge. She turned with an air of seriousness, commanding my full attention. "Sarah?"

"Yeah?"

"I just want you to know that I'm really proud of you. I know it's difficult to listen to your head when your heart is hounding you, but you're doing a great job. And I think, in the long run, Kevin will think so, too."

I sure hoped so.

"You know how I can get. I worry. It's my specialty."

My mom gave me a soft, understanding smile. "You know what to do with it."

Cast your burden on the Lord, and He will sustain you.

"I know. It's just hard."

"Practice makes perfect."

She couldn't be refuted. Things had a tendency to remain difficult the longer you tried to handle them without God. How the faithless got through their daily lives, I could never understand. It broke my heart to think that Kevin lived that way his whole life, shouldering all of his flaws, and struggling with all of his cares alone. No wonder he had turned to the things he said he wasn't proud of before.

"Love you," my mom said, pressing a kiss to my forehead. "Keep me posted, will you?"

"Sure thing. Love you, too, Mom."

Not long after that, my friends arrived. I bid farewell to my parents on the way out, now realizing how excited I was to be spending a night with the girls again. Hopefully, Kevin was feeling better about our time apart, too. Of course, I missed him, but there was a sense of joy in that feeling. I was looking forward to seeing him again.

Sammy was driving her cherry red Kia Sportage, elbow hanging out the window. "Heeyyyyy," she cat-called from the driver's side. Birdie had her phone in hand and briefly glanced up from it with a smile.

"Hello, ladies." I tucked into the back seat and buckled in after throwing my duffel into the cargo space behind me. Birdie held up her phone and instructed everyone to squeeze in and say *'hot water cornbread!'*

"Ew, what?" Sammy balked.

"That doesn't sound better than cheese," I agreed, both of us messing up Birdie's picture.

"Y'all don't know whatcher missin'. Now, just hold still and let's try this again."

Once we had sufficiently "selfied," Sammy kicked the car into gear and rolled out.

I opened my music app and handed the phone up front. "Here, put this on."

"What is it?" Birdie eyed my phone suspiciously, like it might bite her if she touched it.

Sammy put immediate death to my request. "No way, girl. I love you, but I can't stand your old lady jams, sorry not sorry."

"Yeah, yeah." I sat back against my seat, partway between laughing and pouting. Outvoted again by my friends and their modern preferences.

The air whipping through my hair gave me a taste of how it would be at the beach, and I couldn't wait to get there.

"So, where's Mr. Wonderful today?" asked Sammy, as we crossed over the JKF Memorial Causeway Bridge. Almost there.

"Yeah, not that it matters now, but we almost didn't invite you because we figured you'd have plans with Kevin," added Birdie.

Frowning, I leaned forward. "I'm sorry, guys. Have I been blowing you off?"

"Girl, please. If you think we can't handle you having a man, you're wrong," Sammy insisted.

"Besides, we know you'll always love *us* best," Birdie said assuredly, smiling all the while. "You *could* always invite him, you know."

Could I?

Once at the beach, Sammy stopped short of the little spot where Kevin and I had parked the other night, and a jolt burst from my heart and traveled all the way to my fingers and toes. How different it looked in the light of day, so open and not secluded at all, contrary to how it felt then.

I blushed to myself, hanging my head out the window to feel the ocean breeze cool my face. Sammy put on four-wheel-drive in order to park on a small sandbank parallel to the shore.

After squirming out of the back seat, I saw Jared, Dan, and a few others setting up a volleyball net. "Jared's here?"

"Oh, crap. I'm sorry. Is that okay?" Looking panicked, Sammy's inquiry was hesitant.

The group of guys were working away, laughing and setting out coolers and putting on music. Before Kevin, I never would've questioned it. This kind of casual fun was my scene. These were my friends. While that hadn't changed, my perspective now included more than just myself.

For now, I saw no reason to object. "It's fine. He deserves to be here just as much as I do." These were his friends, too.

As if my attention summoned his, Jared turned and looked my way. He stopped what he was doing, stood up straight, and waved. Giving him a light smile, I waved back.

Birdie and Sammy lugged their stuff out from the back, and then Sammy turned to me. "Do you think Kevin would totally freak?"

Lending them a hand, I took hold of a clump of towels cinched up in a mesh bag. "Maybe. Everyone takes their own time to forgive. We haven't really brought it up again since it was all aired out."

"Why don't you invite him?" Birdie nudged, reiterating her earlier suggestion. "I bet those two would have the sweetest bromance ever if they gave it half a try."

There was that idea again. "Maybe." As nice as it was beginning to sound, I didn't know how Kevin would react to an invitation to hang with my friends and me after being told I needed space. But the idea did have me thinking.

"Up to you. And, anyway, just because Jared's here doesn't mean we have to hang out with him."

"We're all here. I'm not gonna make things awkward. I'm already over it all."

After our canopy and tents and net were all pitched and everyone was good and tired, I crawled onto my sleeping bag and checked my phone, letting my feet dangle out the tent opening to keep the sand off my stuff. My heart skipped upon finally seeing a message from Kevin.

KEVIN

Morning.

It wasn't the most lively of messages, but it was welcome.

At first, I typed up a text questioning why he hadn't called me last night like he said he would, but deleted it. As badly as I'd like to know, I didn't want to start the dialogue with a complaint.

SARAH

Morning! How are you?

KEVIN

Doing fine. How are you?

SARAH

Good. Missing you...

KEVIN

Are you?

SARAH

Yes :) Of course.

KEVIN

You do seem in a better mood. What have you
been up to?

KEVIN

And I miss you, too.

SARAH

:) The girls invited me to a beach sleepover
tonight. I haven't seen much of them lately so I
decided to go.

KEVIN

Oh, wow. That sounds like fun.

SARAH

Are you working today? You could come by if
you want…

Inviting him had just fallen out of me. Why not? So far, this day was like a breath of fresh air and I already felt so much better about things, and keeping my distance amongst a large group in a public place wouldn't be difficult at all. It was possible I didn't need the space I originally thought I did, but rather a different perspective.

KEVIN

What about your break?

I couldn't hear his tone of voice, but I could imagine it. Best thing I could think to do was avoid the direct question and show him I was aiming to move forward.

SARAH

I understand if you're still upset… You don't have to come, but I would love to have you here. Just something to consider if you have time, no pressure. We'll be here 'til sometime tomorrow afternoon.

KEVIN

Okay.

SARAH

I love you, Kevin.

KEVIN

Love you, too.

Heart feeling fluttery from our exchange, I tucked my phone into the hanging pouch on my side of the tent before returning to the others.

SARAH

42

Everyone spent the day singing karaoke, playing volleyball, doing terrible impressions of gymnasts, and hunting down the best seashells. Someone spotted a large Man O' War the tide had brought in, and we all had our fun oohing and awwing over it.

Even if most of us had seen those funny blue jellyfish a hundred times throughout our lives, it was still entertaining to gather around and take turns inspecting it with a stick. I concluded if you enjoyed the people you were with, any mundane experience could become a fun one.

It came natural to picture a young Kevin, exploring up and down the sea shore with a stick and sand pail in hand. Maybe he used to poke the jellies, too, or collect fistfuls of coquinas to watch how fast they could burrow and disappear into the sand.

I had extended the invitation, but he gave no indication if he would come or not. I missed him, but this was my own fault.

When the fire was built and everyone began getting comfortable around it, I pulled on a hoodie and took off down the surf, following the direction of the sunset. Eventually, I reached the spot where Kevin and I had parked. The driftwood heart was still set up exactly as we'd left it. I would've taken a picture, but I patted down my empty pockets and recalled leaving it in the tent pouch earlier.

As soon as I got back to camp, I would check in with Kevin again and share that his wooden heart was still holding strong.

I wrapped my arms around my middle and sat down beside the arrangement, effectively wrapping myself in the warmth of that night. Taking in this display now hit differently. Maybe I'd gotten things all wrong. Who said I had anything to be afraid of? What almost happened between us didn't have to be scary. It was a good thing I'd learned a first-hand lesson in boundaries, if nothing else.

The more I thought about it, the more I just wanted to be near him, to share his company. Even if the enemy wished to exploit our relationship by drawing out our fleshly weaknesses, we could decide to overcome that.

My thoughts were interrupted by oncoming footfalls. "Hey, Sarah." Jared was walking up with his hands in the pockets of his beige cargo shorts, and the Hawaiian-print button-up shirt he wore was open and billowing in the breeze. The soft glow of sunset cast a shadow behind him that stretched on for ages.

"Hey, Jared." I reciprocated his light smile, scrunching the sand between my toes.

"What're you doing all the way down here?"

"I just went for a walk."

"Everything okay?" His words were drawn out with his wariness.

"Yep. The evening was just too pretty to ignore."

He looked out to the fading light, a look of agreement on his face, before turning back to me. "Is it okay if I sit for a minute? I won't linger long. Scout's honor." He held up his hand.

I rolled my shoulder. "It's a free stump."

Jared chuckled before coming to rest with a wide berth between us. For a moment, he sat in silence and browsed around, avoiding eye contact, when his gaze landed on the heart mural in the sand. "That's cool. Did you do that?"

"Kevin did, actually. Just the other day."

He thought for a moment. "I assume things with you two are going well, then?"

"They are, thank you." I wasn't aware of the cheesy grin I let slip with my response. Kevin's and my little intermission couldn't keep me from feeling joy over him.

"That good, huh?"

I was grateful the darkness hid my blush. "He's the one."

"Wow. You believe in that stuff?"

"I do now."

"Wow," he said again. "Then I'm happy for you both. How come he's not here tonight?"

"We're just taking a couple days to do our own things." Details were unnecessary.

"Gotcha." There was another bloated silence. "Listen, Sarah, I —"

"You don't have to say anything, Jared."

"Yes, I do. I haven't been able to let it go, and I really want you to know how sorry I am for what happened that night."

Truly, it was long past water under the bridge. "It's alright, Jared. I've already forgiven you."

He exhaled and hung his head, compressing his eyes with one hand. Then, he sat up and cleared his throat. "I'm really grateful to hear you say that. That night was the highlight of all the dumb stuff I've ever done, that's for sure."

I laughed and patted him on the shoulder. "Oh, I'm sure you

could figure out a way to top it eventually," I ribbed. "Just kidding. Jared, you're gonna be just fine."

"Pfft," he laughed. "With my luck?"

"Sarah?"

Hearing my name, I whipped around, not expecting to see Kevin. "You came!" I smiled, happy to see him. The look on his face quickly changed my mood, and I jumped to my feet. "Is everything okay?"

KEVIN

43

From what I could see, everything was absolutely *not* okay. I dared not move or else I might do some serious damage to Jared. By whatever miracle, I kept firmly rooted in place and managed to not run over to her. "What are you doing?"

"I told you earlier. The girls and I are camping out here tonight."

"Not that, Sarah. What're you doing here with *him?*" The spikes in my tone couldn't be helped. What was she thinking, spending time alone with this guy, of all people? Is this why she wanted a "break"? No good could come from this scenario, and the thought of what could've possibly taken place had I not shown up made me sick. My self-doubt and anxiety wouldn't let it rest. I'd never taken her for a cheater, but what was I supposed to think? And who knew what a slime like Jared would try while they were getting buddy-buddy in the dark? Not to mention, in *this* place? *Our* place where *we* had gotten so close? Why would she have brought him here to be alone like this?

"You can see for yourself. Sitting and talking," came Sarah's simple statement.

"I saw you touching him. It's dark out, and you two are alone together? What would I have seen if I'd waited longer?"

She flinched, annoyed. "Seriously? Were you hiding out watching us?"

"You asked me to come. Don't try to get upset about it."

Her gaze narrowed. "I'm not upset you're here, but if you watched us, then you saw all there was to see. Did you even bother to listen to anything we were saying, or did you just take one look and assume the worst?"

As Sarah was talking, Jared rose to his feet. I forgot all reason the moment Jared stepped beside her. How dare he. How dare *she!* None of what she said explained what she was doing out here with him. Contrary to what Sarah may have assumed, I hadn't been watching long at all. The moment I'd seen them, I called her name.

"It doesn't matter. He's had this coming." I stalked toward him, but Sarah stepped in my path, knocking into me a slight cause for hesitation. "Step aside, Sarah."

"No, Kevin. You're not doing this." She stood firm against me despite my bull-like desire to plow through her. She pressed her hand against my chest, beseeching my calm with her touch. "Kevin."

I looked her in the eye, feeling myself growing wild with fury. "Why are you defending him?"

"You've got it wrong. It's you I'm trying to defend here. He and I have already worked everything out. There are no hard feelings."

"Oh, come on, what kind of crap is that? How can you forgive someone for doing what he did? For what he caused?" Then I rolled my eyes, the truth coming to me. "Never mind. Of course you would. Perfect Jesus lady."

Jared moved around Sarah with his hand raised in disapproval. "Dude, you're being low. Let this go before you do or say something you'll regret. I know a lot about that, trust me."

I sneered at Jared for having the nerve to speak to me. To call *me* out for being low was a brand new form of torture that I just couldn't endure, even with Sarah standing in my way, protesting like she was. She walked into me with her whole body, attempting to force me into taking steps back, but I remained unmoving. Previously, when she'd stood with me like this, we'd been standing together. Now that she was standing against me, the entire experience was different.

"Kevin, seriously, you have to put an end to this. You can't act like a caveman simply because you're upset. Please, just walk away before you do something stupid."

"You want me to leave? Why? So you can spend more time alone with him?"

Jared interjected again into the conversation. "We're all hanging out. The guys and I aren't even staying the whole night."

"I don't want to hear you!" I emphasized toward Jared with the point of my finger. I knew the others had caught wind of the shouting when I heard their murmurs preceding them down the beach. The last thing I wanted was to make a fool of myself, or Sarah, in front of her friends again.

"I'm really sorry, Sarah. I said I was happy for you, but now I'm worried. Rethink this relationship because homeboy has major problems. I'm outta here." Jared moved past her and started toward the oncoming voices. But then he stopped, shaking his head. "No. You know what? She deserves better." He took a step toward me instead. "You should've left her alone, man. Even I can see that."

I struggled to process what he had just said. Sure, I would

freely admit that I wasn't the most perfect guy, and maybe I came with certain issues that made being with me less than ideal. Maybe I had a mother who pretended to hate my girlfriend just so she would run and stay away from me because it would save us both future heartache. So what? I also had some good qualities. Sarah told me that all the time.

Regardless, I've never endangered her life!

"You had one date with her and she almost died, or have you forgotten? I helped her get away from you."

"Dude, you just got lucky. You said so yourself." Jared conjured up my past words of diffidence, antagonizing me further.

"I did what was necessary after you *drugged her!*"

"That wasn't done on purpose, and yet between us, I'm still the better guy for her, so what does that tell you? At least what I did was accidental, and I've apologized for it. What you're doing to her right now is just messed up."

"Jared, please, just stop. You're not helping." Sarah made an attempt, but it failed.

"He's beyond help," Jared scoffed. "But I hope for better for you, Sarah. I really do."

All of Sarah's previous talks of forgiveness on Jared's behalf were forgotten. Everything Pastor Brian said in one of his recent sermons about turning the other cheek flew out the window. I only saw red, and I charged, making good on the vow I once made to ensure Jared paid for what he had done.

The control I managed at the hospital couldn't compare as I charged, and as Jared fought back, I was able to leave all traces of remorse behind.

Various shouts came from every direction, but neither of us

stopped to listen. Soon, I gained the upper hand and, after one solid jab to the jaw, had Jared flat on his back.

When Jared sat up, he spat out a mouthful of blood onto the sand. "Look at that. I guess you win, tough guy. Now, who's gonna save her from *you?*"

I didn't want to let that rest. So badly I wanted to walk the two steps closer and lay Jared out one last time, but my feet wouldn't take me. Instead, a sickly feeling bloomed inside me, stemming from my chest and spreading everywhere. Slowly, the anger seeped away, and that junky feeling was all that was left. I got a small foothold on my control and was too afraid to look at Sarah. *What she must think of me now.*

"You're a jerk, dude," was the best I could do.

Jared laughed then pierced me with a pointed stare from the ground and wiped his mouth with his arm, blood streaking his skin. "That's rich. I'm the one down here. So, if I'm the jerk, what does that make you?"

The answer escaped me, and I didn't want to hang around for someone else to explain it. Taking off toward the parking lot, I turned tail and left without another word or a glance at anyone. I was fading quickly, breath coming in labored huffs. Shame engulfed me from all sides, which only confused me more. Jared deserved it, didn't he? So, why should I feel anything but justified?

From behind me, Sarah called out, "Kevin, wait!" I didn't, but she caught up to me, anyway. "Stop." I felt her hand on my arm, and it took all the strength I had left not to yank it away, feeling unworthy of her touch, but I didn't stop. I had inflicted enough damage tonight. "Maybe you shouldn't drive. You could stay, and the two of us can talk."

"I'm fine."

"You're not fine. Would you please just stop for a minute?"

"No."

"Why do you have to be so stubborn?" Another question I didn't have an answer for. "Kevin!" Her voice faded as she gave up her pursuit, the distance between us growing. That was just as well. The closer I got to my truck, the more the words of my mother invaded my mind, sending me even further into the abyss of guilt and shame.

44

"I'm sorry, you guys." I sat in front of the fire, wedged protectively between my best friends, feeling bad about the way Kevin's appearance had turned out. "Sometimes I don't really understand him."

"I can't believe he still isn't over what happened at the party. I mean, *you* are," Sammy said, motioning to me.

Jenna looked defiantly at Sammy. "Are you kidding me?"

Birdie sat and watched the other two argue.

"What? Jared's already paid for what he did," Sammy said declaratively.

Jenna remained unconvinced. "Did he, though?"

"Yes, he did." Sammy was insistent. "You can't hold on to the past just so you can fault someone for what *didn't* happen. Being scared about the possibilities of something that isn't an issue anymore is no excuse to vilify someone."

Without even knowing she did it, Sammy slammed a huge dose of reality into me. In the murkiness of my own emotional upheaval, I had missed that simple truth.

"And besides," continued Sammy. "It was an accident, remember?"

"Guys, I have a confession to make." The talking ceased as they all turned, their eyes burning holes right through my heart. Before I could chicken out, I knew it was time to let my friends know what was going on. I kept my focus on the dancing flames ahead, ready to block out the reactions of my friends, just in case.

Sammy broke the silence first. "Are you finally gonna tell us about your diabetes?"

Struck by the question, I was momentarily paralyzed. I had completely forgotten that came out, but I definitely had to clear that up, too. They deserved to know. "Make that *two* confessions."

"That's not even what you were going to say?" Jenna probed. "There's more?" Birdie pegged Jenna with a pointed stare. "I'm sorry, Sarah. I don't mean to sound rude. I'm just… How come you didn't tell us? What happened at the party was scary, and we were completely useless. We weren't able to help you at all." The fire bounced in the glistening of her eyes, and she sniffed, rubbing her face as a tear fell. "But Kevin knew…"

Feeling guilty, I pulled her to my side and prayed for composure. "I have had Type 1 Diabetes most of my life. When we first found out, I told a couple of friends at school and it didn't go well. They didn't mean to offend me, I'm sure, but their curious and confused reactions embarrassed me. That's probably only because I was so young and didn't hardly understand it myself. I didn't like being the center of attention in class when I had to leave at lunch so my mom could give me insulin. Being asked question after question by kids who were just as clueless as I was made me feel bad. After that, I never talked about it with anyone but my family and doctors again. Eventually, those who knew forgot, and I had a clean slate."

My stare remained forward as I felt the comforting arms of my friends all around me. I smiled, blinking back tears.

"I didn't mean to tell Kevin, either, but he accidentally found my insulin pack and I was forced to explain. Once I did, I actually felt better. And all this time, I was so worried about feeling like a clueless kid again that I hid important information from those who care about me."

I smiled, blinking back tears. "That's actually why I was late on the first day. I overslept and didn't take my insulin that morning, and by time I got to school, I felt awful. I sat in my car to eat and do my injection."

"I knew there was something more to that morning," said Sammy.

"Yeah, you did." I laughed softly. "I could only tell half the truth to keep myself from lying, but that's how I've gotten by all this time. It's not something I usually need help with, so I've always been comfortable keeping it to myself. I feel silly for it now."

Jenna shook her head. "Don't. Your health is your business. And it really sucks those kids ever made you feel bad about it."

"Kids have no filter at all. That's just one of the many reasons I'm never having any."

"Why? You don't want them to be just like you?" Jenna made a teasing face at Sammy, who rolled her eyes, as unfazed as we all expected.

"Exactly. I'm all the *me* I can handle."

"Do you still want to share the other thing? We are totally here for you whenever, whatever, always." Birdie's assurance was supported by the looks of the others.

Already feeling lighter with their support, I took a deep breath to spill my guts one more time. "Okay, so, Kevin and I had a fight earlier. That's why we weren't hanging out this weekend, and that's probably why he was extra edgy with Jared."

"What did you fight about?"

Birdie bumped Jenna with her elbow. "Quit bein' so nosy."

"No, it's okay. I brought it up because I want to share. I think it's good to be getting all this off my chest."

"Alright, then. We're listening." Birdie smiled reassuringly, putting her arm around me.

"I'm just going to spit it out. Kevin and I almost — *ya know* — and I freaked out about it and told him I needed a break."

Birdie was the first to pick her jaw up off the sand to respond. "You're kidding!"

Jenna's voice was shrill. "You almost *what!?*"

"And where?" included Sammy with a chaff tone.

"It doesn't matter. It didn't happen." The reason I didn't tell them was not because I couldn't trust them, but because that wasn't the only thing that happened that night. Not all of it was bad. I wanted to keep the good parts — the big sparkly sky, the chilly water, and the beautiful conversation — just for Kevin and me.

"So, how did the break and fight and all that come about?"

"I was worried about a repeat incident and thought it would be best if we had some time to cool off."

"I did not know y'all were so close. It's almost kinda sweet." Birdie got that dreamy look in her eyes and lovingly rubbed my back.

"Well, there you go. No wonder he's so upset. He's feeling blue…"

Sammy laughed at Jenna's implication. Birdie chastised her for it.

I shook my head. "That's not what he cared about. Kevin was

so great about the whole thing. I'm serious. He is amazing." My eyes filled as I recalled his assurance that we could jump any hurdle, hand in hand. From the moment I flipped and rejected him, he'd sought only to comfort me. "He's more than amazing."

"Wow." Birdie rested her chin on her knuckles, enraptured by the romance. "You so love him, don'tcha?"

"I so do." I sighed, grateful I had such amazing people in my life. "And I love you guys," I said as all our arms went around each other. I'd wasted so much time keeping them in the dark about my true self when I should've known better. They were so easy to talk to and cared like true friends should. Now, I knew beyond any doubt that they were on my side, no matter what. It didn't matter where our views differed. These were my people.

KEVIN

45

I WAS NOT GOING HOME, THAT MUCH I KNEW FOR SURE. SARAH HAD tried to stop me from leaving, but there was no way I could stay and face her after that. Even now, after half an hour of aimless driving, I still couldn't think straight.

"You should've left her alone, man. Even I can see that."

Jared's words were on replay in my mind, repeatedly working me over. Not that I had expected it, but not a single onlooker, nor even Sarah, had come to my defense. Of course, everyone thought I was no good for her. I had personally grappled with that idea more than anyone. In the beginning, I'd resisted my attraction to her, telling myself I'd only ruin her and she'd only get in my way.

Isn't that what Marie had implied, too?

People like her are too good for people like us.

Even my mom, while trying to look out for me, knew I would never stack up. I'd never be good enough. She had been trying to do Sarah a favor at the expense of her own son. And finally, in the wake of this night, I agreed it was well-deserved.

I hadn't felt this uncertain and low in a good while. Not since before we became serious — when Sarah confessed to me she wanted to be with me and all I had to do was reciprocate. I needed that assurance from her again, that iron will she touted. The love of her Jesus, if that's what it was. I craved whatever would give me back the confidence I'd gained since being with her.

But I wouldn't be forgiving Jared anytime soon, not for what he'd put Sarah through, but maybe for her sake, I could learn to pretend Jared didn't exist. I hoped — prayed? — that it wasn't too late for me to make things right with her. But I couldn't go crawling back to her now, not like this. Not so soon after making a total fool of us both.

Realistically, how much longer could Jared even be a problem? At the end of the school year, I would be out of this town, and Jared would cease to exist in my world. And my unforgiving brain reminded me that the same might be true for Sarah and me, too. In a matter of weeks, our relationship might cease to exist, too.

That particular thought I would deal with later. For now, I needed to not think at all.

Pulling over, I grabbed my phone. My finger hovered over Russ's name, but something impeded pressing "Call." I imagined how it would go if I confided in Russell: *"You should've kicked the guy's rear-end all the way to China."* And I would agree. I was too on edge still to be level-headed, and where did thinking like that ever get him? I needed to calm the storm, not stoke the fire.

To my surprise, the next name I looked for was Tyler's. When the youth pastor had given me a little card with his contact info on it after the fundraiser, I thought I would shove it in my pocket and forget about it, but somehow, his number ended up saved.

Before I changed my mind, I fixed my thumb on Tyler's

number and dialed. One-and-a-half rings later, his voice spoke out, "Hello?"

"Hey… Tyler?"

"Sure is."

"This is Kevin." I swallowed hard, already feeling dodgy.

"Oh, hey there, Kevin! How are you?" Tyler's voice was jubilant, somewhat soothing to my nerves.

The answer eluded me. "I don't really know."

"Well, I was just getting ready to go grab a drink —"

"Oh, sorry. I'll let you go."

"— of coffee down at Cafe Calypso. Why don't you meet me there? I'll bet you've never had good coffee in your life."

"Sure." *Why not?* "Sounds like… fun."

"Right on! I'll see you soon."

And so he would. I pulled my truck back onto the road and made a U-turn, heading to the other side of town. I wondered what Sarah was doing now and if she was spending her time crafting excuses for her friends, or if she joined them in questioning why she was with me at all. I resisted the urge to call her and find out, or worse yet, turn around again to go back to the beach. Neither would result in anything favorable to me.

46

CAFE CALYPSO WAS A TINY HOLE-IN-THE-WALL ESTABLISHMENT nestled inside of Half Price Books, the used bookstore in the heart of the shopping district. They served *the real stuff* as some locals would say. It's definitely not Starbucks, they'd tell you. Popular or not, coffee was still bean bathwater as far as I was concerned. I didn't know what exactly I was there for, but it wasn't that.

The cafe was still bustling after dark, patrons coming and going, most with books in tow. The tables were clean, some with unique mosaic tile designs, while others were decorated with postcards from the Middle East, displayed protectively underneath a glass covering. The cushions on the chairs were fashioned from burlap sacks, for an interesting look. Everything came together like a spread in some eclectic travel magazine, but it was pleasant, if not a bit small.

That's when I saw Tyler sitting at a table in the back, sipping something, looking at a book. Somehow, he was alerted to my presence because he looked up and waved. "Over here, Kev."

I went and sat down at the small, circular table with chipped tie-dye paint. "Hey," I said, unable to articulate anything more substantive. A shred of doubt had me questioning why I'd come here and locked up my mouth.

"What would you like to drink?" Tyler asked. "I've got an artisan blend here." He inhaled and smiled. "Want to try it first?"

I shook my head. "I'm good. Not a big coffee drinker." *Or even a small one.* "But thanks."

"Eh, you just haven't had the right kind yet. I'm going to order something for you. Let's just see if you don't end up loving it. I have good instincts about these things. Remember the BBQ plate?"

Sure, Tyler had been right about grilled meats and classic vegetables, but coffee was gross. I didn't want Tyler wasting his money on me a second time, especially not in order for me to confirm what I already knew. "Please, don't bother. I'm not thirsty."

He waved his hand. "Just trust me. Real coffee isn't about quenching thirst, anyway. It's about savoring."

Before I could object again, Tyler took off to the order counter. I heard him laughing with the barista and watched curiously. The closer I looked, I noticed Tyler wasn't just laughing; he was flirting! It struck me as odd to see a youth pastor flirt. I thought they couldn't date or have wives.

When Tyler came back, he had a big smile on his face. He placed the prepared drink in front of me and sighed as he sat, taking a sip of his own brew. "Go ahead, take a sip."

Reluctantly, I gave my warm cup a gentle swish, scrunching my nose in an inhale, and went for it. Smacking the rich flavor on my tongue, feeling the pleasant heat go down my throat, I wasn't all that disgusted.

"You know," I said, inspecting the drink. "It doesn't suck."

"You see? I knows what I knows."

Tyler's gaze was drawn back to the barista. Then he looked me square in the eyes, knowing the direction of my thoughts without asking. "Her name is Cindie. She's going to marry me someday."

I was taken aback and actually laughed. One second, he was flirting with a barista, and the next, he was declaring a future with her. "You think so?"

"Not just think so, *amigo*. I *know* so." He glanced beyond my shoulder to the woman in question and winked. Without turning around, I heard the girl giggle before asking the newest customer what she could get started for them.

"You must come here an awful lot," I said, unsure of an appropriate way to respond. How did you talk to a church leader about his love life?

"Just enough to keep her interested. I gotta set the pace, after all."

"What pace?"

"*Thee* pace, *amigo. El amor es el ritmo en la danza de la vida, y debo conducirlo con cuidado.*"

I looked on blankly. Almost eighteen years living in a city teeming with Hispanic culture, two required years of Spanish in school, and I still had zero idea how to speak the language. "Say what?"

Chuckling, Tyler translated, "Love is the rhythm in the dance of life, and I have to lead with care."

I nodded as though I understood, but I very much didn't. Sometimes, this guy was so down-to-earth I couldn't believe he was a youth pastor, and others, he was so forward and extreme that I *still* couldn't believe he was a youth pastor.

Tyler laughed, sensing my reluctance. "It's like this: I come in and do my thing, mind my own business, and by doing this we observe each other from a distance. We're slowly getting to know one another with no stress or obligation. By the time I'm ready to ask her out on a proper date, she'll be comfortable and I'll be confident."

"I see," I said, supposing now I did a little. "Makes sense."

"Yep. I've lived, and I have learned, and this, my friend, is the way to go. I'm sure of it."

How much living could he have done, really? "You don't seem much older than me."

"I get my youthful good looks from *mi madre*," he rubbed his stubble-less face. "Nah, I'm twenty-three."

"Oh, wow."

"I know. So ancient."

Laughter bubbled out of me again. The ease with which Tyler joked and held a conversation reminded me of Sarah. I wanted to try it. "Practically one foot in the grave," I said back. "Better not strike up anything serious and leave poor Cindie a widow."

Tyler looked at me with humorous shock. "Oh, okay. *El niño* got jokes." We busted up so much it made my gut ache. When was the last time I'd done that, even with Sarah? Oh, she and I laughed plenty. But this was fantastic.

Tyler cupped his drink with both hands and looked at it pensively. "In all seriousness, bro, I've failed big in love before, and I intend to prove to myself I learned from it."

"I don't follow."

He heaved a sad sigh and leaned back in his seat. "You didn't know I was married before?"

I shook my head. "I had no idea. What, uh — "

"What happened?" Tyler finished the question for me as he sat back up in his chair. "I happened, really. Me, myself, and I got in our way, and as a result, we weren't married for very long."

"That sounds like it sucked."

"It really did, but it wasn't for nothing. I pushed on and have only the best of intentions for marriage now because it's no longer about me. It's God and good sense that power me now. Not to mention, she forgave me and remarried a while ago now."

Forgiveness...

Tyler was praising his bad decisions like they were good ones, and that way of thinking blew my mind.

"You are always so insanely positive. You and Sarah both."

"It wasn't always this way. Things used to be pretty difficult for me, but you live life a little and you learn a lot. Now that I live with more purpose and God's guiding force behind me, I don't have quite so many hard lessons to figure out." He laughed and downed the rest of his coffee. Tyler's gaze returned to me, making me nervous. I quickly realized Tyler wasn't scrutinizing me, but simply trying to connect on a different level. "After spending some time at church lately, have you gotten any glimpses of that guiding force for yourself?"

Now it was my turn to shift uncomfortably, assuming my typical slouched position, pushing against the back of my seat, hoping I could disappear within it. Finishing the last of my coffee, I shrugged, hoping not to offend but not wanting to lie, either. "I don't really know."

Tyler seemed satisfied with my response. "That's fair. How you feel is how you feel."

"Yeah, well. I get the impression you'd know if I was lying, anyway." I laughed, low and contrite.

"You're not wrong." Tyler dusted his shoulder and then laughed at himself. Whatever power Tyler must have to command the mood around me was astounding. Already, I felt better than I had in a while. If I could hold on to that long enough, I was hopeful I could make up for my crappy behavior with Sarah.

The only thing I was no longer sure about was my new job and how long I could keep it up. The more time I spent doing it, the worse I felt about it, even though the pennies in my pocket sure felt nice.

I finished up my evening with Tyler, feeling like we parted ways as more than one person with needs and the other with solutions. Rather than acquaintances, we kinda felt like friends. I hadn't made a new one of those since Sarah, and before that, it was Russell and the others from back in the day. Tyler was nothing like Russell or anyone else I would've naturally been friends with in school or at work, but Tyler's natural gravitational pull had drawn me in. Tyler was old enough to have a lot of good advice but young enough to seem like a viable friend. Plus, he was funny and really nice to me. I supposed that alone was a good enough reason to call someone a friend.

What I needed to do when I got home was calculate exactly how much money was necessary to cover my and my mother's expenses for a few more months and replenish my savings a little. Then, I would quit the new job. If Tanner didn't understand, then I'd just have to find another job altogether to coast by with until it was time to leave for school.

But first, I had to make things as right as I could with Sarah. Everything else could come later.

When I got home, I showered the day away and then fell into bed, feeling grounded and refreshed. And a little nervous, but hopefully that was misplaced. If she held no ill-will toward Jared, then surely she'd already forgiven *me*.

Hopefully.

I composed a new text to Sarah,

KEVIN

I'm really sorry.

Better to keep it simple until I got a feel for her mood.

SARAH

I know you are. I'm sorry, too. You were right. We could have handled everything together. We SHOULD have.

My eyes subconsciously glanced upward with relief.

KEVIN

You shouldn't be sorry.

Immediately, my phone buzzed to life. "Hello?"

"Just accept my apology, Kevin," Sarah said in her most adorably stern tone. "I admit I didn't handle what happened the other night very well. Yes, I was really scared, and maybe I did need some time to process it all, but I was wrong to just cut you out like that."

"Okay, okay. Anything you want," I quickly relented. I could now understand where she was coming from, and it felt fair to let her apologize if she wanted to. All the while, the small guilt-shaped fissure in my heart refused to be ignored. How would my new job fit into our mended relationship? Would there be a better, right time to tell her about it?

"Oh, good. I like the sound of that," she teased.

"I don't mind it, either." Chuckling, I chose my current happiness over dwelling on the work stuff. Best case scenario, I would work a few jobs and then quit, anyway. I certainly wasn't going to keep it up long-term, so in that case, why worry her?

"Can I say one more thing before we drop this subject forever?" She took on a softer, more pleading tone.

My heart smacked against my chest. "Sure."

"No more fighting. Please. There's always a better way to confront conflict. Ways that don't involve hurting yourself or anyone else."

Okay, I really couldn't blame her. At the beach, I knew I was being a jerk the second I opened my mouth, but I just couldn't stop. Didn't *want* to stop, more like. My unresolved hatred for Jared fueled my desire to pummel him once and for all. Afterward, I could see that for what it was, and I wanted to do better next time. I owed it to her. And… just maybe… I owed it to Jared, too?

It felt like a stretch, but who knew?

Regardless, I couldn't solve all my problems by punching them in the face. If only it were that easy. The next time I lost my temper and grew violent with someone, it could cost me a lot more than a fight with Sarah.

I *had* to be better for Sarah.

"I won't," I said, and I meant it. "I promise."

"Thank you. And if you ever feel you might Hulk-out again at any point, let me help talk you down. Okay? We are here for each other, remember?"

Heart swelling, I smiled. "I love you, Sarah."

"I love you, too," she replied tenderly. "So, what do we do now?"

"I think it's okay if you still want to take the rest of the weekend apart. I promise not to act salty about it, as long as you still agree that we can talk on the phone."

Sarah giggled lightly. "It's a deal."

I fell asleep with such ease that night, but my peace was soon interrupted by a new buzzing of my phone. This time, when I answered, Tanner was on the other end.

"Last-minute delivery up for grabs. You want it?"

I didn't, but I wasn't ready to quit just yet. It was just shy of two in the morning. I sat up in bed and rubbed the sleep from my eyes. "On my way." Uncertainty trickled in, but I passed over it and got dressed, grabbing my keys before walking out the door.

SARAH

47

SINCE RETURNING HOME FROM THE BEACH, I FILLED THE REST OF my weekend with little else besides talking to Kevin and my friends on the phone. Somewhere in there, my parents and I watched a couple of movies. My anticipation to see Kevin next was flourishing, and not because my hormones were out of control.

Kevin was taking extra shifts at Tanner's to occupy his time. I understood that money was tight for a seventeen-year-old with as much to pay for as he did. To me, the additional hours didn't sound like a problem until Sunday rolled around and Kevin didn't make it.

"Where's Kevin?" my dad had asked, inspecting his watch with a frown. He, like the rest of us, had come to expect Kevin like clockwork on Sunday mornings.

"He had to work today. It was a last-minute thing. He didn't get a say." I explained away his absence as casually as I could, repeating to my parents what Kevin had said to me, but I still felt disquieted by it. And I could tell by the look on his face that my dad didn't like it, either.

Later that night, to top it off, Kevin informed me he might have to miss school the next day, too. "Another shift came up," he said into the receiver. "I don't see how I can refuse it. I have to keep my job."

"Of course, you need that. But what about graduation? Are you worried this could keep happening and your grades might slip?" Despite my growing concern, I tried to speak as neutrally sensible as possible.

"I'm sure it'll be fine," he said, but I was steadily losing confidence. Blowing off one priority to focus on another didn't seem sustainable for the long-term, and I didn't want to see his decisions blow up in his face. "Just don't tell anyone what I'm doing if they ask, okay?"

"What am I supposed to tell them?"

"Anything else," he said, like none of it was a big deal.

I didn't want to see his decisions blow up in *my* face, either. But I was put on the spot again during the weeks that followed as Kevin missed another Sunday and more days of school.

Twenty minutes into class two weeks later, Hallinger's desk phone rang, interrupting his lecture. I had a gut-dropping suspicion it was about Kevin. Sure enough, when Mr. Hallinger looked up at our table at Kevin's empty seat, he returned to his call with a whisper, and it was all too obvious.

God, You know better than me, but I feel sure I'm not worried over nothing. Please, let Kevin be okay.

Mr. Hallinger was still talking to the class when the bell rang, and he had to yell over everyone's commotion. I was the first one at the door, hoping for a chance to get Kevin on the phone between periods, but before I could leave, Hallinger called to me, "Sarah, can you come here, please?"

I started and turned. "Me?"

"If you could, please. It'll just take a second."

I tried not to frown as I glanced at everyone else pouring out into the hall while I was stuck behind. Birdie and Sammy waved sympathetically as they left. As I reached his desk and saw he looked troubled, my feelings changed from annoyed to anxious.

"Do you know where Mr. Sloan is today, Sarah?"

Cheeks heated, I shook my head. Maybe if I didn't have to verbalize it, it was less of a lie to say no.

"The office called earlier. Apparently, he didn't make it to his first class, either. Do you know if he's sick?"

I shrugged, allowing it to be a possibility.

Mr. Hallinger rolled the end of his pencil between his teeth, looking thoughtfully at nothing. "He and I have an understanding this semester. A clean slate. Missing school with no excuse like this doesn't seem like something our new Kevin would do. Since you're his… lab partner and all, I'm sure he's told you all about it. But I ask you, do I need to be worried about him?"

I sincerely hope not! "I don't think so."

He searched my eyes for a second, and I shifted from one foot to the other.

"Good," he said, accepting my response as assurance. He slapped both hands rhythmically on his desk. "He's a good kid. You're all good kids, but ya gotta be in class to prove it."

Smiling, I had to agree. "Yep, and where would we be without those Punnett squares and double helixes?"

"I shudder to think," he quipped, now occupying his hands with a stack of ungraded papers. "Now go ahead. I don't want to make you late for your next class. Word from the teacher's lounge is I'm no longer the only one around here who locks the doors."

I was starting out when Mr. Hallinger recalled my attention.

"Oh, and Sarah, I hope you don't mind me saying something, but I'm really glad to see you're okay after what you went through a while back."

"How do you know about that?"

"Teachers hear about everything you kids do, and then some." He laughed and shook his head. "Kids these days be crazy."

A laugh slipped out. What an unexpected source of kindness. I felt flushed with humility and appreciation. "Well, thank you. We crazy kids are really lucky to have you on our side. And the next time I talk to Kevin, I'll tell him so."

Mr. Hallinger gave me a nod and smiled before returning to his task. I left, pulling out my phone to call Kevin. Even though it was nice to see someone else extend their care to him, it added to my worry that our teacher was concerned. Especially when Kevin didn't answer.

It felt like forever had passed when I finally heard from him.

KEVIN

Sorry I missed your call. Just working away over here. How's it going at school?

SARAH

Fine. Hallinger was asking about you.

KEVIN

What'd he say?

SARAH

He wants to see you in class. Asked me why you weren't there.

KEVIN

What did you tell him?

SARAH

That I'd pass along his concern when I talked to you.

KEVIN

I see. Yeah, hopefully, I won't have to do this much longer.

SARAH

There's really no one else who can fill in? Someone who isn't in high school, perhaps? Lol…

For a while, there was no reply. My nerves bunched up, and when he finally replied, his text assuaged none of my feelings.

KEVIN

Nope. I'll call you when I'm done.

I never had cause to distrust Kevin before, but on this, something inside would not relent. Because of it, my mind played an endless loop of dangerous possible scenarios.

Rather than going to my last class, I made up a phony appointment, excused myself from campus, and drove to Tanner's. If I was worried enough to ditch school, then my instincts couldn't be wrong. I might end up looking like a ridiculous, untrusting girlfriend for no reason, but that would be fine by me. Anything but the alternative.

When I parked at the end of the lot facing the shop, I noticed right away that Kevin's truck wasn't there. I scanned the area, curious if he might've parked somewhere else. Inside the garage, at least half a dozen guys were working, tending to various vehicles and customers, wearing the same gray t-shirt and dark shorts that Kevin wore. I also saw one man in a tan leather jacket, an older couple, and a couple of young people on bikes, all going past the parking lot. Employees, customers, and passersby alike were all over the place, but *no Kevin.* My chest gave way to the quicksand of doubt, and my heart sank deeply.

It was time to text him. I had to ask.

> **SARAH**
> Where are you?

> **KEVIN**
> At work. Why?

I dumped my phone onto the passenger seat and pressed the heels of my hands to my eyes, suppressing angry tears. At first, I merely assumed he just wasn't telling me everything, but he was actually lying to me! Deep down, I'd known all along that something was off, and now I was afraid of what more there was to find out.

Lord, what is really going on with him?

Taking the phone back in hand, I mentally prepared myself for what needed doing.

> **SARAH**
> Then how come I'm here at Tanner's and you aren't?

There was no stopping now.

Instead of a text, I got a near-immediate phone call. Greeted by a photo of Kevin and me from the carnival, I saw myself holding up my goldfish bag, and Kevin, with his arm around me, a churro-dusted smile plastered on his face. I could barely look at it, and I certainly couldn't answer his call. The phone rang two more times, and each time I ignored it early.

KEVIN

Why aren't you answering??

I didn't answer his text, either. Everything I started typing came out angry, and I didn't want to start this conversation the wrong way. Maybe I didn't know what I was going to say when the confrontation finally happened, but I knew for sure there would be one. Whatever lies he had this quickly buried himself under were officially interfering with his relationships and his strict plan for graduation, and I couldn't let any of that go without a fight.

KEVIN

48

HALF AN HOUR PASSED BEFORE I MADE IT BACK TO THE GARAGE, and that was accounting for a few questionable driving tactics on the way. Sarah had caught me in my lie, sending me into a complete panic, and now she was ignoring me. I could only imagine what she must think was going on, and how mad she must be.

After the beach ordeal, I had worked hard to keep in line, and things between us were going really smooth, but this freaking new job made it hard to keep that up.

I had meant to quit by now. Really, I had, but my first real payday after starting the new gig, my mind was blown. Because of the money, I kept saying yes. Tanner called me out for so many jobs that, between those and my regular shifts, I had no time for anything else. No kidding people were going to notice. Sarah, of all people, was bound to figure it out.

Nervously turning into the parking lot, I saw Sarah's car and pulled up beside her. She was leaning against it with her legs crossed at the ankle and her arms folded against her chest. I lowered my window, not liking her hard, blank expression. "Sarah…"

"Last night, you told me you couldn't go to school again today because you had to work," she said in a low, strained voice. "Last week, you told me the same thing."

Think before you speak. "I did." *Don't say too much.*

"I'm confused about how long you've been lying to me then, since you weren't here working thirty minutes ago when you told me you were." Sarah took a step forward, and her disappointed gaze was like daggers in my chest. "Where have you been, Kevin? What's going on?"

I looked around, sweat gathering at my temples. I didn't want to have this conversation with Sarah at all, let alone right in front of the shop. We could be seen or heard. "I can't tell you."

Her eyes went wide. "You can't tell me? Are you kidding me right now?" After throwing her hands up, she started to leave.

On the verge of panic, I leaned out the window, voice going low and stern. "Get in the truck."

"What? No, I'm going home until you —"

"If you want to know, I'll tell you everything. Just get in the truck. Please." I reached across the empty seat and opened the passenger door.

Sarah hesitated, anger and confusion vying for dominance, but she did as I asked, then turned expectantly. "I'm listening."

"We can't talk about it here." I threw the truck into gear and drove off, parking a few streets down from the shop before readjusting in my seat.

"Sarah, I —"

"Lied to me," she interjected.

"Sort of, but not about working. That is what I was doing."

"That doesn't tell me anything." The irritation in her voice was growing.

I brashly rubbed my hand over my hair. "Okay, remember when we visited my mom, and that guy called me over before we left?"

"Yes, I remember."

Much to my relief, when I reached over to take Sarah's hand, she let me. "He showed me the bill for my mom's program, and Sarah, it was a lot more than I could afford. I also had all the bills from the house to take care of on top of my own... Even if I took extra shifts, sold stuff from around the house, and put in all I had from the bank, I wouldn't be able to cover it all and keep going."

"That sounds a lot more serious than what you told me. You didn't share any of that." Her voice was still angry, but her face was softening.

"I didn't want you to know I couldn't take care of my own sh — stuff. I didn't want to admit it to myself, yet, either."

"So, you shut me out of the truth to spare yourself, under the guise of sparing me? It doesn't seem like you've really accepted that we're supposed to be on the same side of our problems, to help each other. Not hiding them."

There was nothing to refute. She was absolutely right. "I'm sorry."

"How did you get the money, then? What is this secret job you have?"

Deep breath in. Deep breath out.

"Tanner runs this hustle on the side — stolen or imitation parts or whatever — and Russell has been trying to get me to join in for a year now. He was always talking about how great the money was, making a real good case for it, making it sound safe. But I always turned it down. Recently, though, I don't know. I just sort of fell into it." My throat stung when Sarah's hand slipped away. "Sarah, I tried. I really did my best to stay out of it. I had no interest in being associated with this. After seeing my mom struggle with the law, I told myself that would never be me."

"Exactly, don't people go to prison for this?"

"I won't. I'll go back and quit right now. My mom's rehab and everything at home is caught up. I don't even need the money anymore. I can go back to working my regular job."

"Even if you did, that wouldn't magically fix everything. You're missing school again, and your grades are slipping. You've missed another Sunday with my family. My parents are asking about you, and Tyler said you won't return his phone calls. Even Mr. Hallinger is worried about you, Kevin. We all are."

I hung my head, shame rising to the surface. "I never wanted anyone to worry about me."

"The people who love you worry. That's just how it works."

Slumping against the door, I let my head fall on the glass of the window. "I don't know what else to say. I'm sorry."

"Where was your sorry on Sunday when my dad was disappointed you didn't show up for God or his daughter? Where was it today when I had to cover for you at school?"

"I know, okay!" I hadn't meant to shout. Calming myself, I said, "I know. I let everyone down. That's what I was trying to avoid by taking this job."

"How does endangering yourself and your future accomplish that?"

I teetered on the breaking point, and the more she spoke, the less acrobatic I felt. Any moment now, I would come crashing down, and things would get bad again.

Who was I kidding? Things were already bad again. "I know I

screwed up, big time. The plan was to only take a few jobs so I had enough money to go around. Without it, my mom would've been kicked out of rehab. I couldn't let that happen to her, Sarah. She is clean and sober for the first time in my life."

Something in her eyes softened. "You should've been honest with me from the beginning. And what you're doing sounds heroic on the surface, but you shouldn't sacrifice your future for anyone. This job, this money, it's not worth that. There's always a better way."

"What is the better way? Tell me what to do."

"I don't think I really can. God can give you those answers if you'll let Him."

I felt too defeated for a sermon. "Why does it always come down to God with you?"

"God is the only one in the world capable of loving you more than I do, and we both want to see you happy and succeeding. Your heart is in the right place, but this is not the way to take care of your mom. I know this much. You can't set yourself on fire to keep her warm."

Tears assaulted my eyes, and I collapsed forward to hide them, resting my face in my arms over the steering wheel. I had thought I was doing the right thing, but that seemed like another lie I'd repeatedly told myself. In actuality, I had handled things all wrong. Again.

Sarah scooted closer and put her hand on my shoulder to urge me up, but I resisted. Then, when she used both hands to lift my face, her eyes were so full of dismay. It ebbed and flowed like pieces of a shipwreck in the sea. "It's okay, Kevin…"

The moment she spoke my name, I came undone. I buried my face in her neck, my arms clutched around her for dear life. Every tear I had spent half my life holding back sprang forth with a vengeance as the force of my troubles were on full display. I had failed. I'd failed my mom in the long run, because in the back of my mind, I must've known I couldn't keep this up. I had failed Sarah by lying to her and causing her more grief. And I had failed myself. It would take a miracle now to get back on the right track to graduation *and* into the Stevensons' good graces.

During my breakdown, both seemed too far out of reach. For a while there, I had almost forgotten that nothing in my life stayed good for long.

KEVIN

49

I was miserable after my fight with Sarah. Yesterday, when she eventually asked me to take her back to her car, I wasn't sure if we'd gotten anywhere. I could only conclude that I had convinced myself I wouldn't get caught so I could put off feeling like this, but there had been no point in indulging the delusion and lying to Sarah. Just how much crap did I expect a good Christian girl like her to put up with?

And it seemed to me that everything came down to God somehow. *Her* God. The one she and her family believed in, along with so many others at their church, but not me. What did believing in Him have to do with *my* path? Didn't I have free will, anyway? Sarah might think I didn't have a good enough reason to commit a crime, and I realized now I had to get out of it, but this *"job"* saved my mom from being booted from the program, didn't it? I had the utilities at the house paid up, didn't I? And I even had a little tucked away in savings again.

By those accounts, everything was okay, but I still had to admit Sarah was right. It was time to stop burning myself for other people. If she said there was another way, then there was another way.

At least I knew where to start. Tanner's company would survive without me, and I could find another job to deal with the rest. Marie would have to stand on her own two feet again, eventually, anyway. If she had truly changed for the better, as I hoped and thought she had, then leaving rehab wouldn't be the tragedy I feared.

I got myself together and quickly departed for the shop. By the time I was left standing in the parking lot alone last night, Tanner had already gone home. Now, I would go straight down there and tell Tanner I quit for good. I wouldn't continue my regular job at the shop, either. It was best if, from now on, my hands were wiped clean of Tanner's place altogether.

At the shop, Russell and a couple others were already in Tanner's office, waiting as their extra earnings were calculated and their envelopes were stuffed. If I detached myself, it looked just like a regular payday.

Russ and Tanner both looked up. "Hey, kid," Tanner said before returning his gaze to the task. "Good work this week." Then, to Russell, he handed a padded white parcel. "Here ya are."

Russell reached over the desk to grab it and then stood and nodded. "Thank you, sir." When he exchanged glances with me, he bounced his eyebrows and smiled, slapping the envelope across his hand and leaving down the hall. The others took turns stepping up, each taking his own cut and also leaving.

After the last one left, I stepped further into the office, knowing it was now or never. "Excuse me, sir?"

"I didn't forget about you, kid. I'm just about done." Tanner sealed my envelope, then continued scribbling something in his record book. Then he clicked his pen and tossed it down. "That'll do it."

"Sir, I just came to tell you that yesterday was my last day."

Blake Tanner didn't seem to appreciate or understand my words. "What was that now?"

"I quit, sir. I appreciate the opportunities you've given me during my employment here, but I'm going to be graduating and moving soon, so I'm tying up all my loose ends."

Tanner leaned back and crossed his arms over his chest as I spoke. I was grateful the beating of my heart was a private matter, or I might have been embarrassed by my level of fear. Tanner liked me, sure, but how far did that go? He had sensitive dealings to keep under wraps. Some people might do outrageous things to protect that knowledge.

Eventually, Tanner sat forward and used the pads of his fingers to move my envelope toward me. "Gotta do whatcha gotta do. You've been an excellent help, I must say."

"Oh, no, sir. I won't take that since I couldn't give you any notice. But thank you for everything." With that, I backed out and turned away, then heard Tanner's chair scraping along the floor.

"Hang on, there."

I froze, a million thoughts frozen in time with me. I turned, not knowing what to expect.

"Take it, Kevin." Tanner held out the envelope. "I always liked you, and I appreciate an honest man. You earned this, so you go ahead and you keep it."

I couldn't believe it. Tanner's face was light with such genuine admiration, one could almost have called it faith. Blake Tanner, businessman extraordinaire, had respect for — or faith *in* — Kevin Sloan. Maybe it was only faith that I wouldn't squeal, but I would take it. And Tanner wanted me to keep the money I'd earned. Most of it was my real paycheck, actually. Either way, this concluded our business dealings. I was truly done. Might as well take the money. There may not be more of it coming my way for a while.

Admittedly, it felt kinda good for this man, so mighty and powerful in my eyes, to show regard for me. I smiled back and took the envelope. Tanner kept his hand out to shake my hand. "You take care of yourself, kid."

"Thank you, sir." Hurrying out through the hall, I pulled out my phone to tell Sarah.

KEVIN

It's done. I'm out.

I would call her from the truck, and if she'd have me, I would go straight over to her house.

When I got out into the garage, I wished harder than I had ever wished for anything else before, that I'd known what taking care of oneself truly was and had done it sooner.

Waiting for me out in the sunshine, which might've held such bright possibilities for me a second ago, was my worst mistake yet. Half a dozen police vehicles were scattered around the place, their silent sirens blasting blue and red alongside the warm streams of the sun. Looking for Russell, I scanned the area. I was then disturbed to see Russ and the others who'd just left Tanner's office in the back of a black SUV, its flashing lights hard at work on the roof. Russ turned suddenly and moved his mouth, trying to convey something to me that I couldn't discern.

A tall, broad suit walked out from behind a car and came forward, a police officer beside him, gun raised and aimed right at me. "Put your hands up where we can see them," he ordered. I had my arms raised as instructed when the suit came closer and stood in front of me, flashing his badge and introducing himself as Detective Miller of Nueces County Criminal Investigations. "Kevin Sloan?"

"Yes."

"The department has been informed that you and a handful of your coworkers are involved in the purchase and delivery of stolen and counterfeit products."

"I don't even work here," I tried, too stunned to try harder, which was probably a good thing.

"Not usually," he said pointedly. His cop pal slithered behind me and aggressively padded me down. In the process, I dropped my envelope.

"What is this?" asked the detective. I said nothing as Detective Miller picked it up and unsealed it with careful fingers. It seemed whatever he saw inside it was exactly what he'd expected. He spun his hand at the cop behind me, instructing him to proceed. The next thing I knew, cold metal handcuffs were choking my wrists and my rights were being read, bringing me to a whole new level of screwed.

50

Despite my best efforts to be empathetic and all of my prayers for patience and guidance, I was still hurting. I didn't want Kevin to feel like I was ignoring him, but I just wasn't sure what to say yet. How could I be a good girlfriend and a positive light in Kevin's life if I didn't have the right words? God knew how much he meant to me.

The last thing I'd heard from him was a text saying, "It's done. I'm out." He wasn't talking about *them*, right? That was about him quitting Tanner's, not about quitting *us*.

Right??

Downstairs, my parents were watching the news. Breakfast had come and gone, which was good with me because I didn't feel much like interacting today. The cereal was still out, so I filled a bowl and poured a glass of milk and tried to sneak out of the kitchen to go bolus and eat in peace in my room, when the footage playing on the TV caught everyone's attention.

"Isn't that Kevin's workplace?" Mom asked Dad, watching the camera footage as it panned around. They hadn't noticed I was there yet. My dad pointed the remote and turned the volume up.

I put the bowl and glass down on the island, hands suddenly weak, and slowly stepped closer to listen.

I watched in horror as the studio newscaster informed the public, *"An anonymous tip proved shocking this morning as Tanner Automotive, a local auto repair shop, was shut down. At least five employees have been arrested so far in connection to the illegal distribution of counterfeit car parts, including business owner Blake Tanner. More arrests from around the community are expected as this story unfolds."*

My mouth went dry. "Is that live?" My parents turned, their curiosity just as piqued as mine.

"No, it all happened early this morning," Dad said.

Mom put her arm over the edge of the couch, twisting to see me better. "Honey, did Kevin know about this?"

I couldn't believe what I was hearing and I couldn't just stand there. Yesterday, he told me he was quitting, and I believed he meant it, so he couldn't have been there during the bust today. But then, what did his text message earlier mean? I had to find him and ensure that everything was okay.

"Sarah, wait!" Mom called after me, but I was already halfway out. I grabbed my keys from the hook by the door and flew like the wind down the stairs and over to my car. "Sarah!" I vaguely heard Dad's voice, but it didn't really register, not enough to make me stop.

The shop still looked like the scene on TV as if it hadn't been touched since then. All the garage doors were closed, and the whole place was blocked off with pylons and tape, with big locks blocking each entry into the building. Kevin was nowhere in sight. No one was. *Kevin must be at home then.*

En route to Kevin's house, my Dexcom notified me of high blood sugar as if I couldn't already tell. I felt like crud, and after taking immediate notice that Kevin's truck wasn't there, that didn't improve any. I pulled my car kit from the glove box for an adjustment injection. Pulling my shirt up out of the way, I pinched at my abdomen opposite my monitor and injected my insulin. I didn't have time to wait for the boost to even me out, so as soon as I updated my app, I took off toward the house. With that out of the way, all thoughts of anything except Kevin were quickly evaporating.

Nobody answered when I knocked. The lights at Kevin's house were out, even the ones inside. "Kevin?!" I called out fruitlessly, hoping for a miracle.

"You lookin' for Marie's kid?"

My head whipped toward the invading voice. "Yes! Is he okay? Do you know where he is?"

A man I didn't recognize stood on the sidewalk, hands in the pockets of his puffy, tan leather jacket. "Well, that depends on your definition of okay, I reckon."

"What do you mean?"

"According to what I seen, he and a bunch'a others got themselves arrested this mornin'."

No, no, no! Please, not Kevin. "Are you saying he's in jail?"

He made a sympathetic roll of his shoulders, but his face read like he wasn't too sorry about it. There was a flicker of something familiar about him, and my suspicions were raised. "Are you a neighbor?"

"I'm just a visitor."

Kevin didn't have any friends in his neighborhood, and he had no other family. So, how did this guy know him? And he knew Marie by name. I looked around but didn't see any vehicles parked on the side of the road nearby. If he was visiting someone, why would he be walking along the sidewalk like he didn't have anywhere to be?

Not comfortable with his presence, I thanked him and hurried back to my car, grabbing my phone to call Kevin again. His phone was dead because it didn't even ring anymore, but I pretended it did, jetting inside like I was on the phone to avoid further exchange. The guy flashed a disturbing smile and waved as I drove away.

My gaze flicked to the passenger seat where my insulin pack was no longer resting. I leaned to reach the glove box, which was still hanging open, but it wasn't there, either. That man... he'd stolen my insulin?! Seriously?! I checked the rear-view mirror, but he wasn't there anymore. Worried, confused, and now more than a little afraid, I began to cry.

God, please protect Kevin, and please give me the strength I already know I'm about to need.

KEVIN

51

Jail was not for the faint of heart, and I still had trouble grasping that Yours Truly had just spent a night there. I couldn't imagine how much worse prison was. There, unlike in my fifteen-by-fifteen holding cell, I wouldn't be alone. I would share those tight and confined spaces with real, hardened criminals. Actual bad guys.

Nothing like me, of course. I wanted nothing to do with that life. I would have quit last night had I been able to, but I'd gone this morning and walked away successfully, if not unknowingly, right into the long arm of the law. At the time, it had felt like the worst luck in the world, but the investigators believed my story and, apparently, none of the others arrested had said anything that disproved it.

All night spent in that cold, depressing cell, I thought about my "luck." Could it have been Sarah's God that had shown me such clemency? Or was it the leniency of a judge, chosen to decide the fate of a misguided student who was trying to better himself in the big, bad world? It was possible that I was just a nameless face in the sea of troubled youth he saw every day, and he had become jaded to it, thinking no punishment he doled would affect me, anyway.

In addition to working closely with the same social worker as before, Cynthia Henderson, I now had my very own probation officer. Ruben Green sat opposite me at a desk in a small office downtown. He was tall and dark-skinned with a gentle expression on his stark face.

I adjusted in his uncomfortable plastic chair and observed this new court-appointed "advocate" and the bulky ankle-monitor on the desk between us, teasing me. It was already fired up and fully programmed to let me go only to a select few places for the next ninety days. Regarding that, I had a lot of questions. But the one that weighed on my mind the most was, "Can I see my girlfriend, or do I have to be completely cut off while I wear this?"

Lifting it up, Ruben showed the monitor. "With this guy, you can go to school as normal, your nearest grocery store up to two times per week, and that's it. It's going to send every move you make straight to an app that I control right here on my phone." He tapped his breast pocket where his cell phone was located.

"But what about Sarah?" I asked again, desperate to know.

"You can see people, sure, but it's in your best interest you don't associate with anyone who could cause you any amount of trouble. If she's involved with any of the stuff that —"

"She isn't," I rushed to say, utterly relieved.

Ruben accepted this and nodded. "Then I'm sure you'll be fine. And, God willing, if you impress all of us with your good behavior over the next few weeks, Judge Whitaker *could* let you out of the band early to enroll into college on time."

"Really?" Besides being able to see Sarah, that was the best news I could've heard.

"It's no guarantee. In fact, it's probably not even likely, but he's very compassionate to those who put in the effort and try, so it can't hurt to hope." Ruben said. "Unlike your pal, he was very lenient with you for a reason."

"Do you mean Russell Grandy? What happened to him?"

Ruben's expression turned sympathetic. "I'm not really at liberty to say."

"He's been my friend for ten years. Just tell me, please. What difference does it make if you do?"

He exhaled, his back straight, taking on a more authoritative air. "He won't be going home so soon. It sounds like he'll likely be going to state when his trial is over."

"Prison! Why? And I didn't get a trial."

"Some cases don't need one. You were found cutting ties with Blake Tanner at the time of your arrest and showed remorse in front of the judge, and your story was corroborated. Mr. Grandy had been in the operation a lot deeper and longer than you, and he clearly regretted nothing. I'm sorry, Kevin." Ruben picked up my file and dropped the stack's edge on his desk to straighten them out. Then he exhaled sharply, his features relaxing with empathy.

"Me too. Russ really wasn't all that bad. Into some bad stuff, sure, but I always thought he was still a good person."

"And that might be true. Some people just don't know how to make the right decisions under pressure. But it's also possible that, even though you've known him for a long time, you didn't know *him* very well. Even our closest friends can look like strangers when the light is shining on them."

I inferred the opposite must be true, too, when Tyler came to mind. I hadn't known him long at all, probably only minutes before I had grasped his true character. Tyler was the type of person who put himself out there for the world to see and didn't hold back or hide anything, even his flaws. And even though Ruben was one of those state officials I usually had a negative feeling about, I already had the impression that Ruben was genuine. That meant one of two things. Either people were getting worse at hiding who they really were, or I was getting better at reading people.

Still, I couldn't believe what had happened to Russell, and what could've just as easily happened to me. "We grew up together. I'm no better than he is."

"I think you'll find that's not true at all. You are not Kevin from ten years ago or even ten days ago. You are Kevin of today. Don't drown yourself in yesterday's puddle." With the monitor in hand, Ruben stood from his desk and walked around to me. "Well, let's get you going, shall we?" Then he affixed the blinking band onto my ankle, gave me a stack of instructional paperwork to read, which among other important things explained how to always keep within range of my monitor's strict boundaries.

Then, out of nowhere, Ruben surprised me. "Thank you for making this job worthwhile for people like Judge Whitaker and myself. You don't know the grit it requires to deal with some others. Take child-abusers, for example." He sighed. "If not for God's mercies, I don't know how I could do this job. Kids like you make up for it — those who deserve and have a real shot at making it after junk like this. I know you have a solid future ahead, Kevin. Don't blow it, alright?"

"Alright." What could I possibly say to that? More people believed in God than I ever knew.

"Oh, I almost forgot. We know you will need money. After all, nothing in this life is free, and that includes your new fashion piece, so Cynthia has set you up with a transcription job you can do from home. Do you have a good internet connection?"

"I don't know."

"Are you any good at typing?"

I had never really thought about it. "Sure."

"Good enough. She'll be by in a few days to set that up with you."

"Sounds like fun."

"That's the spirit! And if not, at least it'll pay the bills," said Ruben practically.

Later that evening, being dropped off at home with an ankle band and no way out for ninety days felt like such a strange sort of sobriety that I didn't know how to describe, except to say that I saw everything in my life in a bright new way. There was confidence in that and assurance from somewhere I couldn't pinpoint the source of. And I was sure glad to be home, even if it was mandatory I be there. Even if my ankle band was soon to get so itchy, I would become hard-pressed not to slice my foot off for relief. I was home, and I still had a future, so I would take any inconvenience that came with.

Looking around, I realized it was the first time in over four years that I wasn't sharing my home with a monster. After I was settled in and things were cleared up with Sarah, I would start really cleaning the place up. New locks for the doors would be ordered ASAP. Every piece of clothing and each piece of trash that belonged to Craig was going straight to the dump. If Craig ever tried to come sniffing around *my* house again, I would be more than happy to let the cops have him.

I tossed my hoodie and a large Ziplock bag full of my personal items onto the kitchen counter and rested my palms on the edge. I took a deep breath and then fished out my phone, plugged it into a charger, and left it while I took a quick shower to wash away the experience and filth of my night in jail. When I came back, my phone had come back to life and had dozens of missed notifications, most of which were from Sarah.

She still cares, I rejoiced.

SARAH

52

When I wasn't staring wide-eyed at the circling ceiling fan worrying about Kevin, I was plagued with nightmares about what might be happening to him. My anxiety had gotten a hold of any and all worrisome thoughts and preyed on me all night. Once or twice, that creepy guy I'd encountered outside Kevin's house even made an appearance in my dreams to taunt me, sporting black-stained teeth beneath a smile that made my skin crawl.

The only thing I knew for sure was that the moment I could see Kevin again, safe and sound, his trespasses would be immediately forgiven. My loyalty was not soft. It was strong and real, and if there was ever a time Kevin needed me to prove that, it was now.

Little by little, my heart had broken as I listened to the tension in Kevin's voice. I couldn't grasp the level of desperation that had caused his decision to chance the law for money. What really did me in was the way he took his mom's burden upon himself. He wasn't an adult, yet he had all the stressors and responsibilities of one, plus everything a regular student his age already had. It wasn't fair to him at all, and it wasn't something he could manage, as was made very clear.

Wagering his future just to protect his mom from her addictions wasn't right, but neither was lying to me. Nothing could make that okay, but he needed my support now more than ever, and I would see that he had it.

I felt I should've been more willing to truly listen the other night. While he was sitting there holding me like I was his next breath, I'd been too focused on my own feelings. I had told him I needed to go home and process everything, and he had been fair and sensitive to my needs. If only I had not been so blinded by emotion that I misinterpreted his attempt at self-preservation as betrayal. By all rights, I should've taken him at his word, but I was so high on anger at the time. By the time that feeling gave way to sadness, it was too late.

Maybe if I had been more sensitive, more willing to listen up front, he wouldn't have gone back and been arrested. Maybe it was my denial that drove him back there.

Too weak to carry the burden of my emotions any longer, I dropped to my knees. My way wasn't working. *God, please help me be strong for Kevin, to love him well even when it's complicated. Guide him, comfort him... Please let me see him soon.*

In Jesus' name I pray, Amen.

When I rose, accepting the swift peace my prayer provided, the moment was made better by the dinging of an incoming text message. A special chime which only sounded for one person in particular. I scooted to my nightstand and grabbed my phone.

Kevin's message was a reply to one of the many texts I had sent before.

KEVIN

I'm okay. Are you?

SARAH

I am now! Where are you? What happened??

KEVIN

I'm home and have a lot to tell you if you're
willing to listen. What do you think about coming
over?

I turned my eyes upward and uttered, "Thank You, Jesus. He's safe. Thank You! Thank You!" My fingers flew over the screen.

SARAH

I'll be right there.

I fled from my bed, grabbed my insulin, and dressed in record time. Downstairs, I searched for my mom and found her just coming inside with the mail in hand. "Good morning, my girl. You seem much better."

"Kevin is back! I'm heading over there now to talk everything out." I rushed to my shoes inside the mudroom bench and shoved them on. As I stood to lift my bag from the peg where it hung, Mom came over and put her hand on my shoulder.

"Hey, slow down." She took me by the shoulders and urged me down with her on the bench perpendicular to the door. "What's happened?"

"I don't know yet. That's what I'm going to find out. But it doesn't matter. I love him no matter what."

"Well, that's pretty ambitious, don't you think? What if he's really guilty?"

"I believe he is, Mom."

I watched the look on my mom's face change rapidly while she calculated her response. "Then have you considered he might not be the person you thought he was?

"I know in my heart that he is."

"Our hearts can be very deceptive when we want something badly enough."

"I know, but it's not just my heart. My head and my gut are both in agreement. Kevin is a good person, Mom."

"He might truly be, but is it wise to forgive so easily? It sounds like the kind of trouble he's in is very serious. We don't want you involved in that."

"I'm not involved. You have to trust me. I believe what matters most is what comes next. God doesn't stop loving us when we screw up, does he? I know I don't love as perfect as God does, but it's my goal to try. I know I'm supposed to."

Tears pooled in the corners of my mother's eyes. "I don't want to tell you to give up on someone, Sarah, but I can't help but worry about you."

"What are you saying?"

"I am your mother. You're only seventeen. But no matter how old you are, if your heart is involved, so is mine. I only want the best for you." My mom lovingly tucked wayward hair behind my ear. She quickly wiped away her tears and regained her composure with a smile. "You're my one and only daughter. I'm allowed to question and cry."

"That's fair. I just know everything will be okay." I hugged my mom, and it was the greatest squeeze I'd ever felt. "I love you, Mama."

"I know you do. I love you, too. And God *bless* you, baby girl." When she sighed and released me from the hug, she was smiling.

I could see her faith in me. "As long as you drive safely. Just be careful, okay? Don't let your emotions run so high."

"I've got this, Mom."

53

MY SURPRISE PALED IN COMPARISON TO THE FEEL OF HER IN MY arms again. My joy was insurmountable. I guided her into the house so I could close and lock the door. Sarah sat on the couch, and when she angled herself to take me in, I steeled myself for the explanation to come.

Sitting down beside her, I wove our fingers together. Knowing my own transgressions were greatest, I didn't want her to feel sorry. I wanted her happy — only happy — forever.

"I've been an idiot all this time, doing one stupid thing after another. You keep forgiving me, but I'm here to tell you that was the last time you'll have to. Nothing else matters as long as I have you. Not money, not Jared, not school, nothing." I glanced at our coupled hands, reveling in how whole I felt with her there. I had come too close, gotten too near the point of losing her over my bad choices, and I vowed I would never do that again. Whatever I had to endure in order to keep her, I would. If I had to become best friends with Jared, then so be it. If I had to sit through church every single Sunday forever, I could handle it. No problem.

"I need to tell you everything that happened," I continued, feeling braver than I ever had in my life. She deserved every ounce of my truth from here on out. "How much do you know already?"

"Not a lot. We saw the bust at Tanner's on the news yesterday."

"We?"

"My parents and I watched."

My jaw went tight. "I'm sorry, Sarah. I wish they hadn't seen that. I wish it hadn't even happened. Your dad probably hates my guts."

"I haven't talked to him about it, so I can only guess at how he feels, but my mom understands. She knows where we're at, and she still respects you. My dad will come around."

Sarah placed her hand on my arm, appearing thoughtful, and urged me on. "What happened?" She curiously watched me lean down to hike up the hem of my jeans, and then she saw the picture come into focus.

"Long story short," I started, smoothing my pants let back down over the ankle monitor, "I will get to spend the next ninety days luxuriating right here in the comfort of my own home."

"You can't go anywhere for three months? What about school? They can't keep you from graduating. That's not fair!"

I was struck with awe by her vehemence, and it humbled and warmed me. "School is part of my terms. It's pretty much the only place I can go. I even have to start this new work-from-home job next week."

"What about your mom?"

I shook my head no. "I don't have a choice. But I think she'll be okay."

"Have you talked to her yet?"

"No, but the social worker has, so she knows about it."

"That's good. Kevin, I hate that you're dealing with this, but I know you'll get through it, and I'll help you as much as I can. Everything will be okay."

"I think so, too." Sarah had begun leaning in slowly as I spoke. It drew my attention to the curvature of her mouth, causing me to crave a new taste of her lips.

"I know so," she whispered in confirmation, and I kissed her, thinking there was nothing better in the world than her love.

As the evening went on, we fixed something to eat and settled onto the couch to watch TV until she had to leave. During the third or fourth episode of Andy Griffith, Sarah's eyes got heavy and I didn't have the heart to stop her falling asleep. I would wake her in time for curfew, but she could doze for now. Just having her here was enough.

Not long later, the doorbell rang. I carefully raised Sarah's sleep-heavy arm and settled it onto the pillow beside her. She roused only slightly and exhaled the sweetest, lilting sound I'd ever heard. When I opened the door, I was pleased to see my beloved Tacoma out on the curb, just being released from a tow truck.

An upper middle-aged man in a navy blue shop suit and matching baseball cap held up a clipboard. "Kevin Sloan?"

"Yes, sir. I'm sure glad to see you guys." The last time a stranger in a uniform had asked me that, it hadn't been so pleasant an experience.

"Just sign right here, and she's all yours again." He responded to my signature with a friendly nod and then dropped the keys into my hand. "You have yourself a good evening."

I thanked the man and watched the tow truck take off. Sarah was still sleeping, so I quietly stepped out and closed the door.

Quickly, I pulled my truck into the driveway beside Sarah's car, where to me, it looked like it belonged. Despite my current circumstances and the strain it was inevitably going to put on everything, I couldn't be happier. I had been given a second chance. I had learned my lesson, and definitely wouldn't be making the same mistakes again. Not with Sarah and not with the law. I had a heart full of gratitude, even if I had an ankle surrounded by hard plastic. Going forward was my only option.

SARAH

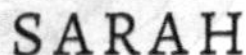

54

"Sarah." I heard my name somewhere in the distance, spoken by Kevin in a light timbre. My eyes opened slowly, and I found him crouched on the floor looking at me.

Rubbing my eyes, I sat up. "Did I seriously fall asleep?"

He chuckled as he rose to sit beside me. "Yeah, a little bit."

"I totally didn't mean to do that. I guess I was more tired than I thought. Sleep was kinda *meh* last night."

"For me, too," admitted Kevin.

We shared the moment, each taking the other in. I couldn't believe the intensity of my feelings for him. I longed for the day we shared one home and one life. It was going to happen. I knew it deep down, but for now, I had a curfew to abide by. "I don't want to leave."

Kevin ran his hand against my cheek. "I wish you didn't have to." A distraction came in the form of the distinct sound of metal scraping metal and shattering glass from outside. "What the heck was that?"

I jumped up. "Sounded like a car crash."

We ran to look out the window. My hand flew to my mouth

on a gasp, in shock. Kevin's truck was parked in the driveway, totally destroyed. Only jagged points of glass here and there remained of the windows. The windshield was a shattered spiderweb of cracks and holes. Dents were pitted into every metal surface we could see, lending a wild guess at what the other side looked like.

"That guy!" I cried, looking in disbelief at the man and his wielded crowbar beside the destruction. "I've seen him before!"

"What do you mean you've *seen him*?" Kevin ground out as the scene outside tested our sanity.

"He stole my insulin bag out of my car when I came here looking for you last night. But I feel like I've seen him somewhere else, too…" The man outside sported a maniacal look. That warped smile of his was even worse than the one from my dream. It was an expression that said he was off in a world of his own and on a psychotic mission. He took swings at the vehicle as he bobbed back and forth, muttering to himself. Even his dusty-brown jacket brought forth a strange feeling of familiarity. "He appeared out of the blue and started talking to me about you. He said he was visiting someone in your neighborhood and told me you'd been arrested. It was weird, though. There's something I didn't like about him and I took off after that."

"Your instincts were right. That's Craig," Kevin spat out. "I've seen him like this before. He must be tweaking."

Craig's rampage momentarily halted, his attention having been caught by our observance through the window. He swayed on his feet, smiling unsightly at his new audience. "I see you in there!" he called eerily. "Come out and talk to me, boy!"

"Lock the door behind me. If anything happens, you run," he said, making for the door.

"No freaking way, Kevin! You are not going out there!" I was adamant, but he'd already made up his mind. Fear welled up inside me as he disappeared outside, throwing the door closed. "Oh, God. Please let nothing bad happen to Kevin. Please keep him safe!" I prayed with all my might, repeating it over and over to myself as I secured the bolt on the door. I ran back to peek out the window, collecting my phone from the couch on the way. As fast as my shaking fingers could manage, I dialed 911.

KEVIN

55

Visibly pleased by my appearance, Craig spun the metal bar in his hand like a baton and hiked his shoulders, his palms facing up. "I'm just here to pay you a fatherly visit. Haven't you missed me?"

Dark feelings surfaced, summoned from years of repressed anger and frightfulness. My truck wasn't the first thing Craig had demolished during one of his trips. Neither was the shed. Neither was our old couch. And neither were my and Marie's bones. Nothing and nobody was safe around Craig on a normal day, let alone when he had consumed his latest poison.

I seethed with something more than rage. Up until now, I had been naïve enough to think we were rid of Craig, but here he was, taking yet another thing away from me. I couldn't tolerate it.

"Leave now." My stern tone carried the weight of my distress. I didn't want Sarah anywhere near this piece of crap, and the fact that Craig had approached her while she was alone both horrified and infuriated me. Because of my arrest last night, I hadn't been here to protect her from Craig. If anything had happened to her…

Craig let his shoulder sag. "Now, what kind of greeting is that for your old man?"

"In no universe are you my old man, Craig. You're not even my mom's husband anymore, so that makes you *nothing*."

Bouncing back and forth on his feet, twisting the bar around in his hands, Craig made a reignited display of his crazy. I wanted to withdraw, to get out of harm's way, but I couldn't back down with Sarah there. I had to protect her now, in all the ways I had never been able to protect my mom. Who knew what Craig would do if I wasn't standing between them.

Steadying my voice, I said, "Look, man, you need to just go. The cops are already coming. It's time you just moved on."

"Oh. *Ooh.* I gotta just go and move on, you say? Big man of the house now, are ya? Large and in charge."

Bigger than you ever were, I thought, hands readying into fists as Craig's toxicity worked its way deeper under my skin. Craig paced with agitation then began shaking his head aggressively.

"No. No, I don't think I will. I'm thinkin' this house belongs to me, seein's how I paid its upkeep for the last six years. You and your good for nothin' mother would be out on the streets where you both belong if it weren't for me, boy. You. Owe. Me." Taking a step forward, Craig squared up. "Or! Maybe I could take what you owe me another way." Craig's twisted eyes moved slowly up the drive, over to where Sarah was watching from the window.

My blood was boiling. With every word that oozed from Craig's mouth, I longed to beat him to a bloody pulp if only to shut him up. "Enough! Get lost, Craig, before I beat you down!"

In response, Craig swiped his nose and laughed, taking a grand-slam swing and sending Sarah's right rear mirror sailing into the side of the neighbor's house. "You know, I have better places to be anyway, but I just had to be here to see how you took it when you finally found out…"

"Get out of here, Craig. Save your breath for Satan."

"…that *I* was the one who told the feds about Tanner's." He snickered and dragged the forked end of the crowbar along Sarah's passenger door, the screeching scrape ringing in my ears, almost drowning out the incoming sirens.

The revelation was on replay in my head. If it weren't for Craig being the evil beast he was, I would have walked away from Tanner completely unscathed. I stepped forward, my arm raising. "You son of a…"

From behind us, Sarah pounded on the glass and shouted at me to stop. Her sobering plea stopped me cold. The sirens were closer, nearly there. Craig was finished. "Hear that? It's over for you, Craig." He didn't matter anymore.

Craig grew more annoyed, growling and repeatedly slapping himself in the head with the heel of his free hand. After taking another swing at Sarah's car, Craig took off, clumsily running through a neighboring yard until I could no longer see him. At least Sarah was safe now, and with how close the cops were, there was no way they wouldn't find him this time.

SARAH

56

Within the safety of the house, I stood anxiously, my stomach in knots. As I watched Kevin's tormentor take on a whole new fervor, a disturbed one I had never seen in a person before, I realized how gravely ignorant I had been about the things Kevin had dealt with. About his entire life in general. Craig's behavior portrayed a person severely unhinged, and the thought of Kevin being subjected to him as a child made me falter.

Tears ran uncontrollably, my heart terrified and broken for Kevin. If this pain was any measure of what Kevin grew up enduring and struggling to protect Marie from, it was no wonder he lacked the faith I had. To live each day in fear of the man I saw right then was to suffer as I never had. What about the others Kevin mentioned who came before Craig? He was the only example I'd actually seen.

Maybe it was easier to be faithful when your life is easy. Yes, I had health issues I was forced to manage, and my family had our own problems. But we were classically normal, myself included. Some might even say I was boring or spoiled.

Or ignorant.

The reality of everything was gross and troubling. Seeing firsthand how a wonderful person like Kevin had grown up was absolutely sickening.

Thank God the police were coming. I could hear them now. Craig could, too, because he vanished between the houses, leaving Kevin alone in the driveway.

I needed to be with him and rushed to open the door. "Kevin!" I exclaimed. He turned just in time to catch me as I leaped into his arms. "I'm so glad he's gone. You don't have to listen to anything he says ever again. They'll catch him. Forget he exists." Giving his arm a tug, I urged him back to the house with me. "It's okay now. Let's wait inside."

Kevin's lead feet finally moved, and he lumbered along, looking frazzled. "I can't believe how close I just came to screwing up probation."

I tightened my fingers around his, reiterating my comfort. "You did really good, Kevin. I'm proud of you." And beyond relieved that it was over, even though my gut told me it wasn't.

KEVIN

57

OH, HOW I WOULD HAVE *LOVED* TO HEAR CRAIG'S NOSE BREAK AND watch the blood and cartilage spew out of his nostrils. I would've enjoyed it tremendously, however depraved that was, in honor of all the horror Craig had inflicted on me and my mom. But something held me back, something more than Sarah's persuasive shouts or her hand on my shoulder now, and I pondered it with awe.

If God loved the world so much He sacrificed His only son to save it, maybe He also loved me enough to stay my hand. Nothing else had ever done the trick, not even the looming threat of losing Sarah's affection, as we'd seen with Jared. To have overcome the deep-rooted desire to give Craig everything he had coming… to resist repaying just a fraction of the evil he'd caused… there was no better explanation I could come up with. And in that bewildering certainty, I thought I might also find some peace.

We were a few steps from safety before Craig reappeared, stepping out in front of us from around the house. The peace I almost felt was close enough to reach out and touch, but apparently, God was ready to let me trip at the finish line. With his metal weapon raised high, Craig stomped forward and lunged at Sarah.

One second, I was at the precipice of something greater, and the next, I was knocked down to the furthest reaches beside my opponent. There was no time to think it over. No more reasoning with an ideology that may or may not have worked out for me in the end. There was only instinct driving me forward, and in an instant, I sent my shoulder into Craig's chest, knocking loose his hold on the crowbar, and catapulting us both to the ground. As fists flew, my wrath was provoked anew.

In the blink of an eye, I lost track of who I had almost become. Instead, I fell back on an old weakness that I used to think made me strong. This time, I did it to protect Sarah like I had never had the guts to protect anyone else before. It didn't matter to me that the sirens had gotten extremely loud, or that Sarah was screaming at the top of her lungs. Nor was it important when I became vaguely aware of additional sets of hands pulling at me. Everything was incomprehensible except keeping Craig away from Sarah, away from my mother, and ultimately away from me forever. Nothing else registered until I was aggressively jerked free of my enemy and thrown down face-first.

A loud, domineering voice blasted into my ear. When I successfully forced myself to calm, I was yanked to my feet, hands clenched behind my back. My chest burned with each labored breath as I took in the hazardous scene around me.

Sarah wasn't where I had seen her last. Now, she was standing between two parked police cars, being held back by cops. Red and blue flashing lights bounced off her wrenched face. With the inconsistent illumination, I saw the tears in her eyes and the pain on her face. She was yelling something. The loud voice was talking, too, but all I could hear was the obtuse pumping of blood that each breath tore through my lungs.

Craig was on the ground, already in cuffs and covered in blood. He was very much alive, and I could barely decide if I was grateful or mad about that, but at least he was *caught*. This would mean the end of Craig's torturous reign in my life and the outside world at large.

A crowd of neighbors had gathered and stood behind a barricade of cops and cars, whispering about the drama. I wondered how many of them had heard Craig terrorizing us over the years, yet never once said anything or tried to help, and my eyes stung.

My adrenaline gave out next. Little by little, I felt every jab to the ribs and each elbow to the jaw and everything between where Craig had inflicted his savagery. For what I had just done, I was surely on my way to lock-up. All I could console myself with was that it would be the last time Craig caused me — or anyone I loved — any pain. If I was going to wind up behind bars, at least Craig was going down, too.

KEVIN

58

THOSE FIRST FEW DAYS WERE A BLUR AS I WAITED TO STAND BEFORE Judge Whitaker for the second time in one week. In the end, I was sentenced to 180 days of incarceration with no possibility of early release. I was to serve three months for the original sentence, and another three were tacked on for assault and battery charges. Although the DA was adamant I be tried as an adult, especially since I would turn eighteen while incarcerated, the judge flat-out refused, decreeing it wouldn't fit my circumstances. Thank God for that small mercy.

Following my release, I would have two years of strict probation, but then my record would be expunged. It was hard for me to be grateful because two years sounded like forever, but I knew I would be in time, and I already recognized I was better off than the others caught in Tanner's bust. I couldn't imagine how Russell's mother was handling her son's fate, the poor woman. And I had no way of knowing how Marie was handling mine yet, either.

Another consolation was the process had been a lot faster

than anyone expected. Now that the Band-Aid had been torn away, real healing could begin. Eventually. Hopefully.

"What an ideal outcome for a not-so-ideal case," Ruben Green announced as he and I walked out of the courtroom, tailed by my own personal bailiff. "Just think, in a couple years, it'll be like this never happened."

I yanked at the stupid tie around my neck, my mood vastly sour when stacked against Ruben's. It was harder to swallow Ruben's optimism when I was the one heading back to a jail cell and Ruben was going home. "Don't count your chickens, dude."

"I *will* count my chickens, *dude*, because I know my instincts are right about you."

"You were wrong already, or haven't you noticed?" *We're back at this awful place, are we not? I just got six months of jail time, did I not?!*

"Don't give me your 'woe is me' act, Kevin Sloan. I've spent a lot of quality time with your file lately, and I know better."

"Whatever. I beat the guy like he deserved. I knew what I was doing."

Ruben dropped anchor, forcing me to stop and look him in the eye. "And what you were doing it *for*, right? Ninety-nine percent of the delinquents walking around this place right now have nothing but selfish motives behind their crimes. They stole because they didn't want to pay, or shot up because they wanted another fix. They broke in because they wanted what they didn't have." Ruben stared intently, his gaze meaning business. "Is that what you did? Acted out of selfishness?"

"I don't —"

Ruben still wasn't done. "Or did you react out of *selflessness*? Ask yourself this: did your actions come from a place of malice or love?"

Shifting on my feet, the weight of Ruben's lecture deflated my lungs. "Both. I didn't have to keep swinging."

"But you didn't swing at all until you had to. See what I mean?" Ruben bumped his knuckles into my arm. "Look, kid. You've got this, okay? This period of your life won't even be a blip on the radar anymore one day, so keep your chin up because I know I'm not the only one rooting for you." With that, I was led back to my holding cell before relocating to my new home for the next six months.

By the time I was settled in at the Nueces County Juvenile Detention Center, complete with a sketchy new bunkmate who went by the name of Badger, I was no longer chomping at the bit to contact Sarah. Ruben's lecture had left its mark on my heart, and I no longer knew what my approach would be when I spoke to her again. I was dying to hear Sarah's voice and fill her in, and of course, I wanted to know how she'd been feeling since my second arrest, but I had trouble facing the music.

The buzz signaling our daily release went off and the cell doors all opened. Calamity rang out as inmates poured through the hallways, each on their own mission. Though I had somewhere to be, I didn't immediately take off as I had intended to, and Badger stepped down from his bunk.

"You chickenin' out?" Badger, whose real name was Derrick Badger, was the outspoken type with a propensity toward nosiness. That being said, I could be a lot worse off as far as cell mates went.

"No." That's what I kept telling myself.

"I was you once. I been here a long time already now, so I know what this is. You got a girl and you too scared to call her, huh?"

Defeated by reality as I was, I didn't see how denying it could help. "That's the gist of it."

Laughing, Badger presumptuously took a seat on my bed beside me. "Yeah, man. I had me one, too. She even came to visit me at first. We wanted to get married, but that was before I got locked up."

"Married? How old are you?"

"I'm twenty. Been in since I was eighteen. Finally gettin' out when I turn twenty-one in a few months." Badger made a steeple with his hands and pressed it against his lips.

"I'll be eighteen before I get out, but I didn't realize people stayed in juvie that long," I said. Still curious, I asked, "So, did she dump you?"

Badger smiled knowingly and nodded. "Yep. Got tired of the waitin'. Can't say I blame her, though. I wouldn't wait for me, neither."

"That sucks," I commiserated.

"It sure did. That's how I know it was real, and why she made it so long before leavin' me. She didn't want to, but she had to. Know what I'm sayin'?"

Maybe. Possibly. "Sure."

"Ain't her fault I'm here, so it wouldn't be fair to punish her, too. But you know what? It's all good, because when I get out, I'm goin' after her."

"Yeah?"

"Yep. And if she won't have me, I can still spin this to my advantage. There's plenty of honeys out there who love a certified bad boy." Badger elbowed me with a smirk then stood up. "Anyway, you goin' to breakfast?"

"In a bit." Hungry though I was, I was still not ready to unglue myself from this bed. The rest of me might fall apart, too.

"Later, bro," Badger said, and then disappeared down the hall.

Somewhere between Ruben and Badger, after sorting through their biases and quirks, I had come to a startling conclusion that they were both right. And that, I now realized, is why I had yet to call Sarah. I didn't want to lose her, but it didn't feel right to keep her, either.

I thought hard about my next step, knowing neither Sarah nor I would like it, but I determined nothing could be as bad as seeing her held back by cops, shouting in distress, while I was painted with crimson regret.

One thought crossed my mind: would Sarah have the same understanding she'd expected of me during a similar conversation? That night seemed like such a long time ago now. I would give anything to go back to that. If only I had known then what I knew now, I could've spared us both. If only the world worked that way.

I mentally prepared as I walked to the phone room. At a rate of twenty-one cents per minute, I didn't have time to waste. After scanning my badge, I looked at the digital timer on the phone unit displaying my available minutes. All together, I had six minutes, zero seconds, so I had to make it count.

The ringer in my ear made my heart do jumping jacks. When her voice came on the line two seconds later, it got even worse. "Kevin? Is that you?"

Deep breath in. Out. "Hey, Sarah."

"Finally! Oh, thank God! Are you okay? What is going on? I've been going absolutely nuts! Nobody will tell me anything."

Five minutes, thirty-one seconds.

"It's so good to hear your voice, Sarah. I miss you so much."

"I miss you, too. I love you. You know that, right?"

I smiled to myself, storing her admission in my heart for later. I would need it. "Of course I do."

"When do you get to come home?"

"Not for a while. I was sentenced to six months."

"No…" Her tremble gave way to more.

If I didn't ignore the sadness in her voice and just spit the rest of these words out, I would not get through this. I cleared my throat, the action sending the sound reverberating through the sterile room. "I don't have a lot of time. The minutes are counting down fast, so I just need you to listen to me right now, okay?"

"Okay… what is it?"

"I'm so sorry for everything I've caused, Sarah. I love you so much and still dragged you through the mud with me, even though I thought I could be better for you, but I don't think I can right now." Marie was right all along. She was right to drive Sarah away. Maybe if I had let her do it then, this wouldn't hurt so badly. Instead, I'd fought and insisted I was better than she expected, only to prove myself a loser in the end. Upon closer inspection, I realized Jared wasn't the only one who had endangered Sarah's life. Look what Craig had done to Sarah's car and then tried to do to her. All because of me.

"Kevin…"

I continued as though her broken crying didn't slay me. I had to. "I need you to step away from all this and just focus on yourself. Don't be waiting for me. Finish school and move on. Can you please do that?"

"What?! No!"

Four minutes, twelve seconds.

"You'll be in pain the whole time if you're constantly focused on me and the fact that I'm in here, and I won't be able to get through this knowing that. Graduate and start college and figure out what you want to do with your life, even if that means I'm not in it. Please, say you'll do this."

"I don't want to!" she refused, her sad voice punching the words through my soul.

"Then do it for me. Give me the same space you asked for once, back when I didn't understand what it meant."

"I won't just abandon you! How can you ask me to do that?"

"Since I've met you, I've changed. I tried not to at first. You witnessed that, but it happened anyway. *You* changed me. I started making decisions that weren't all about me anymore. I learned how to care about my mom again, and I found something in you I never thought I'd have. You've given me so much, Sarah. This is my turn to give it back."

"You don't want me to hurt? Then don't do *this*. Screw whatever I said before, it doesn't apply here. Once upon a time, I was just Sarah and you were just Kevin, but now that we're together, we're not those people anymore. Remember? We have each other. Six months will fly by, Kevin."

Two minutes, fifty-seven seconds. But it might as well be zero because I couldn't endure any more. "This is for the best. I know it is. I love you." With her gut-twisting protest in my ear, I slammed the receiver down. My remaining time flashed in my face before disappearing.

Biting back bitter tears, I slid my ID through the phone unit once more. I inputted my mom's number to check in with her before heading to breakfast. I had to get rid of the rest of those minutes, so I couldn't be tempted to use them for Sarah again.

The next week, I received a letter from her.

Dear Kevin,

Where to start? I love you and miss you more than I thought was possible. I want you to know I'm not upset anymore. I understand why you did what you did. First, you saved me from Craig at the expense of yourself. Then, you saved me from yourself at the expense of us both.

You're so brave, Kevin. I see your sacrifices, and I accept them. More than that, I'm grateful. You have loved me so selflessly, it's the least I can do now to do the same for you.

But if I'm going to do this, you have to do one last thing for me. Focus on you. Take this time to find yourself, Kevin. Reconcile with who you truly are and learn to love him like I do. Like God does.

I'll think of you every day.
Love always + forever,
Sarah

❧

FOR THE DURATION of my lock-up, I kept Sarah's letter folded and tucked underneath my pillow. Sometimes after lights out, when Badger and most others were sleeping, I would take it out and read it again. I had the whole thing memorized. It wasn't very long, but it said a lot. A lot of time was spent wondering how I could accomplish such a thing. How in the world did I find myself when I didn't have the faintest idea where to look?

My mom, now released by choice from her program, was

living in our house again. Each and every Tuesday and Thursday, she would come visit, and the first question she would ask when I sat down was, "Are you getting enough to eat?" I knew to expect it, but it still surprised me. Was this woman really *my* mother? Sometimes, I could only laugh.

Since getting and staying clean, Marie had become the attentive, doting, clear-headed mom I had always been too afraid to hope for. Even her chain-smoking, tough-love exterior had been somewhat diluted. She hadn't quite kicked her cigarettes, and once in a while her words still had a bite to them, but those things, I could accept. If a little tobacco and an attitude were part of who she truly was, then fine. Being clean meant she came by those traits honestly.

Marie had always told me that people never changed, and once upon a time, I even believed it. Now, I thought maybe I understood what was underneath the self-loathing shroud of her vices. The truth was, people changed all the time, but they always remained who they *were*. Ultimately, despite all the odds stacked against her, Marie Sloan had shown herself to be someone I was proud of, so, yeah, I could take the sharp edges of her as well as the new, smooth ones. I would let no one deny her great progress, even me.

At one visit in particular, Marie told me she'd bought a Bible out of the blue. "I haven't gotten past the first page yet, but strangely, it feels good just to have it close by. How weird is that?"

"Not weird at all, Mom." I recalled the peace I had witnessed in Sarah time and time again. If anyone deserved to believe in the redeeming power of Jesus, it was Marie. I felt grateful she had found someone, a "higher power," to look up to and lean on during her recovery.

Mondays were when Ruben Greene visited. At 1:00 p.m. on

the dot. He brought my file, which was growing a little with every visit. I kept him up-to-date on everything going on. All of my academic progress, especially. Over time, I came to appreciate Ruben, although the level of support a probation officer extended to one lowly ward never ceased to baffle me.

Every other Friday, Tyler came. I was incredibly surprised when he showed up that first time. Even though I *did* put him down on my visitors' list upon intake, among various others, I didn't expect to actually see him. Tyler would sit down across from me and begin with the same question every time: "Do you want to talk about anything?"

I knew Tyler was asking about the "faith" issue, but I didn't want to go there. I would pretend to be ignorant and tell him about Badger or how terrible the food was that week. What I really wanted to talk about was Sarah, but Tyler never offered, so I never asked.

But one question, I did… "Why do you come to see me, anyway?"

"Because I want to be here for you, *amigo*, and I enjoy our chats."

From the beginning, Tyler had taken an interest in me that I didn't understand, which left me constantly second guessing his kindness. But the more time I spent with Tyler, the less those thoughts of old crossed my mind anymore. The more time went by, the more I was secure in Tyler's friendship.

It was Tyler who suggested that I look into graduating. Following that advice, I poured everything I had into finishing school. I wasn't sure how, but Ruben coordinated with the school to allow me to test out immediately. The only thing I had to do was take one all-encompassing exam, pass the state-level tests, and I was done. No GED or other equivalent required. And I aced them all, which naturally felt fantastic. So, I wouldn't walk in a cap and gown with my classmates at the American Bank Center, but Kevin Sloan was a high school graduate.

The only downside to this upward momentum was my inability to share any of it with Sarah.

KEVIN

59

THERE WEREN'T A LOT OF UPSIDES TO LIVING IN JAIL. THOUGH most things could be adjusted to as time went on, one thing I never quite got used to was the cold. On three sides, the cells were made of unforgiving cement and stone that gave the whole place a medieval dungeon-like atmosphere. The beds were affixed, sturdy and low to the ground. Mine was nearest the doorway, directly beneath an air vent, which constantly blew out a steady blast of arctic air, regardless of the time of day or year. After breaking down and purchasing extra blankets from the commissary, I ended up sharing them with Badger.

All things considered, Badger was a good guy, but his moniker was pretty telling since he was an incredible nag. Not in the old ball-and-chain sort of way, but in every other way imaginable. Badger could charm, sway, and convince, and he had the soft-core criminal credence to back it all up. He could persuade a millionaire out of his millions as easily as he could a poor man out of his rags, but thievery was his specialty, I learned. He wasn't convicted for most of those crimes, but he'd happily own up to them to fellow inmates if it helped him out. After stealing from the wrong person had come back to bite him in the rear-end, Badger found himself in jail.

One night, the air blowing into the cell was so obtrusive, my teeth chattered like an old wind-up toy. Badger snickered when he heard it and threw his extra blanket at me, and it landed in a heap on my face. As I grabbed it, realizing what it was, I threw it back. "Nah, man. That's yours and you'll need it. I swear they're trying to kill us."

"Not kill, but popsicles are more passive prisoners."

After a moment, I heard the ruffling of linens and the familiar cry of Badger's old mattress complaining about his departure. I opened my eyes in the darkness, the hideous, greenish security light just outside the cell block casting a ghoulish glow on Badger's features through the barred door as he stood over my bed.

"Get up," Badger said. "Ain't nobody can sleep with those noisy teeth of yours. We'll trade tonight. My bed don't get hit as much."

"I'll be alright."

"I know 'cause you'll be over there snorin' away. Get up, big baby," Badger demanded, and I knew he wouldn't relent until he got his way.

"Alright, alright." I sat up and whacked Badger hard with my pillow as I stood up. It was all in good humor, of course, but I put more force behind it than intended. Something glinted in the ugly light, flying across the room, and whatever it was fell to the ground with a quiet, metallic clink.

"Ah, shoot," Badger said.

"What was that? Did I knock out your gold tooth or something?"

"My cross fell off again."

"Oh, man, I'm sorry."

"It's not your fault. Happens all the time." Badger knelt down, scanning the floor.

I got up, sure I heard it land near the sink, and I turned out to be right. When my fingers brushed against it, I carefully held it up to the light. "Got it." The seconds moved in slow motion for me as I held the quarter-sized cross in my hand, really taking it in, before handing it off to Badger. "So, you're religious? How did I not know this?" Sarah had said when you love Jesus, you want everyone to know, but Badger had it hidden.

Sitting down on my bed, well, *his* bed for the night, Badger returned the cross to its shoestring and then tied it back around his neck. "Not really. I don't need no religion, just Jesus." He kissed it before dropping it underneath his shirt, where I had been ignorant of its existence all this time.

"Isn't that all the same?"

"Bro, not at all. That's not how it works. Some folks think you can't have one without the other, but most of the time, those people want you payin' their preacher's car payments. Know what I'm sayin'?" Badger rolled over to face the wall, pulling the blankets up around him with a yawn. "Not saying all churches be like that, but they *are* manmade constructs."

"So?"

"So, a church ain't a building. It ain't a preacher. It ain't none of that fancy stuff. Christ's believers are the real church. To have Jesus is to have it all, man. I could steal *anything* this world has to offer and never get the same fulfillment."

"Then why do you keep stealing?"

Badger laughed lightly then was quiet for a moment. "It's more complicated than we have time for tonight, but the short answer is, because I'm good at it. People outside these walls have expectations for me, needs they want me to meet. I don't always get to tell them no. *They* don't have Jesus."

"What about *'end of days'* and all that stuff?" During the Sunday services I had attended with Sarah, not a lot had come up about that.

"It's not just stuff, and any day of the week is the end of days for somebody. That's what bein' right in your heart with Jesus is all about. You accept Him as Lord and Savior and you are saved. Pretty simple." He yawned again. "Except for the actually having faith part. That's where most folks go wrong, I say. They all talk."

"I'm still confused. What about *'Thou shalt not steal'* and stuff? How can you be saved and still do bad things?"

"You think you know so much, then why are you asking me the questions?" He chuckled sleepily. "I'm human, bro. This life is hard and riddled with mistakes we chose to make, but God has mercy on repentant sinners. At the end of the day, I know where I'm goin'. This dreary slab can't keep me from it. Second Corinthians, chapter three, verse seventeen."

"That's from the Bible, right? What does it say?"

"I'll tell you tomorrow." Badger's breathing quickly sank low and steady, and I knew he was out. Rolling over, I tried to rearrange and get comfortable now that I wasn't shivering, but I was too disconcerted to sleep. My mind hung on every word Badger had spoken and the explanation he'd given for what he'd done in life. How could Badger continue to be forgiven or saved if he continued to sin? What did that even mean?

Those were the thoughts heavy on my mind when I finally fell asleep and slipped into a pleasant dream. Waving goodbye to Badger as he was released from jail, I felt glad for my new friend as well as hopeful for myself. Freedom was drawing near.

I slept soundly and warm, not waking again until early

morning when the first shouts sounded off through the hallway like a siren of myth.

When the emergency alarm fired on, I jerked awake, all traces of sleep having vanished. The flashing lights were bad enough, but that siren was something out of a horror movie. I had only heard it one other time before, early on, when someone from the unit downstairs threw his tray of food at a CO then tried to outrun retaliation. Throwing myself out of bed, I hurried to the bars and saw COs and medical personnel running all over the place. Whatever was going on now appeared to be a lot worse than some kid with a rogue food tray.

"Badger, dude, wake up. Something bad is happening out there." When Badger didn't respond, I turned to wake him up. That's when I noticed the blood I had failed to see before. A small puddle of blood had collected beneath Kevin's bed; the bed where Badger slept. Slowly walking closer, the floodlights overhead illuminated a fatal violence inflicted upon my cellmate — my *friend*. Badger's mouth was foamy with blood and his face distorted by death.

A few short hours later, the details about what had occurred traveled through the ward. A recent transfer had got hold of an empty syringe and gone on a late-night stabbing spree. For some indiscriminate reason, the inmate simply walked down the hall wielding death in his hands, pumping those he could reach through random cell bars full of air. Before triggering the alarm, he'd already caused three deaths, including Badger's. If I had stayed in my own bed last night, *I* would have suffered the embolism. I would be a dead man right now.

For two weeks, all non-emergent visitations were suspended. The morning they resumed, Tyler was first in line to visit me, and thanks to reasons I hadn't yet articulated, I couldn't have been happier to see him. The weight on my heart had grown heavy, and this time, when Tyler asked if I wanted to talk about anything, I actually said yes.

"You have the floor, my friend," Tyler said, setting the stage. Without judgment, Tyler hung on every word as I spoke. I told him everything I had learned about life and faith from Sarah and Badger, and I broke. I dropped my head into my arms on the table and sobbed until my body shook. Tyler reached out, putting his hand on one of my arms, providing his presence and understanding.

Once the shudders ceased, I dragged my hands over my face. Tyler pulled his Bible out of his backpack and set it out on the table.

"I want you to have this," he told me.

"I can't take that."

"You can. And you know I'm not one to push anything, but on this matter, I'm going to." Tyler tapped his hand on the book. "It's served me well, and I know it'll do the same for you. It's my gift to you, so you have no choice."

"Then, thank you." I looked over my new-to-me Bible. My first one ever. It was classic looking from the outside, wrapped finely in brown leather with gold filigree lettering, but inside, there were sticky notes and colored tabs and highlights and notations all over the margins. Tyler brought it with him every time. It was heavily studied and used, chock-full of Tyler's own thoughts and prayers. I felt honored to have it as my own now. Badger would've loved it. Mom was right that there was something special about this book, and having Tyler's well-loved copy made me feel excited.

"Tyler...What if it had been me?" I asked while still eyeing the

Bible, tears barely dry on my cheeks. "According to Badger, if it had been, I would be screwed."

"What do *you* believe?"

I thought for what seemed like a long time, drawing the only conclusion that made any sense anymore. "I believe it's true."

A smile tugged the corner of Tyler's lips. "Well, then, do you know what you need to do about it?"

"Yes. Maybe. I guess I'm not sure."

Pushing the Bible closer to me, Tyler finally smiled. "Read Romans 10 and it'll tell you."

"That's it?"

"That's it, *mi amigo!* The Word provides."

That night, alone in my cell, I opened up my new Bible to Romans, chapter 10, as directed. Reading it carefully, word by word, something clicked into place. Citing verses 9-10, I read the words out loud. As I spoke, something happened deep within my soul. A moment of change had occurred, something I needed only to *believe* in order to achieve. I realized if I had tried reading this passage before now, it wouldn't have been the same. Any other time, those words would have just been words. But in this moment, those words were life. I felt an expansion in my heart, in my lungs, that couldn't have transpired without the belief to back it up. For the first time in my life, I experienced *faith*.

Before closing the Bible for the night, I wanted to read one more thing. I turned to 2 Corinthians 3:17, and afterward, went to bed with a smile on my face.

KEVIN

60

RUBEN HAD BEEN RIGHT ABOUT HIS PREDICTION. I COULD SAY WITH complete confidence that jail had changed me and I was *never* going back, even for the right reasons. I had learned my lesson for real this time, and that lesson had nothing to do with jail and everything to do with freedom.

As I walked out of the front door in the same clothes I walked in wearing six months ago, that freedom had never meant so much. I grinned up at the bright sky on my first day free from physical bondage, knowing my soul was freer than that. I looked skyward beyond the smattering of clouds against the blue sky and thanked God for the salvation I had received. Just as she always knew, I finally found a piece of Sarah's peace after all. And with one last glance toward the Heavens, I bid a final farewell to my friend Badger, whom I would no sooner forget than Jesus himself.

A car honked at the end of the sidewalk, claiming my attention. My mom was already running up the sidewalk, and Tyler was just stepping out of my own truck. Thinking it was totaled and trashed, I was awed to see the old white Toyota 4x4. Both my mom and Tyler had giant smiles when I hugged them as if we hadn't kept steady contact the whole time I had been gone. But their hugs hit differently now that four ugly walls weren't surrounding us.

I was harshly aware that Sarah wasn't there. Was that to be my only conclusion, then? Did her lack of showing up to my release constitute closure? She never came to the jail to visit. She kept true to my request, and there was never another letter, phone call, or even a message from her through Mom or Tyler. And I knew Sarah was still speaking with Tyler because he had mentioned during one of his latest visits that she was helping lead the youth group now. That was the first and only time her name came up between us. How badly I wanted to probe some more, to find out any shred of information that might help me sort through the endless questions I had about our relationship, but I refrained.

It would have to wait until I had the time to handle it, but I would definitely connect with her soon. My heart demanded I find out how she was doing and share everything I went through.

Part of me was still tied to her. Always would be. I was sure that if we talked, she would agree, even if she had already moved on. God had not brought our lives together for no reason. Before the shift, I tolerated what I didn't understand about the Lord, for Sarah's sake. To be able to share all of this with her now seemed like what I needed to do next. What I *wanted* to do next.

Getting a closer look at my Toyota as I approached, I was floored by its condition. Each damaging offense inflicted upon it had been restored. It still looked its age, but the body and glass were made new. I hadn't expected to ever see it again, let alone in good condition. "You got it fixed? I thought it was rotting in a junkyard somewhere. It looks better than it did when I first bought it."

Mom responded with a smile. "You gotta have something to drive to college next semester."

"I don't know what to say." I stepped in to hug her again. "Thanks, Mom."

"It was nothing. You deserve it. Now, how about you take these and drive us home?" She dangled the keys out for me and I happily snatched them.

On the road, feeling the sun and wind, I couldn't articulate my gratitude. Just the feeling of my old, leather-wrapped steering wheel had me feeling some kind of way. And the mere sight of my mother so vibrant and whole like this was the best. She really had changed. It never failed to impress me to see how much.

"Is it like riding a bike, Kev?" Tyler asked, all jokes and smiles from the back seat, jerking me back to the moment.

"Is what like riding a bike?" I asked, confused.

"Being out in the real world!" Tyler clarified.

"I wasn't gone *that* long," I was surprised to hear myself say. Only yesterday, I would've said six months in jail might as well be six years.

"Yeah, but it feels different, doesn't it? A lot can happen in a little time. Everything has changed, but you have yet to see all of it." Tyler's musing made sense, and I realized how much it reminded me of Badger. They both had such a passionate way of speaking about matters of faith, even though they were such different individuals.

Acknowledging what Tyler said was true, I agreed there was plenty of time to re-learn this life and how to do it to best serve God. Though I was still working on an aviation degree, my heart told me I had God's work to do. How or when that would manifest itself, I didn't know, but it would happen. Maybe I could use my art somehow. The possibilities were exciting and seemingly endless. Someday I would figure it out.

After the scenic drive, I stopped at Tyler's place to drop him off first, but not before we made plans to have coffee the following Monday. I still didn't love the stuff, but it was a small price to pay to hang out with my friend.

Tyler said his goodbyes to Mom and then got out of the truck. Before he left, he jogged around to my open window. The hint of a secret outlined his grin. "I almost forgot to share the good news."

"What news?"

"Believe it or not, Cindie and I finally had that date. We've been dating exclusively for two months now."

"Really? Wow. Sure took you long enough. You know, in the big house, we call that the long con," I tittered.

"You can laugh, but there was no conning necessary. I told you my natural charm would do all the work." Tyler smiled and popped an imaginary collar, inciting laughter from us all.

"Why didn't you say something before?" I asked, still catching my breath. "You could've told me."

"It's alright. It's more exciting and dramatic now, don't you think?"

"Sure it is." With so few words, I was completely assured. Tyler had done what Tyler did best. "I'm real happy for you, Ty."

"Thanks, Kevin. I'm even happier for you." Tyler peeked around to my mom in the back. "And you, Marie!"

"You take care, Tyler," she said, nodding and bidding him goodbye.

Her apartment was next.

The week prior, Mom scored a really nice waterfront studio,

leaving our little house on the west side to me. It was already decided that I would live there until I left for school, at which point we would rent it out to supplement my student income.

After the program had set her up with a job, she'd successfully kept it all this time and was doing really well for herself. Between all of her new responsibilities, her weekly meetings, and the joy of her son coming home, she had remained perfectly clean and sober.

Her fourth-floor apartment was spectacular. I admired the view from her balcony, leaning my arms over the rail, watching the sun rays dance over the rippling water. Out there, there was nothing but miles of gulf ocean, sailboats, and the occasional merchant barge. It was nothing like looking at cement every waking hour for months on end. And, as nice as our house had become, and as pleasant as her room at the facility had been, this was unlike anything *she* was used to, either.

I was so proud of her.

Mom joined me outside, stepping through the sliding glass door.

"I'm really happy for you, Mom. This place is awesome," I said, looking over my shoulder at her.

"Don't get any ideas, kid. It's mine. You got the house — no give backs."

Humor warmed my features. "Don't worry. I'm more than happy with this arrangement."

Marie sighed before pulling her cigarettes and lighter out of her pocket. She hit the pack on her palm a few times before pulling one out and balancing it between her lips to light. "Just about anything is better than a jail cell, anyway," she said, exhaling through her teeth between puffs. The smoke wafted into the wind and floated away.

"For sure, but that's not why."

"What do you mean?"

"Since Craig isn't there, and because of all the additional work you've put into it, it feels more like I'm actually going *home* now." She studied me as I spoke, her eyes narrowing and softening at the same time. The end of her cigarette burned bright between her fingers as her hand rested on the rail beside me.

"Kevin, are you sure it's okay that I moved out? Maybe you would prefer not to be living there alone."

"Nah, I'm fine. Jail really isn't that lonely." I chuckled, even as my mind went back to what I'd just left behind. The crowded, humiliating showers, being elbow to elbow in the cafeteria, practically crawling over one another in the rec rooms or outside. Oh, and I *did* eventually get a new cell mate, and he was nothing like Badger. I was *more* than ready to remember what being alone was like.

"No kidding, I know. I've been there. But…" Her contempt faded and she worried her lip, showcasing another habit that was just hers. "What are you gonna do if Craig comes back?"

I narrowed my gaze. "What are *you* gonna do?" I countered, my tone clearly indicating there was nothing *either* one of us would do. We had already tried taking matters into our own hands. Her attempt to get rid of him hadn't worked. Neither had mine. The only thing we could rely on now was the justice system keeping him behind bars, and prayer keeping him behind the power of Jesus. He was no longer any concern of ours.

"Okay, you're right. I just want to be sure you're really okay."

"I *am* okay, Mom. You need to stay okay, too. Don't be worrying about me." I slung my arm around my mom's shoulders, silently rejoicing that her cigarette had reached the butt and burned itself out. "I think maybe all this high-rise ocean air getting to you."

She lightly hit the back of her hand against my chest and shook her head while simultaneously leaning into my embrace. "Don't you sass me, you little punk."

"Where do you think I learned it?"

"Obviously, from your dad," she said, immediately tensing up and utterly surprising me.

I'd never heard her say the "D" word before.

"I think if you aren't nicer," she quickly continued, "I will tell them to lock you back up."

"Since I know you're not all talk, I better do what you say."

"That's right. I'd hate to burn that house down twice, but I will."

I laughed, long and loud, the sound echoing from her balcony out into the shiny world beyond. "Too soon, Mom. Just know, I plan on buying at least a dozen fire extinguishers."

"All jokes aside, I do think it's time you go on home." Mom stuffed her spent cigarette butt into her pocket and cleared her throat, straightening up.

My lungs took in a deep supply of ocean air before letting it out. "I think you're right."

The two of us walked side by side, arms around one another, all the way to the elevator.

"I love you, son."

"I love you, too, Mom."

"I'll come by once you get settled."

"Okay. I'll see you soon."

Last but not least, I pulled into my driveway, and it was an interesting experience. The last time I was there, I had been the most imprisoned, free man ever. My thoughts wandered to the cement under my feet, where there were once splatters of blood, but I didn't bother looking down. It was the same as looking backward. There was only one Blood that mattered now, and it would not be found on the ground.

I let myself inside and was instantly surprised by a familiar face looking back at me from the living room. "Sarah," I said, stupefied.

"You're here," she replied in her calm, soft way, but her intense, glimmering eyes and her twisting hands implied she was anything but calm. She caught onto her own actions and bit her lip, securing her tattle-tale hands behind her back.

"*You're* here," I said, almost not believing it. "How?"

"I had a key," she said, retrieving it from her back pocket. "Your mom gave it to me last week. Tyler, Sammy, and I helped her move." Sarah put the key down on the end table next to her, returning her hands to the safe place behind her back. "Were you wondering why you didn't see me at the jail earlier?"

"I had hoped you'd be there, but I wasn't taking it as a bad sign that you weren't. I knew it was only a matter of time."

She seemed to relax as her hazel-greens performed a search of me. "You're different."

"I wasn't gone that long," I said for the second time that afternoon.

"But it was long enough," she said, a rosy bloom of under-standing growing across her face. "Wasn't it?"

Tossing my keys, I put down my plastic bag of belongings I no longer needed or cared about. Then, from inside the collar of my shirt, I produced a modest silver cross on a shoelace. "More than enough," I confirmed for her, returning her smile.

Nobody was ready to see anything if their eyes were still closed, but I understood now how Sarah and Tyler had hoped to help me see the truth. I had been a fool, feeling my way around blindly, thinking I was alone in a dark grave of the world's creation, when the solution was right in front of me the whole time. All I had to do was look up and live.

To get back here, I'd gotten through the worst of my mistakes and come out victorious, but not alone. And I might not have done it at all if I hadn't met Sarah first. I owed her thanks for her part in introducing me to Christ and ultimately changing my life.

"Oh, I have something for you!" Suddenly, Sarah spun on her heel, forcing me to curiously watch her back as she messed with something on the the other end table, at the far side of the couch. There was a strange noise as she hunched further over, intent on shielding whatever she was doing from view. When she turned around, her eyes were glowing with joy and — flickering candle-light? Looking down at her hands, Sarah held out a single cupcake with one candle stick out of the top.

"Happy birthday," she said. "I made it myself." When a nervous smile spread across her face, I couldn't believe it. She'd gone to all this trouble just for me, and she was still unsure of herself?

"Thank you." Flattered, I stepped forward to take the cupcake. She smiled big and true at my acceptance.

"Now, you have to make a wish," she instructed.

"I don't need to."

"There must be something you could wish for."

I considered all the world might offer, and everything I'd never had, and decided none of it mattered as much as what I really wanted. All I wanted was her.

Holding up my cupcake, I blew the candle out, setting my wish in stone. I took a bite before reaching over and setting it down, planning to return for the rest once we'd talked some more. "Wow. That's actually very, very good."

"Really? Are you sure your taste buds aren't just desperate?"

"Oh, they're desperate. But not for vanilla cake with chocolate frosting."

Her cheeks pinked. "What did you wish for?"

With a hearty smirk, I raised my shoulder. As I teased her, Sarah laughed, too. I thought it should always be like this. The chance to banter with her felt so good. Just being face to face with her felt even better. Was there anything more to wish for than to never have to go without any of it again?

SARAH

61

MY HEART WAS LODGED IN MY THROAT. IT WAS AS IF I WAS SEEING Kevin for the very first time. The real Kevin. The one I always knew was there. And, despite looking a little leaner, which I supposed was to be expected, he somehow seemed taller and more handsome, if such a thing were possible. This moment was worth everything we'd gone through to reach it. All of our decisions leading up to now, all the bad and all the good, had paid off to give us something better. Something the two of us could spend the rest of our lives grateful for — if he thought so, too.

Turmoil was at play within me. "I'm sorry I missed the real deal."

"About that... I got your letter," he said, taking small steps closer.

Fixated on his every move, I watched him, waiting, as butterflies fluttered and battered against the walls of my stomach. My arms dropped to my sides, my mind no longer worried if I was fidgeting or not, but yearning for his closeness. "Yeah?"

"I wanted to write you back so many times." He stepped even closer.

"I know what you mean."

"So much happened."

I went the rest of the way, stopping only when we were merely a breath apart. "I'd like to hear all about it."

Kevin reached, taking hold of my waist, his thumb brushing tenderly back and forth against my glucose monitor. Being under his touch again was so warm and natural, like a dream come true.

"I want to tell you everything," he finally said. "But first, I have a birthday wish to cash in on." Moving one hand to my cheek, Kevin kissed me.

I broke beneath his hold, wrapping my arms tightly around him, my knees almost giving out. Nobody had this effect on me but Kevin. He kissed me like he would never let me go, and that was exactly what I wanted.

The two of us were intertwined in a way that wasn't possible with anyone else. He had done more for my heart and soul and even my very existence than anyone on earth, short of my parents. What I had suffered due to carelessness in the early stages of our relationship was nothing but a distant memory, thanks to Kevin. He had saved my life, and it was no minor victory to know I'd had a hand in saving his.

WHERE THE SPIRIT OF THE LORD IS, THERE IS FREEDOM.
2 CORINTHIANS 3:17

EPILOGUE

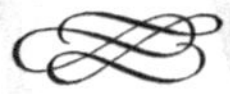

I SAT NERVOUSLY ON THE STAGE BESIDE MY GIRLFRIEND AND observed the sea of people smiling up at me and the rest of my graduating class. The commencement speaker spoke about life after graduation and a great deal about personal responsibility, but all I could focus on was my overwhelming gratitude. Inside, I prayed, thanking God for my success and the enduring love of a beautiful woman, Sarah Stevenson. We both now had earned Bachelor's degrees, me in aviation and Sarah in education.

I had a job waiting for me at the Corpus Christi Aviation Academy, where I would be logging more flight hours for my eventual Airline Transport Pilot (ATP) license. It would just take me two more years until I could finally fly commercial airliners like I'd always wanted. Based on all the education, flight hours, and certifications I already had under my belt, I was probably the most well-trained student pilot in all of Texas.

Calling on her time assisting Tyler with the youth back home, partway through our first year, things finally clicked for Sarah. She realized she wanted to teach. Now, she planned to open up a homeschool co-op program through her old church. Tyler still worked there and had endeavored to help her get it going.

All of our post-college plans were swiftly coming together, and soon, we would be moving back home to put our freshly minted degrees into practice. And, if things went the way I hoped, we would be doing so as husband and wife.

I smiled back at Sarah as she squeezed my hand before looking again at the audience. My mother, with her small oxygen tank situated on her left, was looking up at me with red eyes and a blotchy face, still beautiful beneath her nasal cannula. I knew she was especially proud of me today, and not just because I was proposing to Sarah. I hadn't told anyone I was doing it today.

Last night, I felt a tugging at my heart saying it was time to ask her to marry me, instead of waiting to propose at the water-front back home like I originally planned.

During our final summer break spent in Corpus Christi, I officially asked Jonathan Stevenson for his permission to marry Sarah. He'd been joyously forthcoming with his approval, saying he already considered me a son. When I went to the rest of our friends and family to let them in on it, the support I received was incredible.

Back when I was struggling in my young life, I didn't know what it was like for a respectable man to pat me on the back and say they were proud of me. The idea of my mom wrapping me in her arms and crying happy tears over my milestones was a foreign concept. A lot of time had passed since then, with many similar acts of love from them all, and that was sure to make my proposal today even better, because they'd all be there. As soon as the speaker finished his speech to the whole stadium, I had one of my own to give just to Sarah.

So many times leading up to this moment, I had been tempted to just pull the ring out and hand it to her. I could hardly wait to see how her eyes sparkled when she saw it. There was no doubt in my mind that she'd say yes, but I had spent too much time on my graduation cap to ruin it with impatience. While Sarah had embellished hers with flowers, colorful squiggles, and sequins, I had carefully constructed mine for this moment.

As the cheering picked up where the speech at last left off, everyone leapt to their feet and threw their caps in the air, as was tradition. Everyone except for me.

"We did it!" Sarah cheered, throwing her arms around my neck. Not remembering where she was or just not caring, she kissed me, deep and long. Everything about this moment was ours.

When we separated, I tucked stray hairs behind Sarah's ear. "Your cap is gone, flown away with the others."

"That's why I decorated it so heavily, so I won't lose it. Nobody is going to mistake my cap for theirs with that junk all over it."

"I decorated mine, too."

"You did? When? I didn't notice." Sarah lifted to her toes, trying to peek.

The wait was over. "Want to see?" I carefully pulled my cap from my head and presented it to her. There, in sparkly painted letters, read my plea for her to be my wife. As she read it and realization cast a shadow of shock over her features and tears formed, my heart seized. Until I heard her next words, I feared I might never breathe again. I could have all the confidence in the world, but until I heard that one little word...

Jesus, give me strength...

Lowering to one knee, I drew the attention of people around us and triggered the gasps and anticipatory stares of our loved ones in the stands. Pulling the tassel around, I revealed the next part of my proposal. An emerald-cut diamond engagement ring was tied carefully to it.

"Sarah Something Stevenson," I began, teasing her with a memory from long ago. "You have let me love you for over four years, and because of the love you've given me in return, I've been able to grow and achieve things I never thought possible. I know I'm by no means a perfect man, but just as you did once, I now believe that I'm the perfect man for you. And if you accept me now, I promise you that —"

"Yes!" Sarah blurted out her acceptance before I could finish the request, as if she had known her answer to this question forever.

I laughed. She had beaten me to the punch like this before. "Aren't you supposed to let me ask first?"

"Well, then, go ahead," she hurried me along, exactly as she had in the past.

Fist to mouth, I cleared my throat. "Sarah Lucille Stevenson... Will you marry me?"

"Yes!" she shouted louder, to which the onlooking crowd cheered again. I stood on shaky legs with my chest puffed up and caught her effortlessly when Sarah flung herself into my arms. Then, removing the ring from the tassel, I slid it onto her finger. Her tears left a faint trail of black mascara in their wake, but with the promise of our future securely on her hand, she had never looked more beautiful. I wiped them away before finally throwing my cap high into the air, letting it fly away with the others. *She said yes!*

Sarah leaned in and lifted her voice to my ear. "Just so you know, I'm gonna need you to get that cap back for me. Someday when we tell our kids this story, they will want to see it."

"As you wish, wifey dear."

When the chaos was over, we made our way across the aisles to join our people. Tyler was the first to insert himself into our embrace, reaching one arm over each of us. *"Felicidades, mi amigos! Two major celebrations in one. What a blessed afternoon."* His pregnant wife, Cindie, extended her congratulations before the two of them stepped aside.

Next came our parents. Sarah jogged to her mom first, who was bawling like a baby as evidenced by her own wet cheeks. First thing Lynne did upon releasing her from her rib-cracking hug was hold up Sarah's left hand and examine the ring.

"Isn't it beautiful?" Sarah asked her mom.

"It's more than beautiful! It's perfect for you. And you can't imagine how happy I am to not have to pretend I don't know about it anymore!"

Sarah's eyes went wide with laughter. "Seriously!? Who all knew?"

"Everyone," the group said in unison.

"We've all known for a long time, actually," Jonathan Stevenson clarified, stepping into the conversation.

In the beginning, I only had Sarah to thank for bringing these wonderful people into my life, but then they stayed because they loved me, too, and I loved them just as much in return. I was so proud of the community I had helped to build.

Going toward Jonathan for a handshake, I got pulled in for a hug instead. I could count on one hand how many times he'd done that in the last five years, so this felt extra special. His eyes even seemed mistier than usual.

"You suddenly develop allergies, old man?" I teased him.

Releasing me, Jonathan merely smirked. "I'm so proud of you, son. And so happy for you both. I had a feeling you wouldn't hold out for the waterfront."

Chuckling, I said, "Thank you, sir."

Then Mom stepped forward. She was smiling despite the pain she must've been in and made no sign of it at all. She just wanted to be happy today, she'd told me that morning. Her doctors were trying to keep her liver from failing, and her stats were on a steady decline, but she adamantly refused to miss out on today. Yellow clouds threatened to chase away the shine in her eyes, but she didn't let them. "My boy, a college graduate. I knew you'd do it."

"There were times I didn't think I would be able to."

"Well, doubts or no doubts, you did it."

When she was right, she was right. "I really did."

She grabbed me and squeezed as only a mother can. She was shaking, and I knew it was from more than just excitement. "I love you, baby boy."

"I love you too, Mom. I'm so glad you're here. Thank you."

"For what? You did it all."

"Not alone. I couldn't have done any of it without all of you."

Marie's eyes welled afresh.

"Neither could I," Sarah agreed. She had her turn hugging everyone and their tears finally subsided. "Let's go home," she announced to the group. Of course, she was eager to tell Sammy and the others back home about our engagement. "We have a wedding to plan!"

Once upon a time, I worked hard to just get by. After making a host of bad choices that took me far from my dreams, I had served many months behind bars, paying for them. Yet, even during my worst, God's grace had brought me through to becoming my best. As promised, two years after my release from jail, my record had been expunged. Even though I had come from a childhood of darkness, I knew God had been leading me to the light all along.

In the end, I was saved, with a wonderful co-pilot to fly with through life, and nothing but clear skies ahead.

Thank you for reading!

I sincerely hope you enjoyed your first encounter with Kevin and Sarah of the Renewed Hearts series. Their journey is the first of more to come!

Be sure to never miss an update by subscribing to my newsletter. Visit HeatherCamacho.com to get started.

God bless & happy reading!

- HEATHER CAMACHO

ACKNOWLEDGMENTS

First and foremost, thank you, God! His guidance was essential in writing this book. For more years than I care to admit, I mulled and stressed over countless incomplete stories. I loved the characters, I loved the plots, and I loved writing them. So what was going wrong? I'll tell you what. They didn't glorify God at all.

It wasn't until 2021, when a Kari Jobe song on the radio knocked me to my knees, that everything clicked. Jesus had my attention and I finally understood that it wasn't a problem with my creative life, but my *entire* life. A relationship with Him is more than just believing, and now my stories allow me to express and share that.

Of course, special thanks go out to my husband next. My real life book-boyfriend. Pickle, life with you has been a dream come true in many ways. Here's one more piece of evidence. Dis book; *is nieth.*

To the wonderful, strong mamas with equally strong, amazing children who understand Sarah's struggle first hand: Annissa, Amber and Nicole. Thank each of you for offering your input and knowledge so I could do her story justice.

To my wonderful beta readers: Anna, Maria, Jim, Philip, Alyssa, Kristen, Katie, Lando, and Summer. Every word you all read was a part of my heart and soul, and your care and attention was vital. Thank you for all your comments, critiques, and encouragements.

To Amanda, for making me redo the opening chapters. You were right.

To Ruben, for providing invaluable insight into the heart of a probation officer, and for lending my character your name.

And to my fellow Wordwarrior Princesses: Aimee and Missy. This finished book in your hands is the culmination of many, many accumulated words, over the course of many, many Wednesday Write Nights. This is what true support leads to. I love you guys.

Thank you Jessica Welch, for providing me with your editorial expertise and camaraderie. Your skillful eyes were the first to help shape it into the masterpiece it *obviously* is.

Thank you Allison Wells, for your wonderful editing, advice and friendship. It's all meant the world to me. I'm so happy I found you, long lost twin!

Thank you Kendra Gaither, for taking my book to the finish line. Thankfully that one chick (lol) introduced us, because I couldn't imagine publishing this without your final hour fixes. Bless you!

Thank you Emilie Haney, for your *beautiful* cover art. I waited half a year to publish because I wanted you on my team. I'm so glad I did!

God knew what He was doing when he brought each and every one of you into my life. To *everyone* who gave this book, or me, their time and energy, thank *you* so much! *From Graves to Gardens* is here today because of you.

Lastly, to all my supportive readers who understand that sometimes things slip through the cracks. Editing can be an on-going process in life as well as in writing, and I thank you for your patience in that.

LOVE YOU ALL & GOD BLESS — HEATHER

ABOUT THE AUTHOR

HEATHER CAMACHO'S mission is to tell stories of love and faith, dedicating her craft to sharing the testimonies, truths, and promises of the Word with readers worldwide.

A Midwesterner turned Texan, she resides on a small ranch in the southern coastal region with her husband, three kids, and their many animals.

When she isn't writing, reading, or homeschooling, she enjoys sewing clothes for her children, making quilts for her friends and spending time with her horses.

WWW.HEATHERCAMACHO.COM

facebook.com/HeatherCamachoAuthor

instagram.com/heather.author

threads.com/@heather.author

amazon.com/author/heathercamacho

goodreads.com/heathercamacho

tiktok.com/@heather.author